CHAIN OF SOULS

Other Books by Dan Armstrong

Taming the Dragon
Prairie Fire
Puddle of Love

CHAIN OF SOULS

A Novel

Dan Armstrong

Mud City Press
Eugene, Oregon

Chain of Souls

Copyright © 2010 by Dan Armstrong

Published by
Mud City Press
http://www.mudcitypress.com
Eugene, Oregon

This is a work of fiction. Names, characters, places, and incidents either are the product of the author's imagination or are used fictitiously.

ISBN-978-0-9830045-0-9

Printed in the United States

To Parker and Jean

ACKNOWLEDGMENTS

The love and support of my wife provide the foundation for all my writing. She is invariably my first reader, best editor, and primary source of feedback. Thank you, Judith.

I must also thank all the early readers, Amy, Ed, Patti, Lonn, Lisa, Brian, and Judy. As usual, this novel involved a process of writing and rewriting that took several years. Without the comments and support from those readers, this book would not be in your hands right now.

The story told in *Chain of Souls* was in part inspired by the work of W. Y. Evans-Wentz, specifically his masterpiece *The Tibetan Book of the Dead: The After Death Experiences on the Bardo Plane, According to Lama Kazi Dawa-Samdup's English Rendering*. A few short portions from the "Bardo Thödol" recitations, as translated by the Lama Kazi Dawa-Samdup, are quoted in the novel. All of these passages come from the 1973 edition of Evan-Wentz's classic (published in New York by Causeway Books) and have been modified only slightly to fit the context of the story and to enable easier reading.

I have used several terms in this book that are of Hindu, Tibetan, or Sanskrit origin. They are printed in italics in the text. If the meaning of these words is not made obvious by the context, there is a glossary at the end of the book where all of these words are compiled with their definitions.

Lastly, the image on the cover of this book comes from an engraving of the city of Haridwar in the 1850s, a time when the British were building a small diversion dam on the Ganges River. The original drawing was made by the artist S. Prout.

At midnight on August 14, 1947, two hundred years of British rule came to an end with the partition of the Indian Empire into two independent nations—Pakistan for the Muslims, India for the Hindus. It was a highly polarizing resolution to a difficult situation, and the relocation of the populace became a nightmare of upheaval and violence as individuals, families, and whole villages migrated east and west across the divided empire. In the end, some one million people lost their lives during this process.

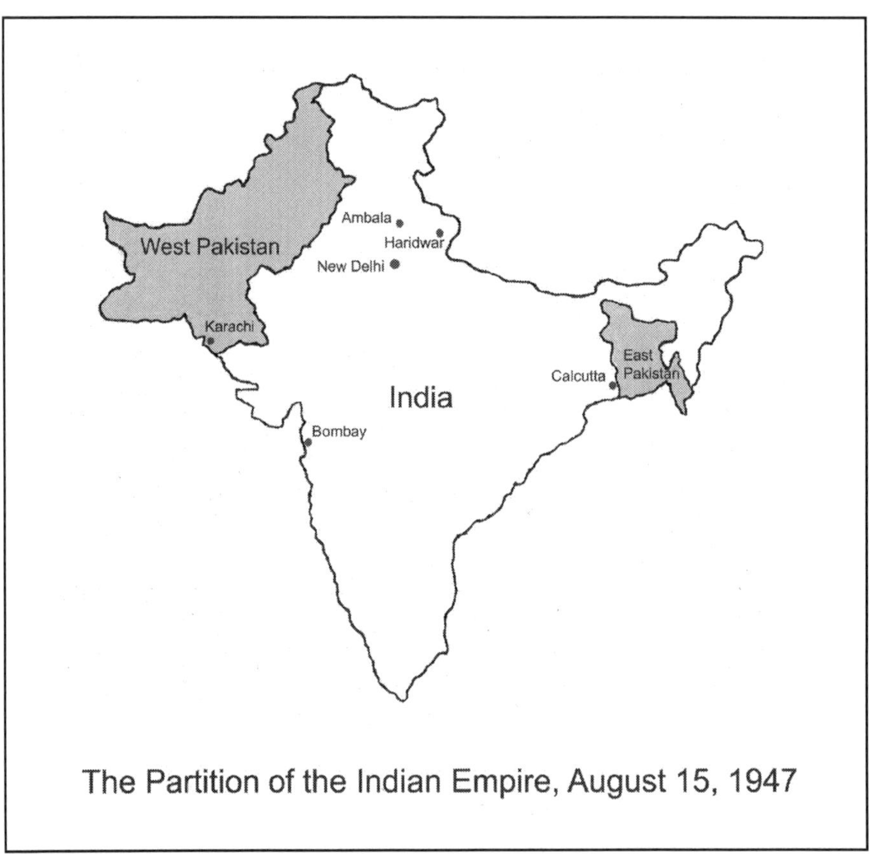

The Partition of the Indian Empire, August 15, 1947

PROLOGUE

There was probably no more dangerous place in the world than along the independence day parade route in Karachi, Pakistan on August 14, 1947. And that was foremost in Roger Taylor's mind as he rushed along, pushing through the noisy crowd, trying to stay just ahead of the lead car in the motorcade. Taylor was part of the British security team working the parade to protect Muslim leader, Mohammed Ali Jinnah, and Britain's Governor-General to India, Lord Louis Mountbatten. The two dignitaries stood side by side in the back seat of a black Rolls Royce convertible, waving to those packing both sides of Bundar Road to celebrate the creation of the first Muslim state.

Taylor cursed at the insanity of the entire affair and damn Mountbatten who felt it was so important to take this ride through Karachi with Jinnah to prove to all the world that the subcontinent—against all evidence—was safe for anyone. Taylor paused briefly to look over his shoulder at Mountbatten in the slow moving Rolls. Despite the scorching heat of midday, the handsome naval officer stood proud and regal in his white dress uniform, but also clearly alert to the movement of the security officers hustling along on either side of the troop-lined, three-mile parade route. Taylor made brief eye contact with Mountbatten, then was back battling the crowd, hissing a litany of vulgarities, looking for anything that seemed the slightest bit irregular.

At six foot two, Taylor scanned the movement of the anxious crowd as from above, keying on individual motions within the seething mass. He fastened on a figure in a black burka pushing with decided purpose toward the edge of the street. Despite the significance of the day, there were few women in the crowd, and those who were there stood out because of their hoods and covered faces—but it was the urgency in this woman's effort and her height that caught Taylor's attention.

Taylor hustled ahead for a better appraisal. At close range, he caught an unmistakable darting in the woman's eyes. Suddenly he knew what was coming as clearly as if it had already happened—and he began shoving people out of the way, ignoring the protests shouted at him from all sides.

With the Rolls only a few meters away, the man—*who was disguised as a woman*—withdrew a package from beneath his burka. Taylor made a final surge through the crowd and tackled the man, now fumbling with the wires of a homemade bomb. They both went to the ground with the man still trying to ignite the bomb, but Taylor was far too quick and strong. He yanked the bomb from the man's hands and immediately began pulling out the wires—at the expense of his grip on the man, who scrambled to his feet.

Taylor made a futile attempt to grab at the man's ankle and caught only a handful of burka. The man stumbled then pulled free from the garment. Beneath he was wearing a wrinkled black suit and an armband emblazoned with an orange swastika. The man turned full face to Taylor still sprawled on the ground, swore an oath of mortal revenge in Hindi, then dashed unimpeded into the crowd.

Amid the cheering and confusion, neither the soldiers nearby nor those new Pakistani citizens there to catch sight of Jinnah passing in the Rolls noticed what had transpired on the ground. But as the big black car motored by and Taylor stood, his trousers torn, his khaki shirt stuck with sweat to his back, and a long scratch across his face, Mountbatten acknowledged Taylor's actions with the slightest nod—then Taylor was pushing out of the crowd to get rid of the explosives he'd wrapped in the black burka.

Eight months later...

CHAPTER 1

Roger Taylor woke in the dark of early morning to the ringing of the phone. The phone rattled again as he groggily untangled from the sheets and reached through the mosquito netting and around a half-empty bottle of whiskey to the receiver. "Taylor here," he said softly, trying not to disturb the maharani in bed beside him.

"Captain Stevens from the Governor-General's office, Taylor. You're to be here in New Delhi as soon as possible. There's a ticket for the six-thirty Central waiting for you at V. T. as I speak."

Taylor looked up at the ceiling fan issuing soft periodic chirps as it churned through the thick tropical air like butter. "That's six-thirty this evening, right, Captain?" As his eyes gradually adjusted to the darkness, he watched Naija Kocchar turn on her side. Her hair fell across her shoulders like a yard of black silk. The wonderful contours of her hips beneath the sheet caused a stirring in his gut.

"No, Taylor, that's two hours from now," said the voice on the phone. "This is urgent. Tell the C.I.D. nothing. The Governor-General wants you in Haridwar in two days."

"Haridwar," muttered Taylor, the stirring suddenly gone. "What is this?"

"That's all I can tell you. Utmost discretion, Taylor. Utmost." Taylor looked at Naija. "Of course." He replaced the receiver in its cradle.

Naija spoke without turning toward him. "You're going to Haridwar?" The Hindu princess sat up and faced him. Even in the pre-dawn light, the contrast between the white sheet crumpled at her waist and the glossy mahogany of her bare torso was stunning. "Roger, please don't tell me you're running out on me at such a difficult time as this?" She spoke English with perfect enunciation. High-strung, beautiful, and wealthy, she spent her summers in Paris and her winters anywhere she pleased.

They were four months into an affair that had taken both their breaths away, and last night, just eight hours ago at a big state department dinner,

Naija had informed Taylor that her husband, the Maharajah of Gwalior, had discovered that her recent series of trips to Bombay had been to see him. Taylor knew immediately that the torrid affair was over, but hadn't said anything at the time, knowing he would have a heart to heart with Naija some time today. This phone call meant it would have to be now.

"I'm sorry, Naija, but I must go to New Delhi," said Taylor, sitting on the edge of the bed, staring at his bare feet, wondering how to start. "And it's likely this will be my last official mission in India."

Naija reached out and clasped his hand, playfully pulling him back down on the bed. "But you'll be back? We'll be together again," she said with a smile as seductive as her body.

Taylor denied her steamy gaze. "I've heard how jealous the Maharajah can be, Naija. I think we've played it out."

Naija pushed herself up on one elbow. "You have nothing to fear, Roger. My husband is a coward. Fidelity is a joke to men as wealthy as he is. He knows I've had many lovers. And he the same." Naija leaned into him and kissed up his neck to his ear. "You must have a little time before you leave?" she hissed, snaking up close to him, laying her leg over his.

"Unfortunately, I don't. I'll barely make the train as it is." They'd made love twice already since midnight. Taylor knew what was going on now was a game and he wasn't going to play. He sat up despite her leg.

Naija's eyes narrowed. "Maybe it's you who are the coward, Roger."

"Please, Naija, you know as well as I do, it's over. This is the end we both knew would eventually come. I'm headed for the far northeast of India and after that a position in some other British commonwealth." He reached out to touch her cheek. "Can't we part as friends?"

Naija turned away from him, leaving his question hanging in the void. She stood from the bed and gathered up her clothing from the cane chair in the corner, then strode naked across the apartment in a way that made Taylor's libido ache. The bathroom door banged shut. He heard the water turn on. He went to his dresser and pulled on a shirt and some trousers, then set to packing a small suitcase.

Before he was done, Naija exited from the bathroom dressed in a gorgeously embroidered red silk *sari*. He turned to face her, but she wouldn't even grant him an ugly look. "Naija, please. We can be courteous." The door slammed as she left.

"Christ," he said to himself. He should have just played her damn game.

An hour an a half later, the sun just peaking over the hazy Bombay skyline, Taylor climbed out of a taxi at Victoria Terminus. Though he was running late, he took a moment to appraise the huge railway station across the street.

Built in the 1880s, V.T., as it was called, was the product of a time when ambitious young architects came from England to take advantage of cheap materials and even cheaper labor to build name-making monstrosities, just because they could. Often referred to as the center of the British Empire, V. T. was a strange animal, like the Raj, huge and awkward, yet still somehow alluring.

From a distance, the train station resembled a long sprawling cathedral, superficially gothic in appearance and so populated with sharp spires, turrets, gargoyles, and sculpted dripstones it overwhelmed the eye. On closer inspection, the detail revealed embossed elephants and fine tile inlays. On either side of the main entrance sat two full-size feline sculptures, on the right the Imperial Lion of England, on the left India's Bengal Tiger. Taylor sarcastically called them the jaws of death. He'd waited too long for too many trains in V.T.

Crowning this sprawling architectural mutant, hundreds of feet above street level, was a colossal masonry dome that reminded Taylor of Tom's Tower at Oxford; a fourteen-foot allegorical statue of Progress stood on the top, arm upraised to the triumph of steam.

Taylor hurried across the street and bounded up the stairs. He acknowledged the two great stone cats as he passed between them and entered the building. If the exterior of this overwhelming edifice was the image of British rule in India—strict and formal; then the interior, decorated with local stone and Indian artwork, reflected the long lost pastoral soul of ancient India. A sweeping staircase dominated the central lobby. It was lined with Corinthian columns of polished granite and lit by walls of filigreed stained glass windows. All manner of beasts, birds, and foliage twisted about the banisters and trestled arches. High overhead was the dome, ribbed in ornamental wood. Its groin-vaulted ceiling was painted a brilliant azure and dotted here and there with stars of gold. Below, the floors were tile, glazed in the luminous colors of Hindu religious art.

Through the doors of this monument to British colonialism, the diverse masses of India blended into one nameless ocean of consciousness, a kind of *sangsaric* way station, only to be separated into individuals again as they exited out the back to the innumerable boarding platforms and trains headed to all parts of the subcontinent. This was British-India in a stone shell, thought Taylor as he collected his ticket at the will call booth and dashed off to catch his train, a strange yet impressive beast—now coming to an end—as was his time in India.

CHAPTER 2

A warm hissing rain was falling as Roger Taylor hurried out of the Tilak Bridge railway station in New Delhi. The twelve hundred kilometer trip had been long and slow, almost thirty hours counting the late departure from Bombay. Taylor stopped momentarily beneath the awning of a newsstand to read the headlines on the *London Times*: GANDHI'S ASSASSINATION LINKED TO HINDU RASHTRA DAL. He already knew the story but bought a paper anyway just to see how wrong they'd gotten it. He read the first paragraph, grimaced in disgust, and put the paper in his suitcase for later. He took a darting glance over each shoulder then stepped out into the wet crowded street to wave down a taxi.

A battered black and yellow Fiat skidded to a stop in front of him. Taylor climbed into the back seat amid a waft of burnt oil. The driver was a turbaned Sikh. Taylor addressed him in Punjabi. "The Viceroy's Palace. And make it fast. I'm late."

Though he knew the sudden summons to see Mountbatten was a compliment of the highest order, Taylor could do without the compliment. After ten years on the subcontinent and the affair with Naija now an unsettling and raw memory, he wished he were anywhere other than India—or the United States for that matter.

It was the twenty-first of March, 1948. India's independence from England was eight months old. It had been the worst period of Taylor's stay. Violent rioting and mass killings, one ethnic group against another, the increasingly troubled British Commonwealth had become a war zone. To make it all worse, Taylor's act of heroism that August afternoon in Karachi had made him a target for the same radical group that had just killed Gandhi, and though his life as a plainclothes detective in the British Criminal Investigation Department had always contained an element of cloak and dagger, it had never been like this. He'd become a man of disguises, the reason for his recent beard, and an

7

unhealthy edginess had corrupted his sleep and increased his drinking and womanizing to a level bordering on suicidal. He needed out.

The taxi sped down the length of the King's Way and pulled up alongside Jaipur Square across from the Viceroy's Palace. Taylor paid the driver, then unfolded himself from the back seat of the little Fiat. He pulled up the collar on his jacket and surveyed the huge copper-domed building across the street. It stretched out for blocks like an enormous version of the Pantheon. Head down, he hustled across North Avenue to the entrance of this grand edifice that served as the Governor-General's palatial home and the seat of British operations in India.

Taylor climbed the stairs two at a time, pausing in the portico to straighten his collar and appreciate how big the place really was. More than twenty two-story columns stretched across the front of the building. It was the largest residence for a head of state in the world and arguably more impressive than Buckingham Palace. Taylor shook his head at the extravagance and entered the building through the security check at gate thirty-five. The halls were as oversized as the building and packed with bustling bureaucrats, striding military officers, and dark-skinned, bicycle riding messenger boys. He continued straight ahead until directly beneath the enormous dome in Dunbar Hall.

Lord Mountbatten's office was off to the left, and as Taylor reached the oversized teak doors, a soldier wearing a brigadier general's uniform and smoking a pipe was coming out. Taylor recognized General Vincent and extended his hand as he approached. The general hesitated.

"Roger Taylor, General," he said.

Vincent removed the pipe from his mouth, took a closer look, then suddenly smiled and accepted a handshake. "Ah, Taylor, America's undecorated diplomat to India's nonrationals." He laughed, loud and full of himself. "Didn't recognize you with all that hair on your face. How are you?"

"Couldn't be worse," Taylor replied with like humor. "Should have gotten out of this vile county in December when I had the chance. What's Mountbatten got for me?"

"Haven't the slightest, old boy. Doesn't tell me a damn thing. Cheerio."

Taylor entered the Governor-General's luxurious reception room to the lingering fragrance of Vincent's tobacco. It had fourteen-foot ceilings and was paneled in teak to match the doors. A military aide was seated at a desk dwarfed by the size of the room. The young lieutenant looked up as Taylor approached.

"Roger Taylor, Poona, C.I.D. I'm here to see the Governor-General."

"Yes, Taylor, he's been expecting you all morning." The aide stood and led Taylor to a second set of teak doors. He opened one. "Your lordship, Taylor's here."

"Send him in," said a strong, confident voice inside.

Like the reception room, the Governor-General's office was extravagant, but the ceilings were even higher and the excess so complete as to verify the pretense. A thick Persian rug stretched to the four corners of the massive office. The wall to the left contained a fireplace and a large portrait of King George VI and Queen Elizabeth mounted in a gilded frame. To the right was an even larger painting of Robert Clive and his makeshift army marching into Arcot in 1751. There was a sense of royalty and tradition in all the décor. Mountbatten fit right in. Handsome like a movie star, suave and distinguished, with a manner as smooth as silk, he was posed, somewhat dramatically, by one of the windows, peering out at Jaipur Square when Taylor entered. He smiled broadly at the sight of his guest and came forward to shake hands with the man who had saved his life eight months earlier. "Taylor, a pleasure to see you," he said with real enthusiasm.

"The honor is mine, your lordship." And it really was for Taylor. This was a cordial welcome from one of the most powerful men in India, maybe in the world. A highly decorated admiral in the Royal Navy, Mountbatten had been installed by Prime Minster Clement Atlee a year earlier as Viceroy, a position that's title changed to Governor-General the day of India's independence. His job was to oversee the transfer of power as India transitioned into an autonomous republic.

When Mountbatten first arrived in March of 1947, the state of affairs in India was ugly at best. Political action seemed the enactment of anarchy and had been that way since the end of the First World War. The previous Viceroy, General Archibald Wavell, made no headway with the mess in his four years, and increasing frustrations between Indian leaders and the English Parliament led to Wavell's replacement. Despite its power and prestige, Governor-General of India was a position no one wanted, yet its importance to England could be judged by the man selected to fill it. Lord Louis Mountbatten, second cousin to the King, was one of the most capable and respected individuals in the

English hierarchy. Uniquely dynamic and highly personable, Louis Mountbatten responded more out of duty than desire. Only through a superhuman effort did he manage to arbitrate the insanity and bring about a difficult, if only marginally honorable, separation of the British from Indian affairs. As it was, India's independence was achieved August 15, 1947, but only at the cost of partition, something almost as unpopular to some Indians as the Raj—and an ensuing transition that brought more upheaval than anyone but Gandhi could have anticipated.

"That beard looks good on you, Taylor," said Mountbatten, clearly trying to take some of the formality from the air. He knew Taylor was an American who had studied physics and philosophy at Oxford and showed him due respect. "Never did like the feel of a beard myself."

"I don't mind the feel, your lordship." Taylor lowered his eyes. "It's the reason I've grown it that bothers me." An understood silence hung between them before Taylor lifted his eyes to continue. "The RSSS has had a mark on me since Karachi."

Mountbatten nodded. "I've heard. Any more trouble?"

There had been an attempt on Taylor's life in January. He turned his neck uneasily, remembering the garrote. "No, but I've been followed off and on throughout the last six months. I need to get out of India, your lordship. I'm more a liability to the C.I. D. than an asset."

Mountbatten pondered this a moment. "I'm of another opinion, Taylor. We've got a little problem brewing in the northeast. It might be nothing, but I need someone I can trust to look into it—someone with a very light hand." Mountbatten took a seat at his desk. Taylor took one of the three black leather armchairs across from him. "And I believe that could be you."

Again this was a tremendous compliment from Mountbatten. Taylor still disagreed. "But I've only got two and a half more months in India, sir, and I don't want to extend my stay the slightest."

"Take care of this problem, Taylor, and I'll have you out of here as soon as it's done. And give you two months leave on the Riviera if you like. You could be there in two weeks if things go well."

Taylor knew as well as Mountbatten he couldn't say no to the mission, but the prospect of leaving early would surely ease the pain. He leaned forward. "What do you have in mind, sir?"

Mountbatten smiled. "You familiar with the city of Haridwar?"

"It's at the source of the Ganges."

"And a sacred city to the Hindus. They call it the gate to Vishnu or some such thing. The waters there are said to hold the nectar of the gods. The devout often go to Haridwar to die." Mountbatten lifted a gold cigarette case with the family monogram on it from his desk and popped it open. He extended the case to Taylor.

"No thank you, sir."

Mountbatten took out a cigarette, tapped it twice on the desk, and lit it with a monogrammed gold lighter. "According to one of our contacts, there's a woman on a death fast in Haridwar." He snapped the lighter shut with a sharp click, exhaled, then sat back in his chair. "She's doing it as some kind of statement about Gandhi's disapproval of partition." He took a long drag off his smoke, then turned away to exhale. "A month after Gandhi's assassination, the woman began the fast to honor the Mahatma's dream of Indian independence with unity. Now as the fast enters its fourth week, it seems she's enlisting others to continue with the fast after she's died."

Taylor nodded, though still unclear on the Governor-General's point. The past two decades had been full of civil disobedience, boycotts, fasts, and solidarity marches. What was the urgency of a fast in Haridwar? Off to the far side of Mountbatten's desk was the only piece of Indian artwork in the room. It was an ancient hand carved jade phallus, about twelve inches standing upright and embossed with naked humans coupling in all manner of sexual combinations. The image of Naija striding across his apartment to the bathroom the day before replayed in his mind.

"One death fast right after another, Taylor. They're calling it a chain of souls." Mountbatten took another pull off his cigarette and exhaled. "It isn't much now. Maybe it never will be. But I don't want to take any chances. We don't need another martyr in this country—much less a whole chain of them." Mountbatten looked out the window behind him, again rather dramatically. He turned back to Taylor and lowered his voice. "The celebration of Kumbh Mela will begin the first week in April. It's one of the largest festivals in India. Several hundred thousand pilgrims will be gathering in Haridwar to take part. What may seem like the actions of a crazy zealot to you and me could turn into something political if it gets any momentum. We'd hate to see this little number slip down the Ganges to Calcutta. I want this chain of souls broken one way or another before the beginning of the festival."

Mountbatten's anger at the nonsense of it all grew as he spoke. "India is like a ship at sea with a hold full of dynamite, Taylor. This woman is an ember on the deck. I want you to go to Haridwar and put this ember out before it blows the whole damn nation out of the water." He paused, staring down momentarily at his cigarette. "Maybe I'm over reacting, but it's my job to get us through the next six months with as few problems as possible. Part of that is anticipating even the slightest ruffle. I want this one smoothed out now."

"You're not asking me to kill this woman, are you, sir?"

"No, of course not. That would be a horrible mistake. Even worse should a Muslim or the RSSS get involved." Mountbatten crushed out his cigarette half-smoked like it was the ember he spoke of and leaned forward. "I want you to talk the woman out of it. I figure you could charm a vulture off a corpse if you had to." He smiled sardonically. "Especially if it's your quickest ticket out of this hellhole."

Mountbatten stood up and turned to face out the window, gazing through the floor to ceiling drapes into the gray afternoon. It was a signal that the meeting was coming to an end. "The Great Eastern leaves for Ambala tomorrow morning at five-forty and connects to Haridwar in the afternoon." He turned around. "My aide has your ticket and some cash. Pay the woman off. Convince her to put it off for a year. I don't care. Whatever it takes." He waved his hand at nothing.

Taylor stood. "Make it go away."

Mountbatten sighed through his smile. "You report only to me. The aide will give you the number of a secure line here and a contact in Haridwar. If you get into any trouble," Mountbatten's eyes paused absently on the piece of ancient art on his desk. He looked at Taylor as though he knew about his recent affair. "You're on your own. I don't know you exist. And no one else does either."

"Yes, sir."

As Taylor turned to leave, Mountbatten stopped him. "I don't believe I've ever properly thanked you for your bravery in Karachi. You covered that bomb with your body to save my life and Jinnah's—and who knows what other violence in the city that day."

"I thought he only had a gun, your lordship." Taylor lowered his eyes. "I didn't know it was a bomb until I was already on him." He looked up. "It wasn't bravery, sir. It was just what happened."

"You're much too modest, Taylor. Bravery is rarely a forethought. It's invariably, as you say, just what happens."

CHAPTER 3

The five-forty Great Eastern steamed out of New Delhi an hour late. A gray dawn woke through the window of Roger Taylor's compartment as the long train labored to build up speed. He wore a collarless Indian jacket that reached down past his knees, called a *sherwani*, with matching pants that were snug on the calves, called *churidars*, and a blue *pagri*. With his rounded, black beard, dark eyes, and the turban, he could easily pass for a wealthy Hindu businessman. He rode alone in a first-class compartment designed for six. Three cars back passengers were stuffed in to the brink of suffocation. He would dine on linen with fine flatware, while others on the train might not eat at all—that day or the next.

The first leg of the journey was almost directly north to Ambala—about two hundred kilometers. Shortly after the cloud-muted sunrise, it began to rain. Hypnotized by the rhythmic clatter of the track and the silent veils of falling rain, Taylor peered out the window thinking about Naija, beautiful Naija. Educated, free-thinking Hindu women were totally different animals than their stiff English counterparts. They approached sex as a tantric art, and Naija was a master. Would he ever dare to see her again? Would she even allow it?

He pushed those all-seeing almond eyes from his memory and turned his thoughts to the task ahead. The mission was a strange one, but that was the way it always was. Though his position in the C.I.D. was never openly referred to as anything but conventional—a plainclothes detective for the commonwealth, much of what he did was classified. He carried a concealed weapon and of late things had grown considerably more violent. Perhaps this mission in Haridwar would not be so difficult. No, he said to his reflection in the window, almost smiling at the absurdity of such a thought and the blue *pag* on his head, these things were never easy.

Taylor soon found himself wishing again he'd left India December 31st. Like most of the intelligence officers, he'd been given the choice to transfer either at the end of 1947 or in June of forty-eight. Though he had long tired of India, June would give him exactly ten years, but his decision had been more a non-choice at the time because he didn't really know where he would want to go—and because he'd just met Naija. Then two weeks into the New Year, there was an attempt on his life and it had affected him deeply. Now he just wanted out. And still, as he thought about this, the idea of leaving came with a faint tremor of apprehension.

The end of his tour in India should not be such an unsettling thing, he reassured himself, as he rocked along in the coffin-like privacy of his railway chamber. Once this mission was completed, he'd simply be transferred somewhere else, presumably Hong Kong or Singapore. It didn't really matter that much to him. Maybe that was what was unnerving. The change would reassert the seemingly incontrovertible solitude of his personal life—again the image of Naija appeared in his mind—and the lonely fate of an intelligence officer who had given his life over to his profession.

Taylor had never married and had all but purposely cut off contact with his family in Connecticut many years ago. His father was still living, but they'd communicated only once in the last five years. Actually it was a letter he'd never answered at the time of his mother's death two years ago. Thoughts of his past, his ancient past in the United States, sliced edgewise like a knife through his psyche. Pain for a thousand concatenated decisions welled up and dispersed again. There it was. The black seed he'd willfully swallowed when he chose to stay in England instead of returning home after six years of graduate work at Oxford. Now, an expatriate and longtime loner, he rattled northward to the remote edges of India to bring a halt to this "chain of souls," as Mountbatten had referred to it. Just the sort of idiotic thing India didn't need in its first year of independence, he thought, wondering again what might lie ahead.

Though it really was a short distance to Ambala, the trip would take nearly four hours for reasons westerners would never understand or accept. But Taylor had become accustomed to the frustrations of living in a country one hundred years behind, and he stared out the window of his private compartment with a derisive detachment as the panorama of paradox that was India rolled by like film from two different movies spliced together into one.

Now there was an expansive sugar cane plantation. Off in the distance lounged the domed mansion of some fantastically wealthy Indian prince. In the spring, the stillness of long afternoons on the lawn, sipping gin and tonic, encapsulated meditative timelessness.

Then it was a slow, rackety crawl through a crowded city where the morning rain had turned the streets to mud and a plethora of wandering homeless shit in public like dogs. Timelessness there was the bleak prospect of life in the trenches of endless poverty.

Inured by the cold decisiveness of his work, Taylor accepted things now that had once caused pangs of social conscience when he'd first arrived, like the Viceroy's sumptuous palace or the train station in Bombay.

Midmorning Taylor went forward three cars to the lounge for a cup of tea. Afterward, on returning to his compartment, he decided it might be wise to have the lounge bartender "top off the flask a bit" in preparation for the long day on the train. He grabbed his suitcase and headed back to the lounge.

Just as he entered the lounge car, an explosion shook the train with a violent lurch, throwing Taylor like a rag doll against a table and then to the floor, along with every other loose cup and plate and passenger in the railway car.

For ten seconds or more the forces of the train shrieking to a stop dominated. Taylor was climbing to his feet, turban askew, rubbing the side of his head where it had hit the edge of the table, when a conductor ran into the car coming from the front of the train. "A bomb went off three cars back," hollered the Hindu conductor in English to the ten people thrown in all manner of disarray across the lounge car. "The rear of the train is off the track. Several passengers have been seriously hurt. Please return to your compartments for a head count."

Taylor stopped the conductor as he proceeded through the car. "My compartment's in the car that was hit. Where should I go?"

"They'll be disconnecting the train one car back. That's where I'm headed. Stay here until I can find you another seat. Be patient; we need to get the injured on board and on to Ambala for assistance."

Further delay was the last thing Taylor needed. He blinked his eyes several times with an accompanying pain in his head, then sat down and tried to regain his wits. A bombing? Could it have been targeting him? There'd been so many bombings and so much violent since the first days of independence it was only extreme paranoia to think such a thing. Christ, he thought, he'd been damn lucky to return to the lounge when he had. This made him smile.

He opened the suitcase on his lap and withdrew an inscribed silver flask. He unscrewed the cap of the flask and, after gently swirling its contents, put his nose to the lip of the half-empty container. He took a deep breath of the bourbon fragrance to clear his head.

"Better top it off a bit, aye, James," he said aloud, raising the flask in the air to toast the memory of a long lost friend. He tipped it back over his head for a deep swallow. "That's what you call a real friend," he muttered to himself, "saves your life even after he's gone!" Taylor laughed with real relief, grateful for the fortuitous stroke of luck. He took another swig and with it came a sobering thought. He couldn't sit back and wait for the conductor when he might otherwise be using this incident to his advantage.

Taylor went to restroom in the car ahead of the lounge. He removed the blue *pagri* and changed from the *sherwani* and *churidars* into a lightweight suntan suit, then quickly shaved his chin and trimmed his beard into mutton chops linked by a moustache. He put on a red striped tie and combed some talcum powder into his hair and beard for some light graying. Adding a pair of wire rimmed glasses, he looked like an entirely different person. He patted the shoulder holster beneath his jacket and climbed from the train, making his way back along the tracks to the exploded car.

The railcar lay on its side blown nearly in half. There was no fire. Just violently twisted metal. Taylor's stomach tightened. A large swastika had been painted on the top of the car and was running off in bright orange rivulets with the rain. The next car up was off the tracks, but still connected to the one ahead of it. Men were working to open the damaged coupling and free the front of the train so it could move on to Ambala.

There were no medics on the scene yet, just railway employees plying the wreckage for bodies. Three severely injured passengers lay stretched out beside the tracks in the light rain. Several lifeless bodies were pinched within the exploded car. Taylor noted one badly disfigured corpse. It was a male Caucasian. The face and torso were mutilated. The lower part of the body was less damaged. Taylor fished the man's wallet out of his trousers and put his own, minus the cash, back in as a substitute. Then he pulled his blue turban from his jacket, dipped it in blood, and dropped it onto the mangled corpse. Three minutes later he was back in the lounge car where he would ride all the way to Ambala.

CHAPTER 4

By the time the Great Eastern pulled into the station at Ambala, it was no longer raining. Even with the delay caused by the bombing, Roger Taylor would have an hour and a half wait before his connection to Haridwar, which would take him another hundred and fifty kilometers to the southeast.

The injured were hurried from the train first, then the other passengers were let off. His head still aching from the fall, Taylor took his time and tried to mix in with the others leaving the train. Even in a crowd though, he stood out in India. Invariably a head above everyone else, his fastidious dress and distinctive looks only served to separate him from the natives, and if he were still being followed, he'd likely be noticed.

At forty-two years of age, well-tanned and slender, Taylor's most casual actions exposed a cool smugness inextricably tied to his good looks and intellect. Vain and aloof, he often drew glances from men and women alike. Despite his spending the first twenty-two years of his life in New England, he now passed for an Englishman and made no effort to alter that impression. His clothes, his mannerisms, his formal speech, all had been steadily acquired in his many years away from the States.

Taylor headed directly to a small English-style pub tucked in a corner at the north end of the Ambala train station. He took a table to himself against a far wall. A Hindu waiter arrived and took his order, a glass, two napkins, and a shot of vodka. When the waiter returned, Taylor asked him to stay while he used the vodka as a disinfectant to sterilize the glass. He didn't trust the cleanliness of any but the most high-class establishments. Beneath the watchful eye of the waiter, Taylor held the glass with one napkin and used the other, dipping it in the vodka, to sanitize the glass. He handed the waiter the glass wrapped in the dry napkin and asked for a gin and tonic. Whatever ire this might have kindled in the Hindu, it was dispersed by the excessive tip included with the fare when the waiter returned with the drink.

While Taylor sipped his gin, he slipped again into the pensive mood that had crept upon him earlier, prompted by the fact that he would soon be leaving India. He absently passed a forefinger across his mouth, lost to the soft, smooth contours of his lips and thoughts of the seemingly ancient history of his youth.

After a moment, he realized how deeply he was puzzling over the strange course of his life and how it all threatened to fit together. A wave of paranoia washed over him, and he scanned the shadowy room. An attractive young, Caucasian woman with shingled blonde hair and bangs sat alone at the bar with a drink. She was staring at him. His eyes dropped to his glass on the table. An old memory soured in his stomach.

The first fully conscious, adult decision Roger Taylor made in his life was during his senior year at Cornell. He was twenty-two and would soon graduate with a degree in molecular physics. When he returned to his home in Hartford for Christmas of 1927, he proposed, on Christmas Eve, to his childhood sweetheart Carolyn Williamson. He had just been turned down for entrance into the prestigious physics program at Cambridge. It had been his greatest dream to do his graduate work with Ernest Rutherford in the Cavendish Labs. He learned this disappointing news at Thanksgiving. Two weeks later he heard from Oxford, his second choice. He'd been put on the waiting list. Reluctantly, he decided to accept the offer from Princeton, his third choice.

Initially he had not planned to ask Carolyn to marry him until his graduate studies were completed, but now that he would be going to school so close to home, and maybe because his confidence had been given a good shaking, he thought marrying her might be the solution to the biggest distraction to his studies—Carolyn's beautiful form. She'd vowed to remain a virgin until they were married, yet with the engagement and a wedding set for June, she broke that vow New Year's Eve as her most loving Christmas gift.

Provision for the wedding proceeded steadily into spring. Then in May, he heard from Oxford that a spot had become available to him in the Clarendon Laboratory, a full scholarship in theoretical physics. Because his mother was English, the idea of going to school in England had always attracted him. He'd assumed acceptance to Cambridge all along, but now that he'd received word of this position at Oxford, it sounded almost as good as Cambridge and a better choice than Princeton. His resolute decision was that the marriage must be put off, and he would leave for England as soon as the situation allowed.

Taylor looked up from his drink uneasily. That was Carolyn Williamson sitting across the bar, eyes fixed on him. She wasn't really there. It was only his memory staring him down. Long ago he had forced her out of his life. And occasionally when he got maudlin, her memory would impinge upon him—but never before as a full face apparition. He put his hand to the lump that had risen on side of his head, wondering if he could have suffered a concussion. Within the spell of this unsettling vision, his mind raced back twenty years in time to the day he told Carolyn of his changed plans. In a flood of insight, he could see how that difficult conversation led, however circuitously, to this railway station in Ambala.

His first full day home after graduation from Cornell, and with the wedding but three weeks away, he went to talk to Carolyn. He brought roses, expecting the worst. Her mother greeted him at the door. Carolyn was down with a cold and in bed. Maybe it wasn't a good day for this, he thought. But if he didn't do it now, he'd never have the courage to do it again. He climbed the backstairs to the bedroom that had been Carolyn's as long as he'd known her. The door was open and the window curtains pulled back. The room was filled with sunlight. Everything looked bright and clean. Carolyn lay propped up in bed reading a book, not looking all that sick. She grinned hinting of guilt, then smiled grandly as he moved up close to her. She laid down her book, and he gave her a kiss on the forehead, then the roses.

"How are you feeling?" He knew what he was going to tell her would ruin her day, her week, her month.

"Oh, I think I'm pretty much recovered," she said, patting at the hair laying flat across her cheek and adjusting herself in the bed. "Mother thought with the wedding coming up, it might be wise to take an extra day to recuperate." She put her book on the bedside table and pushed the blankets away, as though she might be a little warm. Her gown was bunched up high on her thighs. She gave Roger a playful glance. They did have a luscious secret and this was only the second time she'd seen him since the New Year. "Things are almost ready. My mother and your mother have been working every free moment to get everything just right. God, this is coming on us fast, Roger. What do you think? Are you getting excited?"

What was exciting Roger was just beyond the hemline of Carolyn's gown, but with typical single-mindedness, he got right to the point. "Do you remember what our plans were before I got turned down by Cambridge?"

She looked at him through narrowing eyes. "What?"

"What were our plans before I got turned down at Cambridge?" he asked slowly

and deliberately. Did he really love this girl? he wondered. She did look beautiful there in her bed of white, sparkling of womanhood in the sunlight, the light fragrance of her body thrilling in his nostrils all the way down to his balls. He tried to deny the carnal forces and keep to his purpose. "What were our plans then?" he repeated with a shrug, trying to play it down.

She suddenly pulled up the blankets, laying back and tucking herself in up to the neck. "You're having second thoughts?"

"No, no, I desperately want to marry you, Carolyn." He'd begun to sweat lightly. "It's just that I received word from Oxford. I've been given a position for this coming fall. I thought maybe we should just put it off a while."

Carolyn suddenly sat upright. She glared at him, as vicious a look as he'd ever seen. He thought for a passing instant that she'd snapped. Then she let go. "There's no damn way anyone in your family or mine will ever let you put the wedding off." She was seething.

"Carolyn, don't you remember? We talked about this before. I said if I should go to England for school, I must go alone."

Carolyn gripped the bunch of roses like she wished it were Roger's neck, then flung it at him. One flower struck Roger in the face. Petals from the others scattered like bits of an exploding red balloon all about the room.

"Get out! Get out you bastard!" Carolyn hollered at him with an echoing of deep and convoluted emotion, saying much more than words about the embarrassment of a postponement and the hollow meaninglessness of the precious gift of intimacy she'd given him months before. He understood every tiny nuance of her despair. The web they'd spun between themselves tugged at his mind, his heart, and his groin. For a second, he felt the full weight of the Freudian cloak. It hung about the walls like black drapes, printed with the shadowy faces of his parents and hers and others down the ancestral line.

Vainly he sought to brush away the stringy shreds of web and push back the black drapes to let the light of reason back into the room. "Please, Carolyn, you must understand. I'm not trying to hurt you. What's good for my career will only be good for you in the long run. This isn't just going to school. It's taking part in history. I'll be working under F.A. Lindemann. There will be tremendous pressure for me to achieve at Oxford. It's an opportunity of the highest order. The life there is different. The demands more intense. I can only take full advantage of this if I am alone. I know you know what I'm saying is true."

Carolyn rolled over, face into her pillows, and began to sob. Roger placed his hand on her shoulder. "It will only be three—maybe four years. It will go fast. I will be back." As he spoke, he felt the warmth of her body beneath his fingers. In vivid flashes of memory, he remembered the three times they'd made love and the intimacies they'd shared.

Carolyn swung her arm out, pushing him away. "Don't you ever touch me again," she spit at him. "Four years! You selfish ass, get out. Get out of my sight."

There was nothing he could say. He turned away and with reluctance and relief, quietly made his way out of her room. All the way down the stairs and out the front door he felt the filmy strands of web dragging off his shoulders, pulling faintly and snapping as though he made his way out of a dusty old attic.

When Taylor lifted his eyes, the ghost across the bar was gone. He brushed his hand lightly across his forehead and back over his hair as though trying once again to clear himself of the last remaining filaments of her memory. He pulled on the leaden coat of his undercover self and headed to the gate for the Eastern Express, but not before stopping at the bar and asking the tender to top off his flask for the remainder of the trip.

CHAPTER 5

Throughout the second leg of the trip, Roger Taylor tried to focus on the task before him. He knew very little about what lay ahead other than what Mountbatten had told him. A woman in Haridwar was fasting to death as a stand against partition. The perception of this in India was entirely different than it would be almost anywhere else in the world. Fasting had been an accepted religious practice in India for two thousand years. Gandhi had used it off and on as a political tool, even threatening to fast to death on several occasions to get what he wanted.

Known as *santhara,* fasting to death was not considered suicide. The Jains regarded it as a method of spiritual purification, the highest form of dying, and had advanced it into a science. According to what little Taylor knew, the fast in Haridwar had been going on for at least twenty-one days. Ten days without food puts a severe strain on one's system. Twenty results in an extremely weakened state. Thirty starts taking out bodily organs, and forty is day to day until the end. If the real drama of the fast hadn't started yet, it wouldn't be long.

How appropriate, thought Taylor with irritation. His last official business in India, a continent greedily swallowing lives—one might say a nation committing mass suicide—would be trying to stop a death fast. He shook his head at the irony. The amount of death he'd seen in the last eight months had changed him and what he thought of his time in India. At first it had been an adventure to an entirely different world, a romance of sorts. Now it felt like some blundering kind of escape that he was only beginning to understand as it came to an end.

The train's route ran southeast along the jungled foothills of the Himalayas. The weather was coming in from across the mountains and it began to rain again—harder than it had earlier in the day. Rattling along in his compartment all alone, staring out into the gray afternoon, Taylor could almost imagine he was back at Oxford riding the Waterloo

Railway to a rugby match in Twickenham.

He'd gone to Oxford in the fall of 1928 with the intention of becoming a physicist at a time when physics was truly blossoming. Important discoveries were coming one after another—Plank, Einstein, Heisenberg, Bohr, Schrödinger. There was talk of splitting the atom and atomic energy—even a massive bomb. Instead of taking part in that adventure at the cutting edge of science, here he was chasing down lunatics at the fringe of civilization.

Graduate school hadn't worked out at all like he'd thought it would. He'd had trouble with the lab work. It didn't come easily for him and eventually frustrated him. But he loved England and life at Oxford, and to the disappointment of his father, an engineer, he switched from physics to philosophy midway through his second year, meaning it would take him four and a half more years to get the doctoral degree he sought.

This new life left Carolyn far behind. He didn't go home for Christmas that first year, but promised to be there for part of the summer. That didn't happen either, upsetting his mother almost as much as Carolyn and her family and generating a long critical letter from his father. He didn't care, even when Carolyn wrote to tell him she couldn't wait any longer. He was pushing aside his past like old clothes in a closet. And it wasn't just pulling away from a broken relationship. It was the attraction of the highly stimulating academic life at Oxford and the alluring coterie of the intellectual elite. The old life didn't fit him any more, and there was no sense trying to squeeze into something a size too small.

He never regretted his decision to stay in England, but he knew he'd handled the split with Carolyn poorly, cloaking his first sexual experience with guilt. The situation was further twisted in his mind when he received a transatlantic phone call through a radio link from his mother in the fall of 1929, telling him that Carolyn had been killed in a car accident. His mother begged him to come home for the funeral. He said it was impossible. This twist became an inextricable knot when he learned two months later, in a letter from a classmate at Cornell, that the night of the accident, Carolyn had been seen at a party alone and that she'd been drinking in excess. Already heavily armored with a large ego, Taylor took this last piece of news with frightening detachment. It served as the final ingredient in the psychological recipe of one Roger Taylor, intelligence officer. From then on, everything revolved about him and his work—if it hadn't already.

The recollection of that long distance phone call, when his mother finally labeled his self-indulgence, triggered another memory, his fall from honor in her eyes.

In the days after Roger announced the postponement of the wedding, the Taylor household held a quiet yet building tension. Had Roger's father, Theodore Taylor, been questioned, he might have admitted he was more concerned about his son's education than the marriage, but he never let those feelings be openly known. His mother, Mary, voiced her disapproval immediately then resolved to keep any further thoughts to herself. That is, until Roger's sister Katherine, who was also a close friend of Carolyn's, told Mary about the intimacies the couple had shared. That was the setting this one tense evening when Roger prepared to excuse himself from the dinner table a few minutes after Katherine had already done the same.

Their usually lively family meal had been thick with shrouded anger and silence. Not a word had been spoken between the parents and son since Katherine left the table. Roger felt certain his mother knew something. He'd already assumed Carolyn had revealed too much to his sister, and now he suspected the worst.

"Mother, do you mind if I leave the table?" Roger asked rising from his seat, the smell of an over-cooked pot roast still in the air. "I've got some reading to do upstairs."

Mary, who had willed herself to silence through the meal, turned to him with a look that dropped him back into his seat. As that moment held, she nearly shook with anger. It was difficult for her to speak at all. But she did. She laid her fork on her plate with a distinct clink and softly, but unevenly, asked, "Roger, do you ever expect to marry Carolyn?"

Roger hadn't been reprimanded for anything he'd done since high school. He'd been a model son and a brilliant student. Soon he would be leaving for Oxford and a career as a scientist. But he was on the spot now. And the real question was the one behind this one. "Yes, Mother, of course I do." He looked to his father for help. There was none. "You know what my plans are. I've made it clear how important I feel these next few years in England will be. Were I staying in the States, as was my plan, I think an immediate marriage would make sense. But at Oxford, the situation will be too new. The pressures too great. I think it would be unfair to Carolyn to begin our life together with these types of stresses."

His mother's stolid expression changed not one bit with his words. "I'm fully aware of your reasoning and your plans for school, Roger, but what about Carolyn?" She paused to measure her words. "And the commitment it seems you have made to each other?" With the word **commitment** *still spinning in the air between them,* *full of all its awful intimate suggestion, Mary looked him right in the eye without the slightest warmth or compassion.*

Roger's worst fears were now confirmed. His eyes darted to his father, somber detailer of huge edifices and bridges. His father, the one who had always supported, even pushed him along in his pursuit of mathematics and physics, had turned to stone. Like the face of a building, his window eyes only reflected back to Mary's.

Were Roger a child he might have tried to deny or avoid his mother's quiet rage, but it was clear that as a man he must own up to his deeds. As he spoke, however, he found himself sliding on his honor, justifying instead of admitting. "Mother, it seems that somehow you've gained access to matters private to Carolyn and myself." His eyes dove twice to the table as he spoke, barely able to face his mother. "What discretions we may have enacted were between mature and consenting adults."

*His mother glared at him. "Mature and consenting adults? You are but twenty-two. Carolyn is not yet twenty-one. And these actions are **not** just between you and Carolyn. They include us all—both families and our friends." Her voice gave way to a slight tremble, but she gathered herself with focusing anger. "What if things should change while you're in England? What does that do for Carolyn? Might these discretions, as you call them, not cheapen her in the eyes of another suitor? I don't think you can tell me you've thought of that at all. I don't think either of you understands the deeper significance of these—these lower-class **indiscretions.**"*

Roger understood it now. It was his mother's honor that he'd damaged. And he knew this was not a little thing. It hurt him that he'd hurt her. But he didn't appreciate her attack. Again he looked to his father.

"Don't look to your father," his mother snapped. "He knows how I feel." There was more to what she said than Roger wanted to understand. There was something between his parents here also. Something old. Maybe from their courtship twenty-five years before.

Roger tried to meet his mother's now fiery eyes. He imagined he saw pain through the glare. He needed to respond somehow. All that came was dumb apology. "Mother, I'm sorry if this has hurt you, but I love Carolyn and I do intend to marry her." Even as he said the words, he wondered if they were true.

She must have read his mind. "Maybe it's just that I want you to know something, something you or any man"—Roger felt an unseen tremor pass through his father—"may never understand." The sharpness of her anger had been replaced by some deep psychological resolve. "Roger," she continued, "I know you're a bright and intelligent young man, but there are a few things that I know that you don't. And if I may be so presumptuous, let me try to give you some insight into what it means to be a woman.

"I realize your study of science has drawn you away from the Good Book and

religion. Maybe you don't even believe in a god anymore. I don't know. Still, there is a profound wisdom in the Bible. And because I know no other way to express my feelings, I point you to a passage in Genesis. It's immediately after God has seen that Adam and Eve have covered their nudity. And He knows that they've eaten of the fruit from the Tree of Knowledge. God punishes them both, but it's His punishment of the woman that makes my point. I may not know this word for word—maybe you should read it, but God says to the serpent who induced Eve to eat from the tree, 'I will put enmity between thee and the woman, between thy seed and her seed; it shall bruise thy head and bruise his heel.' Then God says to Eve, 'I will greatly multiply thy sorrow and thy pain in conception, and in sorrow thou shall bring forth children.'

"To me, Roger, there is much suggested in these words, much revealed about the tension that exists between a man and a woman and their intimacy. I can't say I understand all that is implied—you know that I'm no Biblical scholar—but that enmity between the serpent's seed and the woman's and that sorrow in conception make the woman cautious in her relations with a man—when the man is not so cautious with a woman. That enmity and that sorrow are the cost of knowing and, as God intended, deliberately cloak a woman's desire with a tension and a reluctance— in a way that a man simply can not know."

With these last words, Mary Taylor got up from the table and disappeared into the kitchen. Usually she tended to be quiet and let the men lead the discussion, but not this night. And after she'd left, neither Roger nor his father said a word.

Now, as Taylor thought about that night twenty years ago, he realized he had always wanted his father to somehow support him through that confrontation. Maybe it was correct for his father to remain quiet while his mother spoke her piece, but later that night or even in the days to follow, it would have been nice to get a comment of some sort from his father. Maybe not a condoning of his relations with Carolyn, but maybe some hint of compassion or understanding. Like emotion from a stone, it never came.

These were sobering and unusually dark recollections for a man who had spent much of his adult life channeling a self-serving intellectual aloofness. And now, as the uncertainties of his future allowed these types of doubts to seep through his normally impregnable pride, the second-guessing he'd trained himself to expel from his thoughts began to drip like a leaky faucet in the back of his mind. The challenge of India, as he'd seen it long ago, appeared an exile. A hiding. A running away. His switch from physics to philosophy—a failing. His destiny in science—one he'd felt so strongly that morning in Carolyn's bedroom—

a delusion. Even the circumstances that puzzled together into his career in India seemed like some cruel practical joke when viewed from his present perspective.

He could only wonder now how it had come about that he'd allowed himself to drop out of physics. The struggle in the lab was part of it, but that could have been overcome. More disturbing was that his quest for the hard edge of physical science had been transformed into a sophomoric indulgence in philosophy's syllogisms and the lure of metaphysics. Surely part of the blame could be placed on Doctor W. Y. Evans-Wentz, another American who studied at Oxford.

Doctor Evans-Wentz returned from his travels in the orient with what he was calling the "wisdom of the snowy ranges" in the mid-1920s. In 1927, he created quite a stir when he published, through the Oxford University Press, a translation of the sacred Buddhist text the *Bardo Thödol* under the title of *The Tibetan Book of the Dead*. Many rejected it boldface as little more than eastern folklore, yet Oxford gave Evans-Wentz a Doctorate in the Science of Comparative Religions in 1931, Taylor's third year of graduate work.

How differently he viewed the mystic doctrine of the East today, thought Taylor, recalling the excitement and discussion prompted among his contemporaries when Evans-Wentz came to Oxford to speak in the spring of 1929. Now, after living ten years in the culture that had spawned the Buddhist philosophy, he could only consider Tibetan metaphysics a relic from two thousand years past and a fad he'd chased in his youth. The bare truth was, as his father had said all along, real knowledge was applied mathematics and engineering. Knowledge that enables mind to conquer matter by putting a roof over your head, food in your stomach, and electricity at the touch of a finger.

The writings of eastern religion had long been reduced to literary tropes for Taylor, just as Christianity and the Bible had been since his introduction to geometry in high school. Even at Oxford, when these eastern litanies were new to him, he didn't so readily embrace their mysteries as did many of his friends. Deep within, he honored a balanced skepticism, all the while trying to penetrate the eastern meanings, intrigued and wanting to find them true, but also dying for a cold hard fact. This study was the intellectual origin of his switch to philosophy and also his career in India.

As a result of Oxford publishing Evans-Wentz's book, the university sponsored an exchange of scholars with the East in the Michaelmas term of 1929. The first to arrive at Oxford was a Tibetan high priest from Nepal, Tenzing Chogyam. The lama, whose official title was Rinpoche or "precious one," was there as much to study the ways of the West as to impart to those at Oxford the philosophy of the East. As it worked out, Tenzing Chogyam, often called simply Rinpoche, turned down an offer to lecture. He preferred a less formal gathering and instead set up a ten-student seminar that met one night a week for two hours. There would be no papers, no examinations, no grades.

Taylor was one of the ten selected to participate in the two-term seminar. Several of his friends who had delved into Evans-Wentz's work were also chosen for the group, including his best friend James Nielsen. Nielsen was an Etonian from London and two years younger than Taylor. They met the first week of Taylor's first term at Oxford. Nielsen was entering his third year as an undergraduate.

As a graduate student, Taylor spent his first year at New College, and Nielsen's living quarters were directly across the hall from Taylor's. The day they met, the younger man thoroughly enjoyed taking the older American on a first-class tour of the university and the town of Oxford. For the first three weeks, James called him "the Yankee," and they became great friends during their time at New College together.

Interestingly enough, Taylor began studying physics and left with a doctoral degree in philosophy and history. Nielsen began in philosophy and was awarded his degree in religion. Taylor could still hear their arguments on metaphysics echoing up and down the staircase where all decently heated discussions took place. James was part of the reason Taylor never went home during his time at Oxford. James would take him into London whenever there was a "vac." James had grown up in London and knew its every in and out. There was probably no better place in the world for a couple of students to pal around and gather balance to what they learned in books.

In their second year, November of 1929, it was discovered that James Nielsen had leukemia. By the time of the diagnosis, the disease had progressed beyond hope. God willing—neither of them believed in a god—James would live long enough to complete his degree—seven more months. Taylor learned of this only three weeks after hearing of Carolyn's auto accident. What grief he'd suppressed for her death, doubled in his outpourings for James. And in many ways, the ordeal of

James Nielsen's disease would include the most important lessons Taylor would learn in his time at Oxford.

The train came to a stop for no apparent reason. This happened more often than not during any excursion on a train in India, and there was no telling how long the delay might last. Taylor reached for his suitcase and opened it on his lap. He removed the silver flask that had saved him from the bomb. Affectionately he clasped the container in his hands and rubbed a finger across the three words and ten numbers engraved on it: Oxford 16, Cambridge 15, December 12, 1928. It had been James Nielsen's. He was a top rugger and had nearly single-handedly won that rugby match in 1928. It was the only time Oxford beat Cambridge in all the years Taylor was there. James had given it to Taylor his last day, "only because I've gotten full use of it—that is, drinkin' and braggin' about the match." With those words running again through his head, Taylor took a healthy slug from the flask. The American whiskey, possibly his last attachment to the States, was really, if he'd admit it, only for show. He took another, longer drink, thinking to himself maybe he'd fall asleep.

Taylor woke in the dark. He thought he'd heard something. He remained still, lying on his side, eyes wide open, his heart pounding. Ever since that day in Karachi, he'd known he was being followed. A minute passed without a sound. He sat up and peered into the dark recesses of the shadowy room. All seemed as it should. He lay back down and closed his eyes. Suddenly someone was on him and a garrote was wrapped around his neck, the leather thong's large knot on his Adam's apple.

For an instant, Taylor thought this was the end, then his entire body convulsed. The man on top of him was much smaller, and Taylor's surge threw him off balance. Taylor turned sideways on the assailant who still held onto the garrote, twisting it into Taylor's throat like a noose. With one hand, Taylor tried to get his fingers beneath the thong. With the other, he swung wildly at the attacker. His hand struck the night stand. Blindly he grasped for anything his hand could find. His fingers wrapped around the oil lamp.

Clawing at the thong around his throat with his left hand, gasping for air, he raised the lamp with his right and swung it viciously at the man now on top of him. The shade flew off, oil sprayed across the room, and the glass lamp thudded harmlessly against his assailant's side. Taylor's life flashed before him. He bucked again with an adrenaline rush, inadvertently slamming the lamp back into the table, breaking it into pieces. Instinctively he clenched a piece of broken glass in his hand

and focused all his effort into flailing with that shard at his attacker's face. Ten, twenty, thirty times he struck at the shadow on top of him, missing entirely or hitting a shoulder or an arm. Then he caught his face. How satisfying a micro-second, feeling that glass rake deeply through flesh. The garrote loosened for an instant. Taylor slid two fingers beneath and gathered in a breath of air. Then the thong was tight again, strapping his left hand to his throat. He bucked with all his might and threw himself and the assailant from the bed. They hit the floor and rolled, stopping side by side. The attacker clung to the garrote as frantically as Taylor fought for air. For one brief instant he saw his attacker's bloodied face. His eyes reflected all the terror Taylor felt. Then he struck again with the glass. And again and again. Gouging, clawing with the glass shard. Blood seemed to come from everywhere. Gouging, gouging...

The sudden jerk of the train starting into motion woke Taylor from the dream. It was a dream he'd had many times since that night in January when a RSSS operative, Gopal Dutta, tried to kill him in his sleep. Sweating heavily, Taylor took his bearings. Yes, he was still on the train to Haridwar. Yes, it was daylight. The rain had stopped and the train was moving again. Rubbing his neck with his left hand, he looked down at his wet right palm. Three raw, jagged scars were testimony to the attack that had haunted him ever since.

CHAPTER 6

It was after five that evening when the Eastern Express trundled into Haridwar. As the train slowed to a crawl, it passed through a crowded neighborhood at the south edge of the city. Mud huts with tin roofs. Barking dogs, barefoot children, chickens, cattle wandering free. It could have been any place in the subcontinent. Roger Taylor opened his suitcase and withdrew a map. He alternately peered out the window and glanced at the map, getting his bearings and appraising the place where he would be working the next few weeks.

The city sat at the south end of a long tight, heavily forested Himalayan valley. The Ganges came rushing down this valley and slowed into a river at Haridwar, gradually widening as it flowed south across the length of India, some twenty-five hundred kilometers to the Bay of Bengal.

In the 1840s and 50s, the British supervised the building of a dam at Haridwar to divert a portion of the river into a canal and irrigate the land south to Allahabad. A small town at the source of India's most sacred river was transformed into an agricultural center. Sugar cane and tobacco became highly successful cash crops. The entire region underwent a boom in the 1920s due to the bountiful man-made delta that stretched hundreds of kilometers south and west across the vast plain of the Uttar Pradesh. Now the city had almost 40,000 inhabitants and sprawled out along the Ganges for five kilometers and up into the hills behind to the east.

Haridwar was also one of the oldest and most sacred cities in India, with a history dating back to the age of Buddha and beyond. "Haridwar" meant gate to Hari, the Hindu god also known as Vishnu or Krishna. This region was literally the cradle of Hindu tradition. What was said to be Vishnu's footprint was enshrined in a temple on the east bank of the river. Aging devotees came to the sacred city to die, believing that this location was the gate to Nirvana and that the river there could purify and cleanse the soul. This prevailing sense of the sacred in Haridwar meant little to Taylor. It was merely something he'd have to deal with.

The train came to a stop at Haridwar Junction. It was little more than a ticket office and some covered benches in the middle of town. After eleven hours of travel and the whole commotion of the bombing, Taylor climbed from the train ready to find a hotel, a good meal, and a drink—in a town where alcohol and eating meat were banned. Though he felt relatively confident he had not been followed, the bombing had deepened his paranoia, and he decided on a circuitous route to his hotel when he flagged down a taxi.

With Tibet just over the Himalayas to the east and Nepal a few hundred kilometers to the south, a significant portion of the city's mostly Hindu populace was Mongolian and Nepalese. Taylor judged the taxi driver to be Nepalese, but addressed him in Hindi, the most common language in the region. The driver responded with complete fluency, and Taylor asked him if he knew a moderately priced hotel at the north end of the city. The driver said he knew one and headed north on Station Road, Haridwar's main thoroughfare.

It was fast approaching sunset, a traditional time for prayer in India, and the shops and bazaars all along the crowded street were pulling in their awnings and closing down. There were very few cars, many motorbikes, a random wandering cow, lots of bicycles and rickshaws and *tongas* weaving through two full lanes of mixed traffic. The city itself abounded with Hindu shrines, all brightly painted in reds, blues, and yellows, many depicting scenes from the Hindu mythology. Taylor had seen too much of this kind of artwork during his time in India and had long tired of it. But Haridwar took this to an extreme. It had been heavily commercialized because of the income created by its many holy festivals. There was something on every corner, an image of Ganesh, a painting of Kali, a thirty-foot statue of Vishnu. It seemed almost cartoon-like to Taylor, some kind of child's fantasy land and religious theme park rolled into one. He wondered if he could keep his cynicism properly submerged for a week or more.

Sitting in the back seat of the small taxi, Taylor opened a conversation with the driver. "I've heard that there's a woman in town who's on a long fast?" he asked, as though it were only a passing interest.

The driver took a second to appraise Taylor through the rearview mirror. "I've heard of this fast, sahib. But it's of little interest to me."

"It was mentioned on the train. I was curious what you might know."

"What this woman does is no business of mine."

"I heard she was fasting for Gandhi."

"You know more than me."

"Do you know where this woman lives?"

The driver glanced over his shoulder at Taylor. "No, I stay clear of fanatics." Then he made a sudden right turn off Station Road toward the river and into the oldest part of the city. The street was narrow, little more than stone and compressed dirt. Some of the buildings were over a thousand years old, stone temples with painted domes, inlaid tiles, and intricately carved arches. Even to cynical Taylor, it was picturesque.

They took Rishkesh Road to within a block of the river. The buildings there were pressed right up to the river's edge. There was a boardwalk along the bank with stairs proceeding into the river so bathers could dip into the sacred waters. During the coming holy days these *ghats*, as they were called, would be filled shoulder to shoulder with worshipping pilgrims.

"The Hotel Hari Ganga, sahib," said the driver, as he pulled to a stop before a flat-roofed, three-story building, painted bright red with white trim. "The best deal in town."

As Taylor climbed from the taxi, he asked again. "You have no idea where I might find this fasting woman?"

The driver shook his head, seemingly irritated by the question. "Why would you care?"

Taylor ignored the question and put twice the fare in the driver's hand. He stood out front of the hotel and watched the taxi speed away in a cloud of gray exhaust.

Taylor entered the lobby of the Hotel Hari Ganga and took a casual look around. It was run down and clearly a second-rate lodging. He had no intention of staying there. Still he approached the desk and paid two weeks in advance for a room on the second floor. He went to the room and took his shaving equipment from his suitcase. He went down the hall to the bathroom and proceeded to shave. Before the recent beard, he had long maintained a thin, clipped moustache. Today he shaved clean. He was tired of the disguises and knew they would only get in the way for this job. He could only hope that his ruse at the train bombing site had put anyone who might be following him off the trail.

Taylor returned to his room, changed into a white shirt, khaki slacks, a light khaki bush jacket over his shoulder holster, and a gray, wide-brimmed fedora that he had to knock into shape after being flattened to fit into his suitcase. He put his map of the city in his jacket pocket and descended with his suitcase to the first floor stairwell. With a glance over his shoulder, he exited through the stairwell window into the alley behind. It was dark, and he quickly moved through the alley and into the cramped city streets.

He peered down Rishkesh Road to the river. Little lights, like fireflies, were floating on the water. He walked down to the edge of the river to get a better look. The boardwalk was barely a meter above the level of the river, lapping at the bathing steps. The buildings along the river were lit up like Broadway and reflected in wavering colors on the water's surface. At close range, he saw that the fireflies on the river were candles mounted on little paper boats. Every evening after prayers, the river was filled with them, floating downstream—devotees' prayers to be answered.

Taylor was less impressed by the beauty of the scene than his concern for what this same setting would look like in two weeks when the spring festival began. He turned away from the river and headed by foot to the Queen's Imperial Hotel and a room that had already been arranged for him.

CHAPTER 7

Roger Taylor had become accustomed to good taste and first-class accommodations during his time in Asia. And it never ceased to surprise him how many top rate hotels existed in the far reaches of India. The Queen's Imperial Hotel in Haridwar was no exception. Built at the same time the canal was put in, the Queen's Imperial was, not surprisingly, excessive. Except for the ancient temples, of which there were literally scores, this hotel was arguably the most impressive building in the city, and Taylor was genuinely pleased when he entered its elegant lobby.

He didn't sign the register until he'd seen his suite and checked the linen. The Queen's Imperial was clearly not the Hotel Hari Ganga. Still he scrubbed and cleaned his bathroom before he unpacked his bag. Then he bathed and dressed for dinner. Tonight he wore a white dinner jacket and a black bow tie with black slacks.

The hotel restaurant was recommended by the concierge, so he decided to try it. He entered the restaurant at eight-thirty and was seated immediately. Most of the tables were empty. The waiter was Hindu but spoke English. The menu offered both Indian and western cuisine. Taylor ordered the duck and a gin and tonic. The waiter said that though meat was served there—and nowhere else in Haridwar—alcohol was not served in the dinning room, but was available in the downstairs lounge as a special service to those staying at the hotel.

The meal came quickly and Taylor ate only a small portion of what was served, just the breasts of the duck, most of the potatoes, none of the vegetables. Such was the amount of food left on his plate, the waiter inquired if there had been something wrong with the meal. Taylor said the meal had been excellent and asked for the bill. When the bill arrived, he paid it with a generous tip and retired to the basement lounge for a drink.

The Imperial lounge, like the hotel, was targeted for wealthy westerners.

It had the feel of an English club with photographs of England on the walls and cricket bats and polo mallets mounted above the bar. The low ceiling created a dark subterranean feel, and the place was empty except for the bartender, who had a patch over one eye and appeared to be Mongolian, and a young Caucasian couple in evening clothes at a back table, leaning in close over their drinks, whispering and laughing. Taylor took a seat at the bar and ordered a gin and tonic. He watched the one-eyed, barrel-chested bartender go about his work with a cigarette dangling off his lower lip. When the man placed the drink in front of him, Taylor addressed the bartender by his first name.

"Chuluun, perhaps, you have some information for me," he said in English as he paid for the drink.

The swarthy, rather menacing looking bartender had a thin, stringy black moustache that had a gap in the center and an outcropping of about thirty long hairs on his chin. He stroked these chin hairs as he took a moment to measure Taylor. The pause was long enough for Taylor to wonder if he had the right man. "Roger Taylor?" asked the bartender, taking one last drag from his cigarette before crushing it into an ashtray on the bar. Taylor nodded. "Word I got was you didn't make it to Ambala."

"I didn't." Taylor smiled. "And I'd like it to remain that way. Now what do you know about this woman who's fasting? Where can I find her?"

"In a neighborhood almost directly east of here."

Taylor withdrew the map from the inside pocket of his dinner jacket. He opened it on the bar. "Can you show me?"

The big Mongolian peered down at the map, then using a stubby index finger traced out a wide circle on the map. Taylor looked up at him. "Can you narrow it down a bit? Like a street, a cross street, maybe a house number?"

Chuluun looked off uneasily, revealing a long, upraised scar running down the side of his bull-like neck.

"You have nothing more for me?" There was irritation in Taylor's voice. He took a swallow from his drink.

"Only that the woman is fasting and that she's beginning to attract attention."

"That's it?"

Chuluun shrugged. "Sir, you now know all that I do." Taylor just stared at him. It wasn't the first time an intelligence connection had been less than what he'd expected. "Maybe you should talk to Chadi," said the Mongolian like it was the last thing in the world he wanted to say. "He knows where she lives."

It had been a long day and Taylor had no time for this kind of incompetence. "Maybe you should talk to Chadi, whoever he is. And get exact directions from him and get them to me." Taylor swilled down the rest of his drink and pushed his glass across the bar. "How about another?"

The bartender gave Taylor a sour one-eyed look, then took his empty glass. When he placed a second gin and tonic on the bar, Taylor paid for the drink and took it to a table in the corner of the lounge.

As Taylor sat there sipping his drink, the long day of rattling in the train gradually eased out of him and he began to relax. Though he was badly irritated by his contact's attitude, the good news was they thought he'd been killed in the bombing. This caused him to sit back with a smug little grin and ponder what lay ahead. If talk of the woman was in the streets, maybe he could find her himself. Then the question was what should he expect from this woman?

Despite his history with Carolyn Williamson, Taylor had always had an easy time with women. Maybe that was why Mountbatten had chosen him. He was so confident of his good looks and charm he felt he could divest any woman of her defenses with the cast of his eye, a few clever lines, and a smile. He always played the gentleman, polite and aloof, but that was it—that was the flaw he treated like a strength. It was all a game to him. Apparently his mother's lecture twenty years before had made little impression on him. He'd never been close to marriage since Carolyn, though the affair with Naija—once again he saw her striding naked across his apartment in Bombay—had taken him to the edge of his emotional limits. It had only been two days, and he still couldn't believe he wouldn't be with her again.

At Oxford, he tended to feast on the townies. He even set his friend James Nielsen up with his first "all night" date. His religious beliefs matched his approach to love; he was an atheist. The years in India, however, had taken him places he'd never intended to go. Prior to Naija, he'd succumbed to a habit of high-class Hindu prostitutes. He hadn't known a white woman in over five years.

The prospect of trying to talk this woman out of her death fast seemed almost entertaining to him now, as he sipped his second drink in the secluded comfort of the Queen's Imperial lounge. Of course, from his present perspective, he could really have no idea what kind of situation he'd find tomorrow, but for the time being, he basked in the gentle caress of good gin and thought back to those heated metaphysical dialogues that punctuated his days at Oxford when Evans-Wentz's secrets of the snowy ranges were all the rage. Allowing the delusion, he expected something of the same when he confronted the fasting woman.

"Still I can't get myself to believe it." Twenty-four year-old Roger Taylor stood up amid the seminar group. It was the eighth meeting of the informal gathering led by the Rinpoche from Nepal, Tenzing Chogyam. Roger leveled his eyes at the small brown man at the opposite end of the table, dressed in an intricately embroidered saffron-colored jacket and a small round silk cap. "If I've understood you correctly," he said, pausing a moment to get everyone's full attention, "you say you're an initiate to the most profound knowledge of all—immortality?"

Up to this point in the series of meetings, Roger had been unusually easy on the Rinpoche. This particular evening, however, as the group idly chatted away in a manner Roger could only consider philosophic trifling, he decided to try the depth of this none too convincing eastern sage.

"Through rituals and oral traditions passed down through the ages, from guru to guru, you have acquired insights that allow you a will in the workings of the wheel of life and death." Roger's tone was just condescending enough to put everyone in the room on edge. "If you choose, upon your death, through your yogic training in the art of dying, you may either escape entirely from the cycle of life and enter upon a higher level of existence; or, if you so desire, you may be reborn again in the womb of your choice, coming to consciousness in the material world in a new body with some or complete memory of your past life and lives." Roger paused again, allowing the other students to appreciate that he was now on the attack—something they all knew well and had seen in other classes. "I just don't believe that's really possible, Mr. Chogyam. It makes a nice fairy tale, but reincarnation, especially the way you describe it, sounds much too simplistic to me."

The Rinpoche smiled easily, as though expecting all along that such a challenge would arise. He sat in his chair with one leg folded beneath him and the other flat-footed on the seat, so that the knee was up in his chest. He didn't rise to speak. "Yes, Mr. Taylor, you have understood me correctly. Except that it is in no way simple or simplistic. What you have described is the highest attainment for any man or woman on this earth, release from sangsara, the eternal wandering of the unenlightened soul. And mastering the Tibetan art of dying is extremely difficult. It involves techniques of meditation that one must practice every day of his or her life.

"And this material world you speak of," continued the lama, clearly relishing the young man's challenge, "it's just as illusory as the dreams you have at night. All of what I speak of is more easily conceived if you learn to think in that way."

Roger stepped back to the room's wall. "You say this," he rapped heavily on the dark walnut paneling that ran from floor to ceiling in the cozy little study tucked away in the west tower of Oxford's Bodleian library. "This is what dreams are made of?" He grinned defiantly. "Not mine, Mr. Chogyam. Not mine."

Again the guru smiled affectionately. "Until the dream ends, all dreams are as real as this." He pronounced **this** *while spreading out his arms, palms upraised. "For the unenlightened, death is but the end of a soon to be forgotten dream and the beginning of another. For the enlightened, it is an end to these dreams and a conjoining with the Clear Light."*

"Come now, Tenzing. You're evading the real question. We've sat through weeks of seemingly directionless and unorganized gatherings. You don't even prepare for these so called seminars. You just rattle on with quaint stories and descriptions of ancient rites. Albeit many of your anecdotes have been extremely interesting in themselves, and the rituals and various naming schemes contain a certain aesthetic. As for elaborating some profound truth, however, I just don't see it. There is no proof. There are no empirical facts. I may as well believe in Santa Claus as your conjoining with the Clear Light."

James Nielsen sat next to the Rinpoche and across the length of the table from Roger. His discomfort with Roger's attack showed in his face. He had been through this many times himself with Roger, all the way to its logical end, a simple matter of faith. Especially since he'd been diagnosed with leukemia, James had become the group's most outspoken advocate of yogic philosophy. But today, for the moment anyway, James remained quiet.

"I don't find it strange that you have trouble with these ideas, Mr. Taylor. You have been taught differently all your life," replied the Rinpoche with infinite courtesy. Tenzing Chogyam was no charlatan. He was a very wise and intelligent man of forty-eight years. Though he had only acquired use of the English language in the last three years, he was now sitting in on graduate level lectures in all subjects including mathematics and physics. "But the truth of it is that the wheel of life and death has been the belief of almost all civilized men of all times and cultures. Only in a small corner of the world, for only a few hundred years, have men believed that consciousness ends with death."

"Maybe so, Mr. Chogyam, but that small corner of the world is also the vanguard of modern civilization—the most advanced and knowledgeable society of all time."

The lama wagged his head as in doubt of Roger's last statement. "But they fear death and love their material world too much."

"And you welcome death?"

"I have trained for it all my life. I welcome it as a warrior welcomes battle." Tenzing Chogyam allowed an increasing seriousness. It was something he'd rarely shown in the class. A lighthearted grin would more often than not accompany his most profound statements. But this knowledge was sacred to him. He enjoyed teaching it. Even more he rose to defending it. "To the yogic master, dying becomes an ecstatic act."

"If you have trained for this all your life, Mr. Chogyam, then maybe you can tell me what death is? What is it like on the other side?"

Tenzing's eyes twinkled with delight at the question, but he maintained his seriousness. "Can you imagine, Mr. Taylor, what it might be like to be submerged in dark and murky waters, running out of breath, not knowing which way is up or which way is down? With all the reason that is in you, you hold your breath until your lungs are about to explode, swimming this way and that because you are afraid to stay still. That is what the other side is like to those who are not initiates to the Great Knowledge. Unending panic before the unknown."

"And—that's it?"

The guru's smile was full of light. "A dream is often referred to as the shadow of death, Mr. Taylor. It is the reflection of mind in its own mirror. All but the mirror is illusion. Reject the illusion. Know the reality for what it is. Forget thy self. Take that deep breath. Conjoin with the waters."

Roger did take a deep breath, but it was one of aggravation. "Very poetic, Mr. Chogyam, but it seems to me that with lungs full of water this initiate only completes his drowning."

"No, that's the art of dying—letting go. Learning to breathe."

"You mean become a fish," interjected Harry Lanyard, another Londoner, gathering in a few chuckles, but not from Roger.

"In a sense, Mr. Lanyard," eased Tenzing, taking no offense. "The meditations and chants of the yogic masters are, at heart, breathing techniques. When perfected, these techniques can put one in an out-of-body state, much like a trance. The experience seeks the voiding of thought. Forgetting of the self. Mind upon mind. It's literally practice for the experience of death when the self fragments. One must learn how to swim without an ego. To become the selfless fish."

"And this art of dying can be taught?" asked Harry.

"Through dedicated study. Yes."

"Immortality can be taught?" spat Roger, skeptical of the way these metaphors were being tossed around.

*"Yes, absolutely, Mr. Taylor, if you want to look at it that way. It's more accurate to say the yogic aspiration is not so much for immortality as it is melding with eternity. The **Bardo Thödol** is a manual for the art of dying. It contains navigational charts for the mind lost in the fathomless sea. A chart leading to the liberation of one's soul to the eternal bliss of nirvana."*

"Sounds like only so much more language to me. I don't believe it—not without proof that death is more than nothing. Can you prove any of this?"

The lama became still, a seeming quiet ire. All eyes focused on him. His silence hung. The eyes turned to Roger. James Nielsen still chose to remain silent.

Roger stepped up to the table. He put both hands down before him and looked right into the lama's eyes. "Because there is a genealogy of experiments, an epistemology of empirical data, and a chain of logical extrapolations, I can believe in the invisible atom. And I can believe the mystic science of wave mechanics and electromagnetism because I can see practical application of that knowledge. Electric lights work just as they are designed to. Radios work just as they are designed to. This is an engineering of the invisible. And this is proof. We have nothing but hocus pocus about transcendental states or the migration of souls. Mr. Chogyam, all I have is your word."

At this point, Todd Thomas, a Rhodes Scholar from New Zealand, who sported a large walrus moustache, interrupted. "Just a minute, Roger," he poked, "you're confusing me." Todd was Lindemann's brilliant assistant in the university lab, the top of the physics class.

"That's not hard, Todd," sniped Harry Lanyard. "You physicists haven't gotten around to tackling any of these really tough questions yet."

"'Well," continued Todd, "are we talking physics or metaphysics?"

"When you get down to splitting atoms, Todd, I don't really think there's a difference," tossed in James, apparently hoping to break the tension for Tenzing's sake. But it was really Roger's tea that was boiling.

Roger raised his voice. "Drop the semantics, gentlemen. Plain and simple, I can't take the leap of faith. Maybe the purpose of this seminar should be to come up with a concrete proof of reincarnation. How about that, Rinpoche? Can we come up with a proof?" Roger's tone didn't make it clear how seriously he meant this.

"The proof is in the certainty that comes with enlightenment, Mr. Taylor. It can be no other way," said the lama measuring each word as he spoke, neither piqued nor provoked. "I could tell you of the disciple of Buddha, Sobhita, who could recall five hundred former lives. Or I could tell you of the many tulkus I have known who have told me of their past lives with such elaborate detail there could be no doubt of their veracity. Or I could tell you of teachers I have had that literally explained the process of death to me as it happened to them in their last living moments, speaking ana-

lytically as each veil of physical reality dropped away. But that again is only my word. I have no magic tricks for you. I can not make the dead rise. No string of rational arguments can prove that which is beyond logic. Proof of life immortal is in your deepest memories, the softest suggestions of your dreams, your subtlest intuitions."

"That's not good enough," said Roger flatly. He was verging on being very obnoxious. "I want you to bring us back something from the so-called other side."

The guru did not respond. James Nielsen took the cue. "Roger, think what you're asking? If anyone could prove reincarnation empirically, then there would be no question. We'd all believe in it. The only proof is in the initiation, and you must first suspend your skepticism long enough to enter into that initiation, which we students here have barely even begun to do. Besides, I don't recall that the class description mentioned anything about requiring full enlightenment to pass the course."

This brought some laughter, but the humor was getting to Roger in another way. He bit his tongue to keep from getting really rude. James took the chance to diffuse things further. "Rinpoche, how long does it take to become a yogic adept?"

"Each student requires his own time, Mr. Nielsen." Tenzing Chogyam knew that James was seriously ill and had great admiration for him. "Some might take a lifetime. Some, perhaps, two or three lifetimes. Some might need less than a year. For others, it may never come."

Roger stepped back from the table, seeming to punctuate the lama's last remark. He'd have walked out if James hadn't been there.

It was ironic. For all the closeness of their friendship, Roger could not have been more different than his friend James. Roger was dark and moody, analytic to a fault. James, the rugger, was fair-haired and once, before the onset of the illness, a ruddy outdoorsy type, not so tall as sturdily built. He looked and acted more like the American with his easy manner and turn for humor. Where Roger would probably have dropped into deep depression with the discovery of a fatal disease, James had maintained much of his usual calm and levity. Even on this tempting topic of reincarnation, where the dying youth could easily have gone overboard with false hopes, he took a soldier's stand against the bleakest odds of all and somehow measured his acceptance of the new philosophy.

Roger didn't say another word the rest of the seminar, frustrated by his own show of emotion and suddenly worried about the extent his friend was embracing the mystic doctrine.

On his way out of the hotel lounge, Taylor selected a large bill from his wallet and placed it on the bar right in front of the sullen Mongolian bartender. "I'm going to retire to my room for the night. Should you hear from Chadi or anyone else who can tell me where this woman can be located, I would be happy to double this." Chuluun made no acknowledgment one way or the other. "I'm in room 234. I'll be up until midnight."

The long train ride had tired Taylor more than he realized. The two gin and tonics were quickly establishing that. He returned to his room at ten-thirty and fell asleep fully dressed on his bed with the light on. Some unknown period of time later, he was awakened by a rough knocking at his door. He sat up startled, hardly aware of where he was, immediately thinking of the night he was attacked in his sleep. That he was fully dressed confused him further. Another salvo of knocks had him standing and cursing as his consciousness and irritation increased. "Who's there?" he called out.

There was only more knocking. Taylor checked his watch; it was just past midnight. He moved cautiously toward the door, his hand on the Beretta beneath his jacket. "Damn it, who's there?" he called out again, abruptly pulling open the door, dead set to explode. But before he could get another expletive out, he recognized the one-eyed bartender holding a moon-faced Nepalese street urchin by the arm.

"This is Chadi," said Chuluun, putting out his palm. "I'll take the rest of that money now, Mr. Taylor."

"Yes, yes," stammered Taylor, slowly fitting things together, surprised Chadi was a youth. God, he felt awful. His clothes were sweaty and wrinkled from sleeping in them, his brain cloudy from alcohol and travel. And why did this man bring the boy right to his room? "What is it this boy can tell me?"

"Everything you need to know," replied Chuluun. "He says he can draw you a map to the woman's home."

The victim of many false leads in his time, Taylor looked suspiciously at the boy. "How do I know this isn't a trick?"

Chuluun sneered. "I work downstairs four nights a week. If this boy is an imposter, you can find me any time you want."

Taylor reluctantly let them in. The boy babbled something in Nepalese. Taylor recognized a word here and there, but for the most part couldn't understand the boy. He found a piece of paper and a pencil and put them on the nightstand beneath the light. The bartender stood back with his hands on the shoulders of the boy. When Taylor looked at him, he said, "First you pay, sahib, then he draws the map."

Taylor rubbed his chin, still suspicious. Wasn't this damn bartender working for British intelligence?

The bartender said something to the boy. The boy answered. The bartender spoke. "If you don't trust a map, Chadi says he can take you to her home tonight. He lives very close to her."

Taylor knew he was going nowhere tonight. He took his wallet from his back pocket and retrieved a bill. "Have him draw the map," he said as he handed the bartender the rest of his pay.

The Mongolian accepted the money and prodded the boy ahead to the table. As the boy took the pencil in hand, Chuluun turned to leave.

"Oh, no you don't," commanded Taylor, moving between the man and the way out. "You brought the boy. You leave with him when he's done."

Taylor, who certainly would have struggled to prevent the husky Mongolian from going anywhere, received no protest. Meanwhile, the boy was concentrating on the lines he was drawing on the paper. It took him a long time to generate a rather sketchy and suspect map. Taylor brought out his map and had Chuluun show him how they fit together. It seemed the woman lived in the east portion of the city away from the river.

Not wholly satisfied with the map, Taylor led the bartender and the boy to the door. As they were exiting, the boy spoke over his shoulder directly at Taylor in Nepalese, saying the same thing over, three or four times. Not understanding, Taylor merely nodded. Then just before he closed the door behind them, the boy called out in uneven English, "Pipal, she is the woman Jesus."

CHAPTER 8

Roger Taylor returned to his bed attired in silk pajamas. He lay there quite a while unable to sleep with the words *Pipal, the woman Jesus* stuck in his head. When he did finally sleep, it was fitful and dream filled. Just before dawn, he woke from an unusually vivid dream and could not fall back to sleep.

Though it was only five-thirty, Taylor rose and ran a bath. In the tub, he tried to remember the details of this last dream. The setting had been Victoria Terminus during the war. The train station was jammed wall to wall with travelers of every variety. Many were soldiers, wounded and bandaged. Many were Indian natives, sickly and crippled. The place looked more like a hospital ward than a train station.

Taylor knew V.T. like the back of his hand, but in the dream, he was totally disoriented with no idea why he was there or where he was bound. He looked up at the board of train arrivals and departures, hoping for some hint as to which one he was there to meet or take, but the information was written in a foreign alphabet that he couldn't decipher. Just as his anxiety verged on panic, he spotted the Rinpoche Tenzing Chogyam some distance away, dressed in his embroidered jacket and silk cap. Relieved to see a familiar face, he called out to the Rinpoche, but the noise and bustle was too much. The little man with the thin, stringy mustache and chin hair, looking strangely like a smaller version of Chuluun the bartender, was quickly swallowed up in the throng. As he called out one last time to the lama, the crowd in front of him parted and in the opening was a small dog, cut in half at the midsection. Bleeding and dragging entrails behind, the mongrel pulled itself across the opening with its front paws, snapping and snarling at Taylor. Unable to move because of the crowd behind him, Taylor watched in horror as the dog sank its teeth into his ankle.

That was when he woke.

The situation of being lost in V.T. was disconcerting enough, but seeing Tenzing Chogyam in the dream and not being able to reach him struck Taylor deeply and hung in his mind like a dangling detail in a contract signed years ago. He hadn't seen the lama since those days at Oxford and had no idea where he was or even whether he was still alive.

The presence of the mutilated mongrel dog in the dream was almost as disturbing. It brought back an old and forgotten memory of a seemingly inconsequential moment in his life. Taylor would usually push aside unsettling dreams, attributing them to rich food or drink. Today he found himself reflecting on an incident that occurred in 1938.

He was in Burma, then a dominion of the British Empire. World tensions were running high and war seemed inevitable. The British began a steady buildup of military forces in the Far East. Burma was part of this, and Taylor was acting as a liaison between the Burmese government and the incoming military officers.

On this particular day, Taylor attended a military review in Rangoon. He spent most of the morning on the balcony of a Burmese palace, overlooking the city's main thoroughfare with a Burmese prince and a British general, while brigades of soldiers and military vehicles passed below. Afterward, a bit worn by his duty as mediator between two fairly disagreeable individuals, Taylor decided to walk to his residence to clear his head rather than take a taxi.

Somewhat out of sorts, he walked in the same direction taken by the military procession. As the street was widest at the palace and narrowed as it progressed through Rangoon, he eventually caught the tail end of the procession as it snaked through the city to the British garrison at the edge of town. The presence of the military, especially the large artillery moving through the streets, drew the locals out to watch. In the more congested parts of town, this greatly slowed the procession and caused all sorts of hazards for both the soldiers and the onlookers.

Taylor, absorbed in his own perambulations, gave little thought to the situation, except that it impeded his progress back to the hotel where he was staying. He was considering another route to the hotel, when a shrieking yelp sounded out of the crowd. His first thought was that someone, possibly a child, had been struck by one of the many military vehicles rolling through the packed streets. He immediately began scanning the area for signs of an accident.

The cluster of people directly between him and the procession parted, and in that opening, a mongrel dog, cut in half just above the hips, was pulling itself along the cobblestones using only its front feet. It seemed that in the excitement the beast had run beneath the wheels of a caisson. The narrow wheel and the enormous weight had severed the animal cleanly, leaving the rear end laying motionless in the street, while the rest of the dog, motivated by the final throes of shock, yapped and snapped this way and that as it crawled out the final minutes of its life.

Much to Taylor's dismay, the dog, dragging bloody strands of intestine behind, made directly for his legs. Snarling and spitting in pain, the dog was certain to bite anything, animate or not, that came close. With only the slightest hesitation and no where else to go, Taylor strode forward with one step and kicked the dog in the head, sending its half-body across the opening in the gasping crowd. All attention focused on the dog, lying on its side, still alive and panting heavily, one eye closed by the blow to its head. The dog's single working eye caught Taylor full on, seemingly funneling its entire being into one last pleading request—please, finish me off. Though Taylor felt this fully, as if he really had known the dog's thoughts, he denied such sentience in an animal and abruptly turned and broke through the crowd instead of mercifully putting the dog out of its misery. Later on that same day, he had terrible regrets about that moment with the dying dog. In a very maudlin alcoholic state, he imagined the dog's situation as similar to James Nielsen's when he was dying of leukemia. The next day he felt this was a ridiculous comparison and never thought of it again.

That this incident from his first year in Asia should surface in a dream seemed somehow poignant to Taylor. He was not superstitious, but he did believe dreams were telling. And though the interpretation of dreams was not something he considered an exact science by any means, he had read portions of Sigmund Freud's work and accepted that dreams were valuable glimpses into one's subconscious, often revealing latent desires and unresolved conflicts. But with more pressing issues on his mind, he let the vivid dream go as nothing more than a curiosity.

Taylor dressed in a suit and tie for breakfast. He had a single egg—poached, two pieces of rye toast, and a small glass of orange juice. Afterwards he took his time with two cups of tea with cream. Halfway through the first cup, he began to focus on the job ahead. Usually there was a lead man to observe the situation. In this case, it seemed his contact was an ass and his lead man a child. He did not like working this way, coming in pretty much cold, but by his second cup of tea, he had the necessary impetus to get on with this day that he'd been dreading all morning.

After breakfast, he changed into casual slacks, put on his shoulder holster and his gray fedora and his short-sleeved bush jacket. He'd made up his mind at breakfast to use a very direct method with the woman. Disguises and subversion were out of the question. He'd take the pose of diplomat and be as straightforward as possible. If she weren't simply a crazy zealot, which was certainly possible, he would use his charm to disarm the woman. In many ways, he was like Mountbatten. His combination of poise, good looks, and intelligence worked as a subtle lubricant, making things happen that might not otherwise. He took an apple from a bowl in the lobby and set out with the hand-drawn map in his pocket. "Pipal," he said aloud to himself. It was the name of a variety of fig tree that grew in Asia, the same kind that Buddha sat beneath at the moment of his enlightenment.

The low, gray clouds of the previous day were gone. The sun was almost directly overhead and the sky, set against the wooded Himalayan foothills, was a bright, transparent blue. Taylor walked the entire way across town, as much for the exercise as to familiarize himself with the city. It was warm and would get warmer, but it was still a relief from the humidity of Bombay.

Haridwar, like most of the cities of India, was a mixed adventure for the senses. The sharp acrid odor of urine, human sweat, and burning cow dung—the universal fuel of India's impoverished—was a constant in the streets. Here and there this was broken by delicate whiffs of perfumes and incense, jasmine, sandalwood, or warming curry. The dusty streets and earthen buildings, the blank sense of poverty, which could seem so bleak to a westerner, contrasted with the brightly painted religious artwork and statuary that caught the eye everywhere, on the street corner, for sale in the bazaars, hawked by street vendors, even painted on the homes. But above all, the daytime streets were noisy—a non-stop multilingual jabbering, punctuated by sudden shrill yelps, intermittent chanting, the call of vendors, a random car horn, the faint tinkling of tiny talismanic bells, the clattering of wooden wheeled *tongas*—a steady dissonance of everyday activity that died off once the sun went down. Taylor had learned to ignore it all. Instead he noted landmarks and street names, trying to get his bearings and a feel for the street life of a city he'd never been in before.

The walk was slightly uphill, and after a while, offered an impressive view of the Ganges spreading out to the southwest across the vast flat plain of the Uttar Pradesh. Taylor never took the time to appreciate the sight. He was looking over his shoulder, but for things at closer range. He'd make a sudden turn to the right, followed by another turn to the left, trying to determine if he were being followed. For all the effort, however, it was difficult to tell one way or the other with all the activity in the streets.

When he was within a few blocks of his destination, he took things a little slower. The neighborhood was middle class. The streets were wider, not so busy, and even contained a few fruit trees and small gardens. The homes were not little tin covered shacks, but small, well-constructed stone or wooden houses, painted in brilliant colors, squeezed in next to each other like poor man's townhouses. Most were upright two-story homes, two rooms on the ground floor and a few small bedrooms upstairs.

Even before he had identified the house of interest, he could see a large cluster of people ahead, sitting off to one side of the street beneath the outstretched branches of a neem tree. As he got closer, he saw that the group, fifty or sixty in number, was a mixture of downtrodden pilgrims and children, closed in around a young blonde woman in a simple white dress of homespun *khadi*, sitting cross-legged on a rug, talking and gesturing with her hands. He eased up to the back of the group, standing off to one side, watching from a distance as though he might be a tourist who'd happened up the street.

The group was right in front of the house that Taylor was looking for. But because of the woman's youth and apparent energy, it didn't seem she could be deep into a fast, and he wasn't quite sure if this was the woman he sought or not. He was just far enough away that he couldn't hear all she was saying, but she spoke in fluent Hindi and, as he gradually understood, she was talking about techniques for fasting.

For the starkness and simplicity of the setting, there was a sense of casual dignity to the gathering like an outdoor Sunday school class. Several children sat close to the young woman, quietly gazing up at her. Taylor saw that one of them was Chadi, the boy who had given him the map. The others in the group, all very old or invalids of some sort, listened intently like it was a lecture or a sermon. And despite his own deep cynicism, Taylor found himself drawn in and intrigued by the scene, all along wondering if the young woman, who was very pretty, almost elegant in her white dress, could be Pipal. He couldn't help hoping she was.

Shortly after Taylor arrived, maybe ten minutes, the young woman bowed her head and led the group in a Buddhist prayer. Then she rolled up her rug and entered the house behind her. The children leaped up and ran off into the street. Some of the older people also simply got up and tottered away, while about half the group assembled in a line that began just outside the doorway to the house, apparently hoping to have a personal audience with this woman or, perhaps, someone else inside.

If this really was the protest that he was there to investigate, Taylor's rough opinion was that it was not a chain of souls, but a chain of lost souls, and he seriously doubted that the situation was as volatile as Mountbatten feared. Hardly.

Without any show, Taylor took a place at the end of the line behind a short, stout old woman. Every bit of the woman's body was wrapped within a plain, blue cotton *sari*. The loose end or *pallu* was thrown across her right shoulder and draped over her head from the left like a scarf. Only her wrinkled brown face pinched out from beneath the hood created around her head.

Taylor had a talent with languages and for recognizing the various ethnic groups in diverse India, and after a while, speaking in Bengali, he asked the woman where she was from. She had barely looked at him until he spoke and she seemed surprised he would address her at all. "I am from Calcutta, sahib," she replied curtly, also in Bengali, appraising him from within the shadow of her *pallu*.

"Was the woman who just led the prayer Pipal?" Taylor asked, ignoring her clear suspicion, trying to be as disarmingly friendly as possible.

The old woman nodded, still appraising him closely.

"And this line is for people who would like to talk with her?"

The woman again nodded, clearly uneasy with Taylor's sudden flurry of questions.

"Have you had the opportunity to speak with her?" he continued like it was nothing.

The old woman turned her head to one side as though thinking. Her skin was very dark and wrinkled. She had a large face and features with heavily lidded, brown eyes, thick black eyebrows above and a series of pendulous bags below. She gazed at Taylor with a certain aged wisdom, then said, "Yes, I've had an audience with her on two occasions."

"I am curious. What is she like?"

"So many questions," said the old woman, finally becoming more engaged, peering out at him nose first, looking a bit like an old witch. "I am curious too. I know why these others are here. Why are you in line?"

Taylor gave a completely straight answer. "My name is Roger Taylor. I'm here on behalf of the British government. I want to make sure there is no incident."

The old woman frowned. "Mr. Taylor, this young woman is teaching us how to fast. There will be no incident here. You are more likely to cause a problem than any of these pilgrims."

Judging from the state of the others he had seen, old or infirm or very young, Taylor knew the woman was probably right, but he dismissed her concern with an easy smile. "I won't cause any problems. But I thought this woman was conducting her fast as a statement against partition."

The old woman frowned again and looked at Taylor through narrowed eyes. "Pipal is certainly displeased by partition, but her fast is not against this that she can not change. It's as much a demonstration fast for those of us who have come to Haridwar to finish our lives as it is a fast to stop the ongoing violence that partition has caused."

"And this demonstration fast, as you call it, how long will it last?"

The old woman looked around at the others in line, seemingly self-conscious of her conversation with this white man. "Pipal began the fast with a simple statement—for every act of violence between any of the ethnic groups, Sikh, Muslim, or Hindu, she would fast two days—until the terrorism ends or it causes the end of her life."

"I see," said Taylor, thinking of the futility of such an action. The worst of the violence was over, but the little incidences and random disturbances could go on indefinitely. "And where does this fast stand now?"

"Pipal is in her twenty-fifth day." The woman paused. "With one hundred and ten more days of debt to the continuing acts of violence."

"So it has become a death fast?"

The woman nodded solemnly. "And there will be others to continue the fast and to account for the days that have already been promised and those that continue to accumulate."

At this point, Taylor noticed Chadi coming up the street with three other children. The barefoot boy's eyes caught his and lit with a smile. Taylor reached into his jacket pocket for the apple he'd gotten after breakfast and tossed it to him. The boy caught it with both hands, took a big bite, then dashed down the street with the others trailing after him. Taylor turned back to the woman. She had been watching him the entire time. "What's your name, kind woman?"

"Sumitra," she said with reluctance.

"Sumitra, why are you here in line?"

"Some come to pray for Pipal," she said. "Some come to be healed."

"You mean she has some kind of medical training?"

"No, it's just that she has a special knack with herbs and sick children. She can make them better with just a touch of her hands. One child who was lame can now run like those boys in the street."

Taylor couldn't help thinking of Chadi's parting words the night before—*she is the woman Jesus.*

"Some come for the *darshan*," said the old woman.

"And that is?"

"To enter into the radiance of a holy person. To bask in their presence like sunshine."

Taylor nodded.

"And some, like myself," continued the woman, "come to join in the fast. I've asked Pipal twice now to put me at the top of the list of those who will follow her."

"And this fast drew you to Haridwar?"

"No. I came here a month ago to die, Mr. Taylor. Like many of the people who stand in this line, I had no intention but to let go of the burden of life. Now I'm learning a way to do this with dignity and purpose," said the woman with more feeling than she'd yet shown.

"So if I may ask again," said Taylor, "what is Pipal like?"

"She is very smart and kind to a fault. And not yet eighteen years-old."

"Why would such a young woman enter into a death fast? It seems awfully extreme to me."

"You do not know this woman, Mr. Taylor. She was going to school in England, but returned to India when independence was declared. She spent several months at Gandhi's Satyagraha Ashram on the Sabarmati River, then moved back here to her mother's home to teach the art of fasting and one day open a hospice for those who come here to Haridwar to die." The woman's inhibitions were rapidly retreating. She spoke with pride, as though Pipal were a very close friend or her own daughter.

"When Gandhi was assassinated, it hit her very hard. She decided to fast a few days to replenish her depleted spirit. Two days later she pushed her goal to a week. Then, saying she'd reached higher council, she announced to her mother that the fast would continue as long as the violence did.

"The idea of passing the fast on came when the debt to violence reached sixty days. A despairing pilgrim told her she was too young and capable to die, and asked if he, older and less useful, could not take on her burden. Pipal declined, but the man, still intent on joining the cause, said he would begin a fast the day hers ended. The next day another visitor made a similar statement. Pipal had never intended to draw others into her fast, but Haridwar has long been a place for the old and infirm to come to die—and these people were also the first from outside this neighborhood to come pay their respects to her. Instead of fighting it, she understood that this might be a good thing for certain individuals and simply said that only one fast would take place at a time and that she would create a list to determine the order."

Squatting on his haunches in the shadows cast by the houses, making his size and presence less obvious, Taylor continued to draw information from the old woman. "You said Pipal has been schooled in England. How is that?"

Sumitra smiled, exposing her dark and missing teeth. A brown stain from chewing betel nuts ran down a crease at the right side of her mouth. "It was her father's wish. He was an Anglo and an officer in the British army, but he died eight years ago. Her mother, Areena Kaur, was born Hindu and lives here in this house on his pension. She's a fine woman with a saint for a daughter." The woman clasped her palms together and lowered her eyes, then looking up at Taylor said, "I'm not sure what they will think of you."

"It will be fine. There will be no problem," Taylor replied, quite intrigued by the story.

"Pipal's mother is the gate keeper. You will have to get by her," the woman told him. "Some days fifty people might pass through. Others none are allowed in at all. As the fast progresses, I'm sure visitors will be severely limited. Today Pipal seemed strong and spoke for longer than she has in several days." Two pilgrims came down the street and got in line behind Taylor. "The visits end at sunset when Pipal retires for prayers." Sumitra looked down the length of the line. "Not everyone who is in line will see her today. I've been coming here a week and, as I said, have gotten to see her only twice."

The line moved very slowly, each visitor spending ten to twenty minutes inside with Pipal. Hours passed and the sun was just beginning to set when Sumitra entered the small two-story house. Taylor would be next. As he had gathered from observation and speaking with Sumitra, gaining an audience with Pipal occurred in two stages. While one well-wisher spoke with Pipal in the back room, the mother would usher the next in line to a seat in the front room. Thus everyone waited with Areena before they were taken in to see Pipal. This allowed Areena to speak to each person individually and tell them the conditions of an audience with her daughter.

Some period of time after Sumitra went into the house, an attractive middle-age woman escorted an old man leaning on a walking stick to the door to leave. The woman was a native Indian but she was dressed as a westerner in a long gray skirt and a simple white blouse with her black hair pulled back in a tight bun at the back of her head. She appraised Taylor quickly and spoke in English. "We have taken the last visitor of the day, sir. There will be another opportunity to visit tomorrow or perhaps the next day."

After five hours in line, Taylor had no intention of leaving without an audience of some kind. "My name is Roger Taylor. You must be Areena Kaur. Please, if not your daughter, may I speak with you a moment," he said stepping into the doorway before Areena had a chance to close the door. "I've come on behalf of the Governor-General in New Delhi. He wishes to pay his respects to Pipal."

Areena couldn't disguise her feelings. "Pay his respects to my daughter?" she repeated full of skepticism. Her pronunciation was clear and held only the slightest accent. "Why does this seems so unlikely to me?"

"We have concerns for her safety," replied Taylor, taking a glance into the sparsely decorated front room. There was a small table with an oil lamp on it, an old divan, and two high-backed cane chairs. The floor was stained wood and partially covered by a *coir* mat, woven from the fiber of coconut husks. The walls were painted dark green, making the modest room seem even smaller than it was. "These are troubled times in India," said Taylor. "There are those who might not agree with the sentiments of your daughter's fast."

"We have only received the support of others, Mr. Taylor. Your concern is unnecessary." Taylor noticed Areena wore a cross on a chain around her neck. "There's no one here to be feared. I'm more afraid for my daughter's treatment of herself than I am of radicals." She studied Taylor a moment. Her eyes were large and sad. "Your presence here offers more of a threat to my daughter than anything in Haridwar."

Taylor didn't try to defend his position. But enough had been revealed in what she'd just said—*I am more afraid for my daughter's treatment of herself*— to make him think this woman could be his best ally—if, indeed, he decided stopping this fast merited his time.

Areena stepped away from the doorway intent on closing the door, but Taylor took a step forward so that she couldn't. "Please, madam. Just a few more moments with you. Your angst is obvious. I want the opportunity to gain your trust."

Areena glared at him. "Trust does not come from forcing oneself in. Please step away. I will talk with Pipal this evening and determine if she is willing to receive you. I will give you an answer tomorrow."

"We can give him an answer today." The curtain that served as a door to the back room lifted. The young woman Taylor had seen speaking outside appeared in the doorway. "Let him in, Mother."

"Pipal, I can take care of this."

"No, Mother, it's fine," said Pipal with a softness to match her beauty. "This man is someone I would like to talk with." Her voice was clear and confident. Taylor could hear the English education in her elocution. He came through the doorway and she came all the way into the room. Sumitra, two black eyes set deep within the cavern of her *pallu*, was right behind.

In the dimly lit room, dressed entirely in white, Pipal seemed to give off a soft luminance. She looked Taylor in the eye and smiled as though greeting an old friend. "Roger Taylor, my name is Pipal." She put her palms together and bowed her head. "I am pleased that you would take the time to come to my humble home."

Taylor had met many important and powerful people in his life. He'd experienced personalities both strong and subtle. He'd felt an individual's presence change the atmosphere in a room like flicking on a light. And he felt this now, overwhelming so. Involuntarily he put his palms together and gave her a proper bow.

When his eyes lifted to meet hers, she seemed to peer right into him. Her beauty was as much a part of it as was the sense of peace in her voice and the placid depth of her eyes. Her face was oval like her mother's and her skin was a lighter version of the same dark tint. But her hair was a sunlight blonde, long and worn free, hanging in waves over her shoulders nearly to her waist. Her cheeks blushed rose through the tan of her skin, and her eyes—her eyes were large, again like her mother's, though a pale, pale starry blue.

But it was something more than her stunning looks that Taylor was feeling. She must have been a fit woman prior to the fast; the twenty-five days had her very thin, but not gaunt, and her being glowed with the radiance fasting can create in the spirit of a true believer.

Taylor had come to India well aware of the ancient culture and the mysteries that Evans-Wentz brought back to the West. He had maintained a stiff pessimism regarding it all from early on. Yes, the stringy-haired saddhus and ash-streaked mystics who could be found anywhere in the subcontinent were to be given a certain measure of respect, but they were not otherworldly in any profound way other than their ascetic life. But something in this woman was different and penetrated Taylor's cool confidence in a way he was not expecting.

"I'm here on behalf of Governor-General Mountbatten," he said quietly, daring to look into the depth of her eyes. "His lordship wants to express his concern for your health." Her appearance, her pure radiance, distracted him. He wanted to stare at her. His eyes dropped again.

"You may tell his lordship," replied Pipal, "I appreciate his concern." Her tone suggested she fully understood the deeper political implications of the sentiment. "I wish he were as concerned for the health of all the people of India."

Before seeing her, Taylor, admittedly, had entertained the possibility that she might be unbalanced. But that was not the case. From her first words, he had felt the clarity and strength of her mind and her convictions and a maturity much greater than her seventeen years. "Lord Mountbatten is concerned for all of India," he said stiffly. "That is part of the reason I'm here." The words seemed heavy and meaningless as he said them.

"And how is that? To convince me that partition was a good thing?"

This was not the discussion Taylor wanted for today. He could not defend partition. "It was what was necessary and not all the doing of England."

"I fast because of what it is doing to India now, and I fast because I know it will forever scar this region and these people. The creation of an east and west Pakistan separated by the new nation of India is a recipe for disaster. A mutual dislike between Muslims and Hindus has turned into a raging hatred that may never be soothed."

Taylor could not dispute this. "But partition has already happened, and the worry is that your protest will add heat to a pot that is already boiling over. Lord Mountbatten believes it's time to let this be—not stoke the fire."

Pipal smiled. It enhanced the Caucasian in her features. "So you are really here to stop the fast?"

"Yes, I am," said Taylor, glancing to both Areena and Sumitra to measure their response to this admission. Sumitra was too deep within her cloak to read, but Areena lowered her eyes in acquiescence. "India does not need another Gandhi right now."

Pipal's face lengthened with seriousness. "Please, Mr. Taylor, there can be no other Mahatma. My fast is not to emulate, but to honor the Great Soul, to further his philosophy and to serve as a reminder to the people of India that we have let him down." Her face seemed to change chameleon-like with her mood. Now as her passions rose, it was her Indian blood he saw subtly disguising her father's ancestry. "His vision was all Indians united, regardless of race or creed or class. What we have now is segregation, something that heightens our differences, increases the tension. Partition is an insult to the Mahatma's life work, and the hundreds of thousands who have died as a result are only further stains upon his lost dream."

"Do you believe another death will help? Truly, Pipal. Gandhi may have been able to use the threat of a death fast to quiet the people of India, but how can you possibly believe that you can do the same?"

"If my fast gains no audience, then the second fast will, Mr. Taylor. If not that, the third. We will eventually be heard—and the violence stopped."

The conversation was going further than Taylor had intended for a first visit. Retreat seemed a better response for now. "I may not understand your means, Pipal, but there is no arguing that your sentiment is noble. Please forgive me. I only wanted to introduce myself, not upset you," he said bowing humbly. "I've taken enough of your time today. Besides, I believe it's time for your evening prayers."

Pipal's eyes softened immediately. "Mr. Taylor, I'm not upset—only expressing what I believe in passionately. As much as you might want to dissuade me from my fast, I want to convince you—and Lord Mountbatten—of its necessity." She was very young, but her thinness in certain lights could accent the shape of her skull and make her look and seem older than her years. But now she glistened with youth like a flower greeting the morning sun. "I will feel slighted if you don't visit again, and perhaps we can delve this subject a little more deeply."

"I would like to come again—as long as I am entirely welcome." Though Taylor said this to Pipal, it was clear this was also addressed to

Areena—and Sumitra. He turned to both of them. "I don't want to cause trouble for anyone." Sumitra's dark eyes said nothing. Areena again turned her eyes downward.

"There will be no trouble, Mr. Taylor," said Pipal. "And you won't need to carry a gun next time you visit." She placed her palms together, bowed, and said a soft, "*Namaste*," then returned through the curtain to the back room.

This left Sumitra, Areena, and Taylor alone in the front room. Pipal's final remark hung uneasily in the air. Taylor hesitated a moment, then bowed to each woman and walked out the door completely baffled by what had just transpired and wondering how Pipal had known he carried a sidearm.

CHAPTER 9

It was the dinner hour when Roger Taylor began the long slow, downhill walk from eastern Haridwar to the Queen's Imperial Hotel. The streets smelled heavily of burning cow dung, and a thin brown layer of its acrid haze lay over the city. Further off, a crease of pink stretched across the western horizon, casting the wide, flat plains in mauve and causing the distant irrigation canals and holding ponds to shine silver like pools of mercury. To Taylor, the scene expressed the bitter essence of India, a contrast in utter poverty and subtle beauty—much like what he'd just experienced meeting Pipal.

Taylor tried to gather his thoughts as he walked and put the visit into some kind of perspective. Though he'd accomplished his minimum goal—to meet Pipal and gain some trust, he was unsettled because it didn't happen in any way that he had imagined. And the woman herself, Pipal—he said her name aloud to himself—had struck some chord deep within him and he could still feel it vibrating, trembling in his solar plexus. He was attracted to this young woman in some way, but he refused to believe that it was simply her beauty or even a sexual attraction. It was something more and it reminded him of the few times he had seen Gandhi.

Taylor had been in the Mahatma's immediate presence twice in his ten years in India and had also seen him speak once in London. On only one of those occasions did he actually talk to the great man. It was March of 1942 when Sir Stafford Cripps arrived in Delhi from England with one of the many plans for British withdrawal from India that were discussed in those difficult years preceding independence. Much of the world was at war, and the situation had been complicated by the question of India's military responsibility to Britain. Taylor had acted as a security guard for Cripps during the visit and was at his lodging on Queen Victoria Road when Gandhi came to review the proposal Cripps had recently drafted. He needed Gandhi's approval before taking it back to England's Parliament.

Taylor was personally introduced to the Great Soul that day. It was just a meeting of eyes, a brief exchange, and a bow, but that moment had impressed him. There was something tremendously humbling about Gandhi, seeing this tiny man with a bald head and enormous ears, in what could only appear to westerners as an over-sized diaper, commanding the attention of stiff British officials like Cripps. Stripped bare to all the world, a man of few worldly possessions, Gandhi made a good man feel uneasy and an ambitious man feel positively ashamed. Just seeing him, it seemed, could make you regret stepping on an ant.

Taylor learned something of Gandhi's method that day. Despite the spiritual and political gravity of the Mahatma's presence, Taylor knew enough of eastern diplomacy to get some angle on the subtle games Gandhi relied on. The dynamics of *satyagraha* were in a sense a reverse psychology. In this version of nonviolent resistance, the protesters were always very polite, surrendering to arrest and submitting to beatings. The demonstration of courage and conviction was intended to undermine the enemy's position by gaining his respect.

Taylor thought he saw some of Thomas Carlyle's Mohammed in Gandhi. The more elevated the mind, the more sophisticated the confidence games, and there was no out gunning Gandhi intellectually. His clothing was part of it. Certainly he wore what he wore because it was consistent with his belief in non-possession—*aparigraha*, but he was also clearly aware of how disarming his overall look could be. Through appearance alone, he took a clear stand on the highest moral plane.

Taylor could still smile thinking of Gandhi's curt response to Cripps' plan. "If this is your entire proposal to India, I would advise you to take the next plane home." His words were pointed enough, but the way he said them and the tenor of his voice must have devastated Sir Stafford. With the seventy year-old, ninety-eight pound weakling in a diaper simply mocking the man in formal attire, the scene was fraught with a certain ironic humor as well as profound truth.

Taylor figured that he now had the difficult part of Cripps facing a female Gandhi. He felt fairly confident he could play the game with a little more facility than the boorish Stafford Cripps. He would go to Pipal's home every day just like any of the other pilgrims. He would take in the lectures and prayers and wait in line for an audience. Little by little, if he wasn't too pushy, he would make his argument in small increments—and gradually convince her that the fast need not go on.

Night had fallen by the time Taylor entered the lobby of the Queen's Imperial. He stopped at the reception desk and asked the clerk to put a call through to New Delhi and have it transferred to his room. It was almost an hour later that the phone in Taylor's room rang. It was Mountbatten.

"Good to know you're still alive, Taylor. You know we thought the worst after finding your ID in the demolished railway car."

"Yes, sir. It seemed like a good opportunity for me to disappear."

"Let's hope it worked. Now tell me this crazy chain of souls has been broken."

"I'm sorry, your lordship. That's not the case and the situation is much more complex, though perhaps not as volatile as initially thought."

"How's that?"

"The woman is an Anglo-Indian. Her father was an officer in the Royal Army. And she's been educated in England."

"Christ," muttered Mountbatten at the other end of the line. "What else?"

"The woman is only seventeen years-old and resides with her Indian mother—who lives here in Haridwar on her late husband's pension."

"What! England is supporting this fiasco. Maybe we should threaten to cancel the pension."

"The woman has put her life on the line, sir. It would mean nothing to her. And if I may say so, I'm not certain this is such a horribly precipitous affair. It's rather tame in my opinion."

"Wait until the crowds for that damn festival begin to arrive. Tame or not, Taylor, I want this affair, as you call it, stopped. There was more unrest in Calcutta last night. This whole damn independence thing is going to hell. See that nothing comes of this woman's fast. That's all I care about."

"I'll do what I can, sir."

"Get this done right, Taylor, and you're out of this wog-filled country forever. Make a mess of it, and we'll all be here the rest of our lives."

Taylor hung up the phone disgusted by Mountbatten's tone. He paced back and forth across the room for several minutes then dressed for dinner. After the meal, he retired to the basement lounge for a much needed drink. Chuluun was not the bartender, which was all the better. The way Taylor was feeling he was in no mood for the surly Mongolian.

He got a gin and tonic at the bar and took a table in the corner.

The lounge was again mostly empty. There was a table of four, two couples—ostensibly tourists, on the far side of the lounge and two English men, one in a military uniform, the other in mufti, telling stories and laughing at the bar. Taylor finished his first drink and immediately ordered another. Halfway through the second drink, he found himself absently staring at the three scars in the palm of his right hand. They were still tender and he ran a finger over the raised skin thinking again of that night two months ago when the assailant had attacked him. It was the only time he'd ever killed a man, and though it had been entirely self-defense, the brutal act, killing a man with a piece of glass, had been almost as unsettling as the attack itself. And it reminded him of something his grandfather said to him when he was very young.

His father's father, Edwin Taylor, had gone to West Point and fought for the Union Army in the Civil War and afterward on the western frontier. Toward the end of his life, the old man began to talk more and more about his time in the military and exaggerate his exploits on the battlefield. Young Roger was the only one in the family who would listen. One night after a long story about his military valor, Edwin told his grandson there was a difference between a man who had killed another man and one who hadn't. "Not that killing is a good thing, Roger," said the grandfather, "but only after you have taken a life do you truly understand what a life means." Though only six years-old at the time, Taylor had never forgotten that, and it was one of the first things he thought about when he killed the assailant two months ago.

Edwin died in his sleep before Taylor was seven. Young Roger was the one who found him in his bed. His mother came into the bedroom when he asked what was wrong with Grandfather. He would never forget the way she pulled the sheet up over his grandfather's face as one might close a book. It was his first encounter with death. It was hard enough for him to understand that it was final and that his grandfather would never "wake up," but the funeral was traumatic.

Lying in bed that morning, Roger was determined to deny the day had begun. When he didn't come down for breakfast, his father came up to get him. Theodore Taylor was already dressed in a stiff, dark suit for the funeral. Surely struggling with the event himself, he came into the room a bit gruff and didn't understand exactly how distressed his son, now hiding beneath the covers, was.

"*Come on, Roger,*" *he said pulling the blankets back off the boy.* "*It's time to get up and get dressed. Mother's got breakfast on the table.*"

"*Father, I don't want to go.*"

"*We're all going, Roger. Get dressed. Your clothes are right here. Mother laid them out for you last night.*"

"*I don't want to see the corpse.*" **Corpse** *was a word he had just learned.*

"*Roger, it will be fine. The corpse is nothing to fear. It's Grandfather's body. That's all.*"

"*Do I have to look at it?*"

"*Just walk by the casket.*"

"*What's a casket?*"

"*It's the box Grandfather's body has been placed in.*"

"*Will you hold my hand?*"

"*Yes, of course. Hurry up. Get dressed.*"

The rest of the morning was filled with dread. Breakfast was wordless and somber. Even his sister Katherine at four and a half seemed to have been taken in by the quiet mood that had descended upon the household. The ride in the roadster, usually an adventure with the entire family, was thick and cheerless.

Roger had never liked going to church, but pulling into the parking lot that winter morning, the old stone chapel set amid a cluster of dark leafless maples seemed like a forbidden castle. It may as well have been the morgue for the way Roger's young mind painted it. Inside the overwhelming sense of dread thickened. The vaulted ceilings brooding with shadows. The black veils over the women's faces. The wavering candlelight. The figure of Christ writhing on a cross everywhere you looked. It was like going to one's own execution, it seemed then to Roger.

As direct relations to the deceased, the Taylor family sat in the front row, immediately before the imposing black gloss casket, which was open for viewing once the speakers had finished. The walk-by impended like a huge pendulum, hung from the church ceiling's highest point, sweeping back and forth to the slow, monotonous rhythm of the eulogy language.

But when it actually happened, the walk-by was entirely anticlimactic. After the speakers had finished and everyone stood up, his father took Roger's hand and led him quickly past the coffin without the slightest chance to look in, while his mother, holding Katherine's hand, took to it more slowly and paid her respects to her father-in-law.

The rest of the funeral activities, the burial and the tea at the Taylor home afterward, served as a gradual transition for Roger from the suffocating horror of droning eulogy speakers to the harmless chatter of the gathering in his home. He did learn, however, during the tea, that his grandfather had been buried in his military uniform and with his sword. This upset Roger. He'd never seen his grandfather in that uniform he'd spoken of so many times. In the days and years to follow, he would wish he'd had the courage to look into the coffin, if only to see his grandfather one time in his U.S. Army uniform.

Taylor glanced down at his scarred right hand. He wondered for the hundredth time if his killing that man had really taught him anything about life and death that he hadn't already known. When he looked up, the answer was staring him in the face. Gopal Dutta, the man he'd killed in January, sat across the table. Long, wet ragged gashes ran down one side of his face and neck. Blood still pulsed from the gouged artery that did him in. Like the apparition of Carolyn Williamson Taylor had seen in the bar in Ambala, this man was not really there at all—except as a projection of Taylor's mind. He quickly threw down the last of his drink, pushed away from the table, and exited the lounge. The ghost followed him up the basement stairs and across the lobby, but had faded to nothing by the time Taylor entered his room and turned on the light.

James Nielsen's flask stood on the bedside table. He picked it up and, as he often did, ran his finger over the engraving like he was reaching back into the past. After a while he got undressed and climbed into bed, looking for the relief of sleep. But it didn't come. Like the night before, Taylor tossed and turned. When he did slip off into sleep, he'd dream, one dream after another. In the last of these dreams, he returned to Pipal's home.

He sat alone with Pipal on the divan in the front room. The fast was not an issue, and they spoke freely like friends. Taylor asked her what she'd studied in school.

"I always wanted to write poetry," Pipal replied, looking positively radiant. "I studied literature and the romantic poets. Blake and Coleridge. My favorite, though, was Percy Shelley. What about you?"

"I studied physics as an undergraduate in the States. But when I went to Oxford, I got soft," said Taylor with a smile. "I moved into philosophy. From Schrödinger and Planck to Hegel and Kant. What an ass I was," he said laughing freely at himself.

"Why do you say that?" Despite the seriousness in her voice, her eyes sparkled with life and humor. "Only the poet is on a higher level than the philosopher."

"Oh, I see. The poet is the only honest thinker."

"Yes, of course, because only the poet admits that life is emotional as well as intellectual. No true knowledge of life can be as dry as Hegel or Kant."

This caused them both to laugh and in the midst of the levity Taylor reached out to touch Pipal's cheek. She accepted the caress of his hand, and he drew her to him, nuzzling into her neck, pulling her closer. When he lifted his head to kiss her lips, her face was Gopal Dutta's, cut and bleeding. Taylor abruptly stood in horror, but the figure on the divan was not the assailant or Pipal, it was the still form of James Nielsen in his death bed, suddenly receding from him as down a long tube.

Taylor sat upright in his bed, shaken by the vivid and strange nature of the dream. He went into the bathroom to splash water on his face. After drying himself with a towel, he simply stood at the sink staring as his reflection in the bathroom mirror.

CHAPTER 10

After a bath and breakfast, Roger Taylor took his time with two cups of tea. It seemed that Pipal came out each day to talk to the pilgrims about noon, so he set out across town just after eleven.

The sun was out, and though the day would certainly be very warm, the walk was pleasant. He took a direct route and was so eager to see Pipal he never gave a thought to being followed. During the walk, however, the dream from the night before came back to him. Instead of readying arguments for what he planned to be a mild confrontation of her logic, he found himself wanting to ask Pipal the same questions he had in the dream.

Upon entering Pipal's neighborhood, Taylor saw that she had not yet come out to address the pilgrims, but there were noticeably more of them there for her talk and prayer than the day before. The old woman from Calcutta was there, seated near the front. Taylor settled in at the back of the group, trying his best to go unnoticed.

It wasn't until nearly twelve-thirty that Pipal came out, wearing the same simple white dress she had the day before, but her hair was pulled back in a long thick braid. Her appearance brought children running from all over the neighborhood to squeeze into the gathering and get as close to her as they could. She unrolled her rug in the shade of the neem tree and took the lotus position. Before she spoke, she surveyed the group. Like some school boy with a crush on the girl at the front of the class, Taylor felt his heart rate rise as her eyes swept across the gathering and briefly met his. He cursed himself for being so emotionally engaged.

Pipal opened her talk with a short prayer spoken aloud in Sanskrit with her head bowed. Taylor knew many languages but could not follow the Sanskrit. Before she finished the prayer, a boy on a bicycle came up the street, pedaling furiously, as though he were hurrying to join in. A small girl was riding on the back fender. The front tire hit a rut in the street and the bicycle went end over end, throwing the girl over the handlebars. Everyone watched as the girl hit the street not twenty feet from the neem tree. The boy escaped the fall unharmed and quickly gathered up his bicycle, but when the stunned girl sat up, her left forearm was twisted at an impossible angle from her elbow. She took one look at her arm, burst into tears and started howling.

Pipal had already stopped the prayer. She stood and went to the girl with several others who were close by. She knelt down before the wailing child and with a finger to her lips quieted her to a hesitant whimper. She took hold of the girl's arm at the wrist with her right hand and gripped the girl's upper arm with her left. Then she slid her left hand firmly down the length the girl's arm—popping the dislocated elbow back into place with what appeared almost no effort. Pipal helped the girl to her feet, gave her a hug, and led her to an open spot at the front of the group. The child sat there like nothing had happened, and Pipal returned to her prayer.

When she had completed the prayer, Pipal spoke at length in Hindi about fasting, specifically about the method she was using.

"Fasting is an ancient practice," she began, "but the techniques have been steadily improved upon as we've learned more about nutrition and how certain foods or lack of them can affect the body. I approach fasting both as a form of spiritual purification and as a science, and in the oldest tradition, strive to extend the fast as long as possible and in that way minimize the strain on my body."

As Taylor listened, Pipal explained how she had slowly eliminated one variety of sustenance from her diet at a time, starting with the most substantial foods and gradually reducing to nuts and simple grains to just fruit, then fruit juices, and finally to only water. She said she had only reached this part of the fast in the last week, leading Taylor to understand why she still looked as good as she did and that the most serious part of the fast had only just begun. She concluded the day's talk saying that Gandhi always added a pinch of bicarbonate of soda to his drinking water to neutralize the stomach acids that can build up during a fast, especially as juices or slices of fruit can be the very last sources of sustenance consumed.

As she had the day before, Pipal ended the session with a prayer. She prayed in Hindi and addressed the issue of partition, the ongoing violence, and her hope to end this violence through the series of death fasts. Taylor couldn't help but feel that she was taking this opportunity to lay out the complete philosophy of the fast because he was there. It ended with the word *Namaste*. She stood, collected her rug, and returned to her house.

Immediately afterward, those who wished to speak with Pipal formed a line at her door in a process that gave advantage to those at the front of the gathering. Taylor ended up at the back of the line, meaning he would be standing there many hours before he got the opportunity to talk to Pipal for a second time.

Because of her place near the front of the group, Sumitra was well ahead of Taylor in the line. She was talking with a woman behind her and didn't seem to notice that Taylor was there at all. But his presence was not missed by those at the back of the line, and it didn't take long for this to be broadcast through the line all the way to the front. Taylor noticed Sumitra turn his way. He smiled into her gaze, but she showed no acknowledgment.

A short time later, Taylor became aware of a subtle parting in the light foot traffic on the street and a ragged man coming his way. The man's hands, feet, and head were wrapped in thick woolen rags. Taylor understood that the man was a leper. While lepers are usually shunned and segregated in western society, they were a common sight begging for alms in the streets of India.

The leper took his place at the end of the line directly behind Taylor. His dark eyes, just visible between the folds of cloth around his head, darted furtively in gauged precaution. Taylor, for all his effort to bend to the whim of the crowd, struggled with the suggestions of leprosy. He had heard there was a colony up in the hills behind Haridwar, and that was all well and good, but the close proximity of this leper made him uneasy. Though he knew the disease could only be transmitted through close and long-term contact, he felt his psyche cringe and his skin crawl with every movement of the man behind him.

Along with his grizzly appearance, the leper reeked with the distinct smell of rotting flesh. With each little whiff of this penetrating odor, Taylor found himself more and more uncomfortable, becoming almost hesitant to breathe for imagined bacteria conspiring in the air to enter his lungs. In his agitation, he allowed his own darting eyes to meet the leper's momentarily. How could two men share such different fortunes in life? Taylor, handsome, educated, and accustomed to the good life. The leper, last on humankind's list of the unfortunate. The repulsion, the disdain, their vastly separate fates, all of it passed between the two men in a flash of eyes. Not a word was spoken, but Taylor imagined the man's resentment boring into his back, wondering with each step whether the man would suddenly vent his frustrations with the thrust of a knife. While Taylor tried to focus his thoughts on the job at hand, he could not forget the man behind him, and the already tedious progress of the line seemed to slow further to a barely discernable crawl.

When Taylor had passed through about a quarter of the line, he caught sight of the little woman from Calcutta exiting from Pipal's home and heading his way back along the length of the line. She spotted him as she approached, but diverted her eyes when his eyes sought hers. Taylor understood Sumitra's caution—in some ways he was more of an outcast in this line than the leper—still he said hello to her, even then feeling the eyes of the leper on his back. The old woman could not resist the charm of the handsome Taylor and allowed a half-toothless smile as she reached him.

"How is Pipal today?" asked Taylor.

"She's very tired," said the old woman, casually like a neighbor passing in the street, her eyes stalling an instant as she noticed the leper.

"And how are you, good woman?" continued Taylor, trying to establish a level of familiarity in the society of the line and hoping to break the spell the leper had cast upon him.

"I am saved. Pipal has added my name to her list—and she is likely to put me at the top," she announced proudly over her shoulder as she continued on her way.

Three hours later—that seemed like six, Taylor was on the doorstep, next to enter. Across the street were three men in turbans sitting on boxes and smoking bidis. They appeared to be watching Taylor and had been for quite some time. As Pipal had requested, he was not packing his handgun. Now he wondered if that was a mistake. Then Areena was there at the door. She made no sign of recognition when she brought him into the front room. Only as he sat down at the small wooden table, greatly relieved to be free of the leper's presence, did Areena take the seat across from him and look into his eyes. A weak smile momentarily lit her face then dimmed as she whispered, "I can see that my daughter is on the verge of getting sick." She looked out toward the door, then her large, sad eyes turned back to Taylor. "All these people are too much for her."

Taylor took the opportunity to push his own agenda. "Have you thought of asking her to quit the fast?"

Areena's sad eyes sparked with emotion. "I'm her mother, Mr. Taylor. She is a daughter to me not a saint. I'm the last person in the world who would want to witness this fast." She was obviously full of feelings on this topic and had surely struggled for weeks to keep them to herself. Areena softened her tone. "Pipal is just too young to take life so seriously."

Taylor reached across the table and touched the woman's hand.

She drew her hand away. Eyes down, she continued. "Until last week, she would sit at her treadle at least an hour every day. Now she is too weak. Still she rises each morning with the sun to meditate and read the works of Gandhi until she goes out to speak to her followers. All of that is an act now. She gathers up all her energy for those few minutes each day." Areena lifted her eyes, the deep sadness had returned. "It can't last."

Taylor wanted to repeat his initial question, but didn't. Areena filled the momentary silence as though reading his mind. "I can't stop her, Mr. Taylor, and if she is going to die." Welling emotions punctuated her phrasing. "Then I must be here to help with the meditations and lessen the strain of her fast."

"Can you at least support my efforts to talk her out of it?"

Areena looked down at the table, clearly torn by the question. When she lifted her eyes, she simply said, "I'm more afraid that your being here will attract trouble. If your Lord Mountbatten is truly worried about violence, then you would be best staying clear of here." She turned at the sound of movement in the back room. The curtain pulled back. A stooped old woman came out of the room. Areena stood to perform her duties.

Taylor entered the back room amid a rush of angst. Pipal sat up in her bed clearly happy to see him. Her bed was a traditional *charpoy*, a wooden frame strung with ropes covered by a thin straw-filled mattress. It was so completely covered with the multi-colored flowers that the pilgrims brought her she seemed to be bathing in them.

The small room was empty except for the bed, a small *coir* mat on the floor, a hand treadle for spinning cotton, and a nightstand. On the nightstand sat an oil lamp, a pitcher of water, some slices of lemon, a tiny jar of bicarbonate of soda, a bamboo mug, and a once folded piece of stationery—presumably her list. Two windows on the south wall projected bright parallelograms of light across her room. One illuminated her bed of flowers. The other reflected like a mirror off the dark-stained floor. The plastered walls, as in the front room, were painted a gloomy green.

Pipal stood in a cascade of roses and carnations, advancing toward Taylor hand extended. Though her grace disguised her weakness, her plain homespun gown of *khadi* hung on her thin frame like a funeral cloth, and something of her extreme condition hit Taylor all at once. The wondrous vision of Pipal in his dream washed away before the grim reality of the situation. He saw a gaunt and tired woman in her teens, barefoot in remote India, starving herself to death amid a nation of dying. No one would ever notice her passing. The chain would never have a link past her own. She spoke before he'd overcome this stark vision.

"I'm so glad you've returned, Mr. Taylor," she said, obviously trying to impress him with her strength and control.

"I believe the honor is mine, Pipal." He stepped forward taking her hand and led her back to the bed of flowers and clear sunlight. She sat on the *charpoy* and he knelt on the floor.

"I have to ask about the girl who fell from the bicycle. It appeared that her arm was badly dislocated. And you seemed to fix it so easily?"

Pipal smiled graciously. "I don't believe it was as bad as it might have appeared." Her voice was confident and had a soothing quality. "Besides such things are much easier with children. Their joints are very supple."

"Maybe so, but it was very impressive nonetheless."

Pipal shrugged as though it were nothing, then spoke to her own purpose. "After your visit yesterday, Mr. Taylor, I realized that you must be here to chronicle my fast."

"But I'm not a journalist at all. I'm an emissary from the Governor-General. I report only to his lordship and it's not passed on. If anything, I'm here to see that word of your fast goes no further than Haridwar."

Pipal only smiled. The sunlight from the window behind her broke in rays about her head and shoulders. "That may be your intention, but you will cause more to know. While you try to dissuade me, I will persuade you. Beyond the door to this house is a long line containing people from all over India. Even as we speak, word of my fast flows down stream like the waters of the Ganges."

Her optimism frustrated Taylor and he came back with more force than he intended. "Just because these few people have come to see you doesn't mean that your fast is doing what you want it to do. This is nothing, really. Probably no more than a few hundred individuals have been here. If you are dead in ten days, no one will remember. No one will care."

"That doesn't matter," she answered with an infuriating calm. "As I said yesterday, if word of my death does not get the world's attention, then the next fast will. If not that one, the next. Eventually word will get out, and one day the shame of partition, the shame of the ongoing violence, the shame of one of our own killing our most revered leader will be a permanent scar upon the souls of all Indians—and they will live better and more consciously because of it."

"These may be honorable goals, Pipal, but think this through again, please. Yes, your fast has gained some modest attention here in Haridwar. But it's because of your youth and your blonde hair that people are captured by this. When you are gone and the second in line is an old woman or a leper, who will care? Who will come to see them? It won't be the same. It won't. So many have died already—isn't Gandhi's assassination reminder enough?"

Pipal reached for the pitcher on the bedside table and filled the bamboo mug with water. "So it may seem to you, Mr. Taylor, but to me the sacrifice of my life is little compared to what the Mahatma did." She squeezed a little lemon juice into the water, then a pinch of bicarbonate, and took a drink. "Such a fast is an honor, the most profound statement of *satyagraha*—devotion to truth, love beyond the individual self."

What could he say to these kinds of responses? Taylor shook his head in disbelief. He knew he was pushing harder than he wanted, but still his emotions rose. "Pipal, you are deluding yourself. You can not be what Gandhi was. You may admire him. You may even worship him." A small, framed, black and white photograph of Gandhi, sitting legs cross-ed before a spinning wheel, hung on the wall above her bed. "But becoming a martyr will not bring you any closer to him. Can't you see that Gandhi himself would be horrified by what you're doing? You're too valuable to the cause alive. You might have already done irreparable damage to your body. Your liver and kidneys are at risk. Your capacity to reproduce is at stake."

Pipal drew back, laying all the way down and turning to the wall. A haunting memory of Carolyn Williamson—that day he'd told her he was going to Oxford—settled down upon Taylor like a gauzy curtain. Pipal looked back over her shoulder. "Why should I be worried about my body or children, Mr. Taylor? It is death that I seek." She spoke calmly, evenly.

Taylor wanted to scream. "Are you sure? You really want to die? Don't you worry about how much this will hurt your mother? She doesn't want this. Watching you fast is tearing her apart."

Pipal sat up and turned fully to Taylor. "Do you know what it means to die, Mr. Taylor?" she returned with intimation and some volume. "I don't take this lightly. I have died many times before. I have prepared for it in this body more than any other."

Her conviction reminded Taylor of the confrontation he'd had with Tenzing Chogyam years and years ago, but he refused to accept it from her just as fully as he had rejected it from the Rinpoche—because, yes, he did know death. The mere thought of it conjured memories of his grandfather lying still in his bed, of James Nielsen's esoteric funeral in a cottage at Oxford, the bloodied face of the man he'd killed with a shard of glass, and finally an etheric visitation by Carolyn, now sitting in her nightgown on the bed at Pipal's feet.

Before Taylor could properly put these feelings into words, Areena, who must have overheard the last exchange, lifted the curtain from outside the room and stood in the doorway. "How can you speak with such wisdom, Pipal?" She came all the way into the room. "You're a young girl. A smart girl. But a young girl who has not even known the revelation of childbearing. How can you speak of knowing death so intimately?"

As her mother spoke, Pipal seemed to be looking directly at Carolyn's ghost. It dispersed before her gaze, and Pipal turned briefly to Taylor, as though she'd seen the apparition. Then she said softly, "Mother, you are here to give me strength not tear at my spirit. Be proud to have a daughter such as me. You should feel nothing but joy for me. Who is so fortunate as I am? How few can face death eyes upraised and full of faith? You must know this is the highest aspiration given to humankind."

Areena shook her head. "These things are very hard for a very ordinary mother to understand." The pain of it all was evident in her voice. "I'm just not ready for you to leave me this way. I have tried—tried very hard—and prayed, but I must tell you what I think."

Areena said these last words, then turned, eyes tearing, and left the room. Taylor stood, knowing he'd had his few minutes with Pipal and that he'd pushed her further than he should have—for her health and for his success. He wanted to dismiss her as crazy, but he felt too strongly she wasn't. Even more her sincerity was depressing. He'd delved these eastern concepts that Pipal held true many times in his life and despite all his study had never believed they held enough truth to embrace. Still there was something in the timbre of her voice that unsettled his firmest convictions, touching some vague aching memory of his own.

"Don't worry, Mother," said Pipal, barely audible, "it will be a long fast."

Taylor watched Pipal tremble as she spoke these last words. He dared to look into her eyes again. He felt humbled when he didn't expect it. The naive girl he'd seen earlier had transformed before him. Now sitting in the bed of flowers, bathed in brilliant sunlight, Pipal positively glistened with beauty and life and faith. "I'm sorry," he heard himself say head down. "I have disrupted your peace. I am sorry. I have even upset your mother. I shall return only with good wishes. Please, excuse my harshness today."

Taylor backed out of the room awkwardly, looking up to catch her eyes one last time. She smiled. Then it struck him. Possibly what he'd been feeling all along. In her eyes, heightened by her smile, and enhanced with her hair pulled back in a braid, was a fleeting resemblance, maybe just in the blind strength of spirit, to James Nielsen.

"Then I can expect to see you tomorrow, Mr. Taylor?"

"If your mother will allow it, yes. I will be back," he said, suddenly wanting to stay and ask those questions he'd asked in the dream the night before. Instead, he turned and pushed through the curtain, nearly bumping into the leper who was next to see Pipal. Areena stood by the front window looking out at the pilgrims waiting in line. She turned as Taylor passed through the front room to the door. When their eyes met, she allowed the contact, and this time, it was Taylor who lowered his eyes.

CHAPTER 11

It was late afternoon when Roger Taylor returned to the hotel. Still unsettled by his close proximity to the leper, he went straight to his room to bathe and change into clean clothing. Then, instead of having something to eat, he went directly to the lounge.

The lounge was empty, except for the bartender. It was not Chuluun. He would have the evening shift that night. Taylor ordered a gin and tonic and took it to a booth in the corner of the lounge. He drank this first drink too fast, then ordered a second which he took to more pensively.

His thoughts focused on Pipal. For all that he could reasonably allow her, he could not accept the rationale behind her fast. And yet, on some other level, he was giving in to her. That she should evoke the memory of his long dead friend James Nielsen was part of it. Whether there was a real physical resemblance or it was something he was projecting upon Pipal, it didn't matter. He had been invaded by a haunting presentiment and the memory of a night at Oxford he had often tried to forget and now wanted to recollect in every detail.

Two weeks after his critical attack on eastern metaphysics in Tenzing Chogyam's seminar, Roger attended a reception thrown by Oxford's Vice-Chancellor. It was the Chancellor's annual pre-Christmas bash for the dons and graduate students, celebrating the end of the Michaelmas term for the year 1929. The event began with a large banquet dinner in St. Edmund's Hall and culminated in a long evening of cocktails and animated discussion. Traditionally it was the scene of wild debate, where graduate students, fortified with the confidence of drink, took the opportunity to challenge their dons with the full vigor of their youth. Though tensions could rise, it was generally considered a lively time for all. Those dons who might be particularly defensive usually left right after the meal. Those who stayed were there for the spirited exchange. Some even felt that more was learned at this single event than in all the term's lectures and tutorials combined.

Though not a graduate student, James Nielsen attended this reception with Roger. And while Roger had one drink after another, James, whose health had been in steady decline through the fall, nursed one weak drink all evening and policed his Yankee friend who had given in to a measured but somewhat drunken bravado. More than once, James, wise beyond his years with the visage of death staring him coldly in the eyes, had to delicately turn aside Roger's intellectual blade before some unsuspecting tutor found himself skewered. This did not make for an easy evening for James, but it was his first night out in more than a month and he was enjoying the challenge.

Just before midnight, as the evening was winding down and most of the guests were gone, Roger spotted Tenzing Chogyam in a corner of the hall's library wearing his full length silk robes and cap, somehow invisible amid this group in dark suits and academic gowns. Over the last few days, Roger had idly conceived of a metaphysical experiment. He'd never really considered it very seriously until this moment when flushed with scotch whiskey it suddenly struck him as profound. Roger quickly grabbed two drinks from a nearby waiter's tray and headed straight for the Rinpoche, purpose increasing with every step. The lama smiled as he saw Roger approaching with James Nielsen trailing cautiously behind.

There was a large walk-in fireplace in this area defined as the library, really only three walls of books at the south end of St. Edmund's expansive first floor, and with a drink in each hand, Roger corralled the Rinpoche before this enormous stone hearth. He must have appeared some psychic monster to the extra-sensitive lama as he pushed a glass in his face. "Here. Have a drink, Tenzing, and please accept my apologies for my inconsiderate attack on your philosophy the week before last." He raised his glass to the Rinpoche. "Join in with the good old boys of Oxford."

Tenzing Chogyam was not one to drink. Of course, there had been times he'd had wine or fermented goat's milk, but never whiskey. Out of deference to the situation and as a karmic gesture to Roger, he looked deeply into the twisted smile gleaming in his face, glanced at James Nielsen beside him, said no apology was needed, and took a sip of the scotch, not fully aware of its strength.

The ensuing conversation between the three men, silhouetted against a blazing fire, began with the passing of pleasantries and worked its way steadily to the **Tibetan Book of the Dead** *and finally to reincarnation. Nothing was said, but the lama and James could surely feel Roger purposely steering the discussion to this topic and the casual atmosphere of the party gradually giving way to Roger's mounting intensity.*

"You know, Rinpoche, ever since the other day when I voiced my disbelief in the Tibetan doctrine of reincarnation, I've been puzzling over a way to prove or disprove that a mind or a soul, whatever you want to call it, can really travel from one life to

the next. It's just that I've been so deeply steeped in the ways of empirical science I can't make the necessary leap of faith without something concrete. I need a proof of some kind."

James shook his head at his belligerent friend and allowed a capricious grin. The lama also smiled, but said nothing and took a second sip from his drink.

Roger needed no further prompting. "I realize both of you may try to resist what I'm about to suggest. So take a moment before you react. Because I feel that we must do this. The situation is so unique and so perfect, it demands it."

James and Tenzing gave each other a look and Roger pushed on. "Now please know that I make this proposition in the name of higher knowledge and science." He lifted his glass in the air again. "And if I offend anyone's sensibilities, I'm sorry. This idea is offered among friends, and at any time either of you resists, I'll stop."

The lama merely nodded. James raised his glass in affirmation. "Roger, I can't say I know exactly what you're going to propose, but I'm sure whatever it is, it has something to do with my illness." He advanced from a few feet away to the warmth of the hearth and looked Roger in the eye. "Be sure that I will be able to talk rationally about my condition until the very end. Tenzing has helped me a great deal with this already—more than you might know."

"I've seen it, James. I have," said Roger excitedly. "And that's why I have the courage to make this proposal that some might think morbid." He sensed that James had already guessed his plan, so he saw no reason to hold back any longer. "I want to perform an experiment with your life—or should we say death, James. And I want the Rinpoche to be part of it." Roger lowered his voice and moved up close to the lama. "Would it not be possible, for you Rinpoche, to usher James through the Tibetan funeral rites and with great likelihood assure transference?"

*Though Tenzing Chogyam, like anyone within ten meters, knew that Roger was inebriated, the spirit of discussion and debate were always in him, and the little bit of whiskey he'd consumed unmasked his perpetual good nature with a great cheshire smile. But James responded before the Rinpoche could give a direct answer to Roger's question. "Roger, we are way ahead of you. Tenzing and I have already entered into a private study of the **Bardo Thödol.** Nothing is assured." He paused to catch the lama's eyes. "But transference is our goal."*

Roger grinned. "Then if transference is possible, James, why not directed reincarnation?" The flames in the fire fluttered like a flag across Roger's face. "Isn't that something a practiced guru could do?" He looked from James to the Rinpoche.

"Roger, please," said James in deference to the Rinpoche.

But Tenzing took the request in stride. "What exactly do you have in mind, Mr. Taylor?" In his ornamental robes and silk cap, the little man from Tibet looked more like one of Santa's helpers about to fill a stocking at the hearth than a master in the sacred art of dying.

"I want to use the opportunity, if you will, of James' leukemia to prove reincarnation." Tenzing tilted his head as though he didn't quite follow. Roger continued with building enthusiasm. "Tenzing, you act as James' guru during and after his death. Guide him through the ordeal of dying and assist him in finding a womb. If, as you say, reincarnation can be a conscious part of the yogin's art of dying, wouldn't it also be possible for you to help an initiate like James to be purposely reborn, that is, directed to a specific womb? Then, in that new life, could he not remember the conversation we are having now and consciously, even though it might be some unknown amount of time later, find me and tell me he was back? That is, if reincarnation really does happen and if the yogic techniques really work."

James answered for the Rinpoche. "Please understand, Roger, Tenzing and I have already prepared many hours for the Tibetan funeral ceremony. As I said, our goal, however, is transference, liberation of consciousness and a conjoining with the Clear Light—and that is not easy or assured." The caution in his words was not matched by the thrill in his voice. Neither of the other men could have failed to miss that James had been tempted by Roger's suggestion.

Tenzing turned away from Roger and James to look full face into the fire roaring in the hearth. He breathed in the smell of the burning oak and allowed his thoughts to meld with the leaping flames. When he turned back to his students, a somber ashen mask had replaced his cheshire grin.

"The rites of death are a sacred art, Mr. Taylor. They have been opened to the West in the spirit they were conceived, not as magic, not as spectacle, but as profound belief. The power of the **Bardo Thödol** *can not be bottled and sold as most things of meaning in the West.*

"You must know that the decision to publish the **Bardo Thödol** *was not looked upon favorably by all eastern scholars. They feared it would be diluted and profaned. They feared its power would fall into the hands of so-called black magicians who would try to use it for personal advantage. Many like myself ignored those fears. We felt that the real essence of Tibetan philosophy was inherently safe because it demands such complete dedication and surrendering of the self. It will only avail itself to the pure of heart and intention. The knowledge is more than just the words and rituals. It's a sobering insight into the transience of this thing we call reality and the sham of our worldly ways." With the fire at his back, the lama's face was haloed but dark, while the faces before him flashed with the light of flickering flames.*

"As much as I would like to bring the spirit of James back to the living world for you, Mr. Taylor, and for me," continued the elfin sage, "what you imagine runs counter to the current of the belief."

"Then what you're saying is that there is no reincarnation?" snapped Roger in a

way that made James cringe.

Tenzing stared at Roger for some time before responding. "No, that's not what I'm saying, Mr. Taylor. The concept of self—Roger Taylor or James Nielsen—is just a temporary constraint of perspective, a kind of training device on the ladder to higher consciousness. As long as one thinks of self as the ultimate expression of life, he is bound to earth and can have no real understanding of the ocean of consciousness and the Clear Light that is the godhead. All astral migration occurs in that selfless sea."

Roger began to sputter, but James put a hand on his shoulder to quiet him, and Tenzing went on. "The **Bardo Thödol** *teaches the most basic method of transference or the liberation of consciousness, face-to-face deliverance through hearing. The art of finding a womb and bringing about a directed reincarnation is really only secondary to those teachings. Enlightenment through liberation is the highest goal. To come back to a body is dubious acclaim and is usually only for religious men like the Dali Lama who come back to earth as avatars to promote the advancement of the sacred philosophy. There are consequences for this kind of action. There are karmic costs. If there is a black art, misuse of this knowledge is it."*

"But wouldn't a proof of the Tibetan beliefs serve to further the knowledge more than the efforts of a lone Tibetan holy man?" followed Roger, not giving in the slightest to the increasing intensity of the guru.

Though clearly captured by what Roger was saying, James defended the Rinpoche's position. "Roger, I think it's evident that Tenzing is rejecting your experiment. For what it's worth, he and I have spoken many times about the challenges of the Tibetan funeral. He feels confident that with his help I should be able to attain liberation. That alone is a worthy goal. There is no need to press it."

"But what is liberation of consciousness, James?" returned Roger, taking James by the hand and speaking into his eyes. "Just a blank acceptance of the void. You may as well have no belief at all. Even the acceptance of Jesus Christ into your heart seems more transcendent than that. It's the idea of coming back that addresses the real question—knowledge of death. **That** *is a goal worth seeking, not mere ecstatic acceptance of the null."*

"You're chained to western thinking, Mr. Taylor," countered Tenzing. "You speak with the blindness of ego. You're trying to seek material rewards from the wisdom of spiritual transcendence. It's similar to wealthy Christians expecting to buy their way into heaven by giving to the church. Besides, what you ask is not only bordering on sacrilege, but it's also extremely difficult. Even the most adept have trouble following the torturous route to rebirth while maintaining a kernel of self from the previous life. Memories of their other lives are faint. Only the most significant memories, and those often shrouded in our dreams, are available, except in the rarest

cases like that of the Dali Lama."

"Then let's seek the rarest case," protested Roger. "What have we to lose?"

The guru looked at James when he answered. "There is much to lose, Mr. Taylor. Should we attempt the nearly impossible task of directed rebirth and fail, then there may be no successful transference either. That would be a major loss."

Though he had grown close to the guru in the past month, James' friendship with Roger was longer and deeper and he was caught by the temptation. "I would risk transference, Tenzing," said James softly in a discussion that's volume had steadily increased.

Tenzing Chogyam gazed into James' eyes as though measuring the sincerity of the young man he'd grown to like very much.

"It's a rare chance that we could perform such an experiment, Rinpoche," coaxed Roger. "You could become a major contributor to the science of the West. Think what it could do for the Great Knowledge."

"Being part of western science means nothing to me, Mr. Taylor," replied the lama soberly. "Such a proof would never occur to an eastern sage. This thinking is inverted. Eastern metaphysics begins with faith. Western science begins with doubt."

"I accept your position entirely, Rinpoche," said James. "We are asking you to do something contrary to your teachings, but I can't deny what Roger is saying—not that I want so much to direct my reincarnation, but that my death, which does seem like such a shame, could have a purpose and open a door that has long been closed to the western world."

Tenzing turned away from both men and again stared into the leaping flames. For expanding minutes he remained silent with his back to James and Roger. The young men exchanged a glance—could it be they had angered or insulted the eastern sage? Still Roger would not give it up. "What if I wager you, Tenzing? My life against James'."

"Roger, please," pleaded James. "It's clear he's had enough of this."

"Let me finish, James," said Roger as the reluctant lama turned around to face the two young men. "Should we perform this experiment, if and when the time comes that I meet James in his new being and the proof is made, I will dedicate the rest of my life to spreading the wisdom of your beliefs." Roger turned to his friend. "James, would you accept these conditions?"

"Such a strange temptation to place before your friend, Roger." Tears began to form in James' eyes. "I know you as well as anyone, and for all that I care for you, you are a man deeply centered upon yourself. Good or bad, it's who you are and I accept that. But for you to find selflessness—and teach it—would be worth any risk I might take."

Tenzing stepped forward. "Roger, your arrogance is disturbing. Your disdain even worse. To turn such a mind as yours would be significant and more important to me than a place in western science, but let's up the ante. I will take the wager, if you will also agree that upon finishing at Oxford to travel to the East and spend ten years in the shadow of the Himalayas—to observe the people and know their lives and the origins of these beliefs—so that you know fully what you must become when the awakening occurs."

"To spend ten years in the East, Rinpoche—that's a tall order."

"Compared to what?" said the lama.

Roger turned to his ailing friend. James lowered his eyes. "Very well then." Roger reached back and threw his empty glass into the fireplace. "I'm game," he exclaimed as the glass shattered against the wall and the pieces fell into the fire.

Tenzing approached James and touched his arm. "And you are willing, James?"

James looked at both men, bewildered by all that had transpired, then hesitantly said, "Yes."

"Then we begin preparing tomorrow." The Rinpoche put his palms together and bowed. "Good night, gentlemen."

Neither James nor Roger had expected this sudden acceptance. It seemed too much to comprehend. For several minutes, not a word was said, but their hearts raced. It was almost as if the lama had told them he had a cure for leukemia.

Taylor sat in the lounge for a long time nursing one drink then another, reliving this memory and pondering the wager he'd made years earlier. It was part of the reason he'd come to India—but only a minor part. After that night at St. Edmund's Hall, it was four and a half more years before Taylor finished school and received his doctoral degree in philosophy. By then the emotional impact of James' death and his own interest in eastern metaphysics had waned. The wager seemed something he'd done in a fit of melancholy on an evening he'd had too much to drink.

Upon graduation, Taylor decided not to return to the United States to pursue a teaching position at an American university. Instead he took a lesser job at an English boarding school teaching introductory physics. He remained there for two unremarkable years until a classmate from Oxford suggested he interview for a position with the British Secret Intelligence Service. Mostly out of boredom, though certainly related to the trouble brewing in Europe, Taylor set up an interview and got a desk job in London. He liked it. A year later he was offered a position with the C.I.D. in India. India in the 1930s. A land of romance and fantastic wealth. The gem of the British Empire. It sounded like a great adventure. That he would also be addressing the promise he'd made in

1929 was no more than a passing thought at the time.

After ten long years in India, it all seemed a bit silly to Taylor now. Yes, he had greater insight into eastern culture, but it had only made him more cynical—not more open to the beliefs. Taylor took another sip of gin and recalled the talk he and James had immediately following the wager he'd made with Tenzing Chogyam.

The festive feeling in St. Edmund's Hall had vanished. It was as though the seriousness of the challenge Roger had placed before the lama only became clear after the wager had been accepted and the Rinpoche had gone. James and Roger left the party very soon afterward and began the long trek back to New College.

The night was beautiful, clear and cold. High above, the moon was full and bright. They walked for quite a while without saying a word until they both suddenly stopped and dared to look each other in the eye.

"Roger," said James softly. "What have we just done?"

"It seemed such a logical extension of all that was happening. I had to ask. I never thought the Rinpoche would accept."

"I could never have asked such a thing of him for myself. I still don't know what to think of it."

"Do you really believe he can do it?" asked Roger as they began to walk again. "I mean, it is intriguing, but we've been told differently all our lives. I must admit I have my doubts."

"No false hopes—of course. But you know what?" James broke into a wide, beaming smile, lighting his blue eyes from the inside out. "I've become entirely convinced there is something to the **Bardo Thödol***, Roger. I don't mean every little detail of the rituals themselves, but the overall concept—as an artful approach to the inevitable—as a way to accept and embrace dying—it* **is** *a profound teaching. And the Rinpoche is teaching me this sacred art! As to the transmigration of souls, it does seem unlikely, but not impossible to me any more."*

James' optimism was beautiful. Roger envied his friend for his faith. "Can you imagine the look on my face when you first find me in your new life? Who knows ten, twenty, thirty years from now?"

"What am I supposed to say? How will we know? Will it be obvious? Should I have a password?"

Roger shook his head and chuckled at James' seriousness. "I don't know, James. Somehow I think we'll just know."

"Probably, but if there should be a need for some kind of clue or verification, it should be simply saying the name, **Tenzing Chogyam***. Nothing else could be more appropriate. He is the magician."*

They reached the Ashmolean Museum of the History of Science, one of Roger's favorite buildings at Oxford. A wall surrounded the museum, capped with the busts of famous scientists—Newton, Galileo, Hooke, Boyle, Huygens, Copernicus, Kepler, Bacon. Their faces stood out white in the moonlight.

Roger stopped and motioned down the length of the wall with an open hand. "It seems to me, James, that all of these great men of science were really searching for one thing—the conquering of matter by the mind. Whether it was a steam engine or electricity, the net effect of their work was a lessening of the physical burdens for mankind.

"Mind over matter," continued Roger, "that's what they sought. Newton and Bacon pushed that to its logical limit. The Great Work—the philosopher's stone— the elixir of life—immortality. Newton's work in physical science and mathematics was so tied up in his alchemic work that he, at least, probably considered them all part of the same endeavor. Not to mention old Elias Ashmole himself."

James laughed. "Can you believe it? Now we have entered into the illustrious search for immortality in the tradition of Mr. Ashmole."

"And I just bet ten years of my life on it," continued Roger laughing. "I must be out of my mind."

"Not necessarily," said James suddenly serious. "Think about the part of you that is of such stuff that it can't be touched. Our body must eventually grow old and decay, but not our mind. Mind, thought, consciousness is of a finer fabric. It is to our body as an electromagnetic field is to a magnet or an electric current."

"Perhaps."

"Faraday told us that when an electric current is cut off, the electromagnetic field it induced detaches and exists on its own for some unspecific time as a damped oscillating field. So it could be with consciousness also. When the body has become cold, the last thought, an electromagnetic event of firing cerebral synapses, separates and oscillates eternally, never the slightest bit damped because of the fineness of the medium through which it vibrates."

"And?"

"And the art of dying and yogic techniques are, in a sense, a training and tuning of the oscillations of your consciousness. The Tibetan sage believes that there is a proper vibration to establish at the moment of death."

"Sounds like a lot of void to me," said Roger with a chuckle.

James looked down at the ground, then lifted his eyes to Roger's. "Maybe I will never convince you while in this body, but what of your commitment to Tenzing? Can you honor that?" There was heat in his voice. "Will you really spend ten years in the East?"

This caught Roger off-guard. Rarely did James ever put anyone on the spot in this way. He hesitated a moment, knowing deep down that he had been rash to make such a promise. "Yes, certainly, I will," he answered. But even then, he knew he didn't mean it. And he sensed that James could feel that as the words were spoken.

CHAPTER 12

It was late in the evening when Roger Taylor left his table in the basement lounge. Chuluun had taken over at the bar. There was a brief meeting of their eyes as Taylor walked out. He should have said something to the Mongolian, but he'd had too much to drink on an empty stomach and felt like hell. He ordered a meal from the dining room to be delivered to his room. By eleven he'd eaten and was in bed. As had been the case many nights of late, he slept fitfully and dreamt heavily. One dream woke him in the middle of the night. He lay awake afterward thinking about it. It was nearly identical to the dream he'd had two nights before.

He was in Victoria Terminus during the war, not really sure what he was doing there or where he was going. Very early in the dream, however, he realized that *he was dreaming* and that he'd had this dream before and seen the Rinpoche. Knowing that he might suddenly waken, he began looking for Tenzing Chogyam. He spotted his mother rushing through the crowd towing Carolyn by the hand behind her. They hurried past without seeing him, but walking slowly in the opening left behind them was the Rinpoche. "Tenzing! Tenzing!" Taylor shouted making his way through the crowd to the Tibetan sage. "What's going on? Why are you and I here?"

Tenzing stopped and smiled at the sight of Taylor. Beside the lama sat the mongrel dog-half from Rangoon, holding itself up with its front legs, seemingly at ease with the guru, but wary of Taylor.

"Why are we in this dream?" asked Taylor again.

"Had you taken the *Bardo Thödol* more seriously, Roger, you might have a better idea how to cope with these crowds. I know it helped our friend James."

"What? You've seen James?" Taylor sputtered, feeling things spinning around him and the dream fleeing. "Was he reincarnated?" he asked, an eye on the mutilated dog, now perceptibly growling in a low gurgle. "Is James here?"

"If he were reincarnated, he certainly wouldn't be here," answered the lama. "But I'll give you a little hint." He pointed to the many tunnels leading to the loading platforms. "Try taking a train."

It was at this point that Taylor woke. The dream bothered him more than it had the first time. His running into Tenzing Chogyam and then asking him about the dream was extreme even for a lucid dream. But the sight of his mother with Carolyn jarred loose an old regret about missing both Carolyn's and his mother's funerals. This second incident marked his last communication with his family. It was a letter from his father in the winter of 1945, telling him of his mother's death and asking him to return for the funeral. The timing had been bad for Taylor. He'd just received orders to go to Calcutta. He passed it off in the hurry of the moment. A week later he reread the letter and knew he'd made a bad decision.

The letter provided a one-two punch. It opened with the news and details of his mother's sudden death. She'd slipped on some ice outside the house and hit her head, resulting in a severe concussion. Two days later, a blood clot in her brain killed her. The second part of the letter lapsed from sadness into praise for the recent success of the atomic bomb and the advent of the atomic age. Taylor read the passage over to himself several times before he'd finally tossed the letter away in anger. He could still remember part of it word for word. "I can't help but think you really missed out on something when you gave up on physics," his father had written. "You might have been part of this new era of discovery."

Even after leaving science, Taylor had closely followed the work of the scientists who engineered the splitting of the atom. Lindemann's work at Oxford had been instrumental to that success. Several of his classmates had contributed. He'd often had second thoughts about his switch from physics to philosophy, but after his father's letter, it became a recurring regret—and a sour note with which to begin this day. It didn't help that he'd had too much to drink and too little to eat the night before.

Though his last visit to Pipal had been an unsettling one and his doubts about the mission itself had grown, Taylor still intended to stick to his plan of visiting Pipal every day—because, for reasons he hadn't fully admitted to himself, he did want to stop her fast. He had a large breakfast in the Queen's Imperial dining room and three cups of strong tea to get him going. About eleven, he headed across Haridwar to Pipal's home.

When he reached her neighborhood, there was no cluster of people beneath the neem tree waiting for Pipal to come out and speak, only a long line at her door. Taylor quickly learned that Pipal had canceled her talk due to physical weakness, and with no other choice, he took his place at the end of the line and did his best to fit in with a group of people he couldn't have been less like.

He saw the little girl who had been thrown from the bicycle the day before. She was running and playing with the other children, showing no ill effects of the accident. This seemed so remarkable Taylor felt it was more likely he had misjudged the severity of her injury, as Pipal had said, than that it had been so easily fixed and healed.

A short time later, there was some commotion in the line ahead of him. Taylor was too far away to determine what was going on, but it ended almost as quickly as it began. He thought nothing else of it until the old woman from Calcutta walked up along the line after her visit with Pipal. She didn't return Taylor's smile as she approached, but slid up close to him as she passed. From within the hood of her *pallu*, she whispered quickly, "There is talk of you in the line—beware." Then she moved on down the street and was gone.

Taylor now understood the problem in the line earlier was because of him, but nothing else came up until he reached the doorstep several hours later. Across the narrow street from Pipal's home sat the leper, his face wrapped except an opening for his eyes, which stared out malevolently at Taylor. Next to him were three other Indian men in loose turbans leaning against the building and talking loudly. These were the same men Taylor had seen the day before smoking bidis. One pointed purposefully at him, gaining a nod from the leper. Taylor could only imagine that the leper had overheard his conversation with Pipal the day before and was passing the story along to others—saying he was there to stop the fast.

Then Areena was at the door to usher him in. She was quiet and withdrawn. Taylor asked her if anything was wrong. "Has something happened? Is it me?"

Areena looked into his face. The strain was evident in her eyes. "I simply can not bear this much longer. That is all. Please make your visit short. Pipal is very weak."

Nothing more was said until Areena led him into the back room. She remained in the room, standing beside the curtained doorway as Pipal stood from her bed of flowers and advanced toward Taylor, beaming. "My friend, Roger Taylor, I am so glad to see you."

Today her hair was worn free. It fell in cascades around her shoulders like spun sunlight. Her beauty and radiance struck Taylor dead center. Flushed with emotions he couldn't contain, he knelt to one knee and took her outstretched hand. Like a self-conscious youth, he fumbled for something to say, only to rise with her hand and usher her back to the bed of flowers.

"It may be that I am wrong to be here, Pipal," he finally said, deeply captured by the presence of this far from ordinary woman. "I come trying to talk you out of your fast and you greet me like a long lost friend. You seem to have me at my own game."

"Mr. Taylor, you forget I am a student of Gandhi's. His most important lesson was to wish even your adversaries well. Gaining their respect is the first step to gaining their support."

"Then you consider me an adversary."

"No, Mr. Taylor, you have become a friend. I can see it in your eyes right now." When her eyes met his, it felt like she was reading his innermost thoughts, increasing his turmoil.

Humbled, Taylor knelt beside her bed. While her grace and kindness were so fluid and natural, a leaden jacket of formality cramped his every move. He bowed his head. The dream from two nights before when he'd touched her cheek came back to him. He looked up daring to meet her eyes again. In the otherwise dimly lit room, sunlight from one of the room's two windows filled the space between her face and his like an ethereal mist. And in that mist, he saw James Nielsen's face—tired and thin, near the end—hovering over Pipal's face like a transparent mask. Stunned by the sight, he dropped his eyes momentarily, then, looking up, the apparition still there, he blurted out, "Pipal, why must you be the one to take on this burden?"

Pipal touched his hand. "Roger, I am more of the other world than this one," she said with a soft smile. "Trust me in this; I am ready to die."

He wanted to scream at the nonsense of her words, but for a suspended instant, it seemed that everything else was stripped away. It was as if it were just him and her—no, just his mind and her mind—and impossibly James' also—conjoined in the bright space between them. He was overwhelmed by the thought that Pipal could be James Nielsen reborn. It was too much for him—more than he was able to believe. Like an initiate at his first séance, startled by a psychic presence, he fought the moment of transcendence and, in haste, stood up, breaking the spell, frightened to face what he couldn't understand.

Areena still stood beside the doorway. Taylor stared into her face like a man who'd just seen his own ghost, then, in confusion, turned back to Pipal. Though she was actually below him at the level of the bed, Taylor had the overwhelming feeling that she was looking down on him from above. Her smile was gone. Her eyes sat deep in their sockets. The thinness of her face accentuated the shape of her skull. A death mask stared directly into his heart. He backed out of the room in emotional disarray and hurried out of the building.

Taylor strode, head down and distracted, back along the length of the line. Several people shouted at him. He quickened his step. A rock struck him heavily on the back and several others just missed. He doubled his pace and two men began to run after him, waving sticks, throwing rocks, and shouting at him. In the confusion, he collided with a child on a bicycle and fell to the ground. The two men behind him were suddenly on him, beating him with their sticks. Bystanders crowded around in a circle, taunting him and egging his attackers on.

Taylor had been trained in self-defense and was much bigger and stronger than his assailants. He struggled to his feet, used his left forearm to deflect one man's stick, and countered with a powerful right cross to the nose, sending the man to the ground in a spray of blood. Taylor caught the second man's wrist as he tried to strike him with his stick. Taylor put a knee to the man's stomach, then lifted him off his feet with a uppercut to the chin that left the man sprawled on the street. Amid hooting and hollering, curses in who knows how many languages and dialects, Taylor grabbed his hat from the ground and pushed out from the ring around him. Seething with anger and adrenalin, like some mad animal, he stalked down the street, no one daring to touch him or get in his way.

CHAPTER 13

When Taylor returned to the Queen's Imperial, he went straight to his room, bathed, attended to the scrapes and lash marks on his arms and face, dressed in clean clothes, and headed to the basement lounge. He found a table in the corner and ordered a drink. He knew a call to Mountbatten was in order, but what would he say? He felt embarrassed, defeated, humbled, and mostly quite lost. He, Roger Taylor, diplomat to the nonrationals, had become nonrational. There was no denying it. Not only had he become a victim to his emotions, he had caused just the kind of disturbance he was there to prevent.

Determined not to simply drink the day away, Taylor ascended to the dining room for dinner after his second gin and tonic. Following the meal, he returned to his room to reassess and be alone. For quite some time, he just sat on the bed, perplexed by the events of the day and haunted by the ridiculous idea that Pipal was James reborn. He reached for James' flask sitting on the bedside table and held it close to his chest, as though hoping to absorb some of its good spirit.

During this moment of fleeting calm, Taylor recalled the incident of the bomb four days earlier on the train between New Delhi and Ambala. Sinking into sentimentality, he reaffirmed to himself that the flask had saved his life that day. This thought and fond memories of James tended to buoy his spirits. He undid the cap and took a swallow of bourbon from the flask, then holding the flask out before him, recalled the last time he'd seen James drinking from it.

It was a week after the Vice-Chancellor's bash celebrating the end of the Michaelmas term. Christmas was still ten days off and holiday spirits at the university were running high. The rugby season had wound down to its last match, the always hard fought battle with Cambridge. Though his health was rapidly deteriorating and his doctor prescribed rest and quiet, James confided to Roger that he would like to attend this last match in Twickenham because he'd never have the opportunity again. Roger, of course, agreed to accompany him.

As it turned out, word got out of James' intentions to go to the match, and several of his friends wanted to be included. At first Roger had resisted this, thinking it would be best to minimize the excitement of the excursion, but when he mentioned his reservations to James, it became clear that James wanted to make it a party.

Despite the extra effort, James turned down the use of Harry Lanyard's automobile and requested they all take the Waterloo Railway for old times' sake. It was the way Oxford men always went to matches at Twickenham. The group numbered five—James, Roger, Harry Lanyard and Todd Thomas from the Rinpoche's seminar, and another rugby player, Timmy Broadhurst, who had damaged his knee during fall practice and had been forced to sit out the rest of the season. Though James had kept the seriousness of his illness concealed from many of his friends, all in this group knew the leukemia was terminal and understood the sentimental nature of the trip. None, but Roger, knew of the wager that had been made with Tenzing Chogyam.

The day of the match was a blessing. The sun was out and it was unseasonably warm. It was really a perfect day for the match, especially considering James' precarious health. They met at the train station full of fun and vigor, but something of the sadness of the event was in the air. The good-natured ribbing and joking died out very early in the train ride, and a stiff solemnity cramped all further efforts at lighthearted conversation. Clearly, Roger, Tom, Harry, and Timmy were languishing before the inevitability of losing one of their most cherished friends. James did not miss this, but as was so typical of him, he chose to ignore it and rouse his friends out of the doldrums without letting on how much he felt their melancholy.

About halfway to Twickenham, amid what was slowly becoming a very depressing ride, James decided it was time to appeal to higher spirits to liven up the group. He'd brought a small knapsack with him on the train, and he delved into it while the others, peering forlornly out the windows at passing scenery, seemed to be lost to their own thoughts.

"Anyone interested in a drink?" inquired James, allowing a slight smirk, as he produced a nearly full bottle of Glenlivit scotch from his knapsack.

Before anyone said a word, Todd, Harry, and Timmy turned to Roger. Drinking and rowdiness were always a part of attending rugby matches. The festive atmosphere was already spreading through the train filled with Oxford students. But Roger had asked them all to refrain from drinking in James' presence because James was restricted to no more than a social sip or two. Seeing the questions in the others eyes, Roger warily took the lead. "Yes, James, I think I'll have a nip." And he took the bottle that James had already opened.

The others could not have been more pleased. They were all struggling to make the day a pleasant one and the alcohol was just what was needed. As they each took a full swallow and passed the bottle on, James pulled his engraved flask from the inside breast pocket of his jacket and with studied ceremony undid the top and took a sip himself. "The bottle is yours, gentlemen. I topped off my flask earlier, and seeing how we're headed to the match I won single-handedly last year." He smiled broadly when he said this, as he was never one to boast. "I will take to this trophy," he lifted the flask, "by myself."

"What do you mean, single-handedly?" gibed Timmy as he handed the bottle to Harry. "Seems to me I had two good knees a year ago and I was part of that scrum."

James grinned. "Maybe so, but look who's got the flask."

They all laughed at this, and sure enough, the liquor worked steadily to turn the mood of the group around—only dark thinking Roger lagged behind. He took his regular turn at the bottle, but feeling responsible for his soul mate James, he resisted intoxication.

*Not too long after James broke out the bottle of scotch, the train pulled into the station at Twickenham. It was only a short walk from the railway station to the rugby grounds, and almost the entire load of passengers, close to three hundred rowdy Oxonians, bustled along the walkway from the station to the stadium. The sunshine and fresh air brought color to James' face and a radiance to his being that had been waning steadily over the last month. Walking backwards and talking excitedly, he led the group of five down the path to the stadium. "Boys," said James, "I think this is my real church." He grinned impishly. "You know what I mean, Timmy? Where else but in the heat of the match do you feel so alive or completely involved? All else in the world is pushed aside and, as a child again, you just **are**—running, kicking, yelling—your spirit infused with vital fun. There is probably no better therapy for the soul than a good rough and tumble scrum."*

"I couldn't agree more, James," answered Timmy. "Damn, if I don't wish I was suited up and out there right now, warming up with the ruggers. Especially against Cambridge. Gad, James, they need us."

Good-natured James scoffed. "They'll have us, Tim. We'll be yelling for 'em. We'll be there."

Harry and Todd joined in with the fun, but Roger still wrestled within himself. Despite the obvious thrill the trip was giving James, Roger couldn't enjoy it as he should. He smiled when it was appropriate and even pressed himself to laugh, yet the specter of death hung upon his shoulders like a heavy black cape which he could not push off.

After they entered the stadium, James and Timmy separated from the group and went down to the field where the rugby squad was gathered for a final talk from the coach. Watching from the stands above, seated with Harry and Todd, Roger could see, almost feel, the emotion James' arrival inspired in the team. They all knew he was fighting some illness, but only the coach and two other players knew it was fatal. Hiding his sadness from Harry and Todd, Roger verged on tears as he saw the ruggers gathering around his friend, patting him on the back and exchanging wishes for good health and a victory on the field today. One of the players took James aside and gave him a hug; every nuance of the emotional goodbye was taken in from above by Roger. Lastly, the coach came up to James and clasped his hand. Roger imagined he could read the older man's thoughts as he spoke to James. Then there was a great hurrying as the teams prepared for the opening scrummage. Timmy and James bid the ruggers good luck and headed for their seats with the others.

The first half of the match was marked by inspired play by both teams. Cambridge was the favored squad, but Oxford made several good tries and converted on two long kicks in what was an unusually high scoring match for these teams. Oxford actually led 18 to 17 when the first forty minutes of play were over.

The furious play and steady nipping at the flask had James entirely involved in the match, screaming and cursing with every turn of fortune, yelling the names of players, calling out encouragement and instruction. It was not the same for Roger. He took his turn at the bottle as it was passed about, but with too much concern for his friend, he cringed a little each time he saw James reach into his jacket for the flask. He felt as though he were watching someone taking poison, and he feared that every sip took a day of life from his dear friend.

There was a twenty minute break between the first and second halves of the match. During that time, James and Timmy provided their expert commentary on the action—foul plays, a noticed limping in Oxford's top forward, and the one extremely long field goal by Oxford just as time expired in the half. James was feeling no pain. Timmy had surely risen to the occasion with him. Harry wasn't far behind. Todd was trying, but more than once, stroking his mustache down around the corners of his mouth, he allowed an eye of concern to meet with Roger's. Roger had no choice but to gradually give in to the drink, taking bigger and bigger swallows from the bottle, hoping that he could somehow enjoy the match, despite the heavy weight upon his shoulders.

Just as the second half was about to begin and the ruggers were taking the field, James unsteadily stood up on his seat. He lifted his arms over his head to gather as much attention as he could and began singing one of the rugby team's jocular fight songs. He had a beautiful tenor voice, and though the words of the song didn't seem to fit the lilt of his singing, James silenced the crowd all around him with awe and humor. When he finished his spirited display, which the Oxford ruggers below did not miss, the entire section of fans exploded with a roar of approval and laughter. Timmy, Harry, and Todd were as loud as the rest, and Roger, containing himself throughout, found himself staring at James as he stepped down off his seat. James caught his glance and read Roger's thoughts as though their minds were one. He shrugged and made a funny twisted smile, as if to say through the noise of the crowd, "It's okay, Roger. This is really good for me." Roger finally got it. James was drunk and so what? He was having a good time.

Roger took the half-empty bottle of scotch and with his first real smile of the day raised it to James. James pulled the flask from his coat and returned the gesture. Then both took hearty swallows. The black cloak slid from Roger's shoulders and he proceeded to join in with unrestrained vigor, finally feeling the full spirit of his phenomenal friend James.

Unfortunately the Oxford rugby team could not maintain the level of its play. The second forty minutes were all Cambridge, resulting in a lopsided 33-23 Oxford loss. The group of five hardly noticed. With the drink and increasing good spirits, led by James, they all were laughing and screaming throughout the sloppy second half of the match.

Afterward they decided to take their time and not rush to get the first train back. There was no need to hurry. The day was still bright with sunshine, and they would let the crowd thin and catch the second or third train returning to Oxford. Harry, Todd, and Timmy took the opportunity to venture to a nearby market and procure some food. They all needed something in their stomachs to help shake off the effects of the alcohol.

While the others were gone, Roger and James sat on the grass outside the stadium and reviewed the match. Having taken to the scotch heavily after the half, Roger pulled the bottle from James' knapsack, hoping for one last swig, only to discover that the bottle was empty. A little cockeyed, he held the bottle up before him, as though fully taking in the reality of its emptiness, causing James to chuckle at his friend's obvious state.

Roger twisted his head around in the direction of James and dropped the bottle to the ground. "This is a fine fix, James. You wouldn't be thinking of sharing your trophy flask, would you?"

"Why surely. Have at it," said James, betraying a slight grin as he reached into his jacket and produced the engraved flask.

Roger took the flask, unscrewed the cap, and tipped back his head for a long swallow. As soon as the fluid entered his mouth, he abruptly spit it out, looked quizzically at the flask, and passed it under his nose. "What? James, this is water."

James compressed a guilty smirk. "Sorry to disappoint you, Roger. But I'm on strict orders from the doctor not to drink."

"But? But..."

James let go a laugh. "I just thought it might help everybody forget about me and enjoy the match."

"But I would have sworn you were drunk. God, especially when you stood up in the crowd and sang!" Roger's mouth hung open in disbelief.

James shrugged his shoulders in the same way he had after singing and made that same funny smile that had broken through to Roger before.

Roger shook his head and laughed and laughed. "You beat all, James. I can't believe it. But you did it. One by one, you got us. Lastly, the most difficult one of all, me."

Taylor had just indulged himself one last reminiscent tug from the flask, when there were three heavy knocks on his door. Though he hadn't spoken with Chuluun since the first night, Taylor's initial thought was that it must be the bartender, who he knew was working a shift that night. Two more knocks sounded as he approached the door.

"Who is it?"

"The Haridwar Police," said a heavily accented voice in English on the other side.

Taylor hesitated, then opened the door. Three Indian police officers stood in the hall. Two were tall, bearded Sikhs in black turbans. The third, standing in front, was a shorter man, a Gurkha in khaki shorts and wearing a wide-brimmed, felt terai hat, pinned to his head by a strap beneath his chin and tilted at a radical angle to the left. This man spoke. "You're Roger Taylor?"

"That's correct. How may I help you?" Taylor's haughty tone matched his mood.

"My name is Captain Havildar Rantanbir." He was a small, wiry, dark-skinned man. With his hat, wire rimmed glasses, and wide, black mustache, he looked like an Asian version of one of Teddy Roosevelt's rough riders. "There has been a complaint filed against you by two men on the east side of the city for assault and battery." As the man spoke, he appraised the welts on Taylor's face. "I would like you to come down to the police station to answer a few questions."

"We could save the trouble by talking right here, Captain," said Taylor unimpressed.

"Trouble, Mr. Taylor?"

Taylor rolled his eyes. "All I meant was there's no reason to go all the way to the station. The mishap this afternoon can be easily explained."

"Mishap, Mr. Taylor? There's a man in the hospital with a dislocated jaw and another who was treated for a broken nose."

"I was attacked, Captain. I was defending myself."

The police captain strode into the room. "Do you mind if we search your room?"

Taylor was fit to be tied. "Go right ahead," he said full of sarcasm, then stood back as one Sikh went to the closet and the other to the chest of drawers.

Rantanbir approached the bedside table and picked up the flask. An infuriated Taylor watched as the man noted the inscription, unscrewed the top, and passed the flask beneath his nose. He looked at Taylor. "You do know alcohol is prohibited in Haridwar? This alone," he lifted the flask, "is grounds for arrest."

"Come now, Captain," snapped Taylor, just loose enough with drink to get belligerent. "They serve alcohol right here in the basement. That's where I got that whiskey."

Across the room, one of the other officers lifted Taylor's shoulder holster and handgun from the dresser drawer. Rantanbir's eyes swung from the gun back to Taylor. "I believe we've found that trouble you were trying to avoid, Mr. Taylor."

Taylor wagged his head in frustration, all set to explode, then suddenly collected himself. "Captain Rantanbir, please. I have a permit for that gun. I'm undercover C.I.D." Taylor reached for his wallet, realizing as he opened it he'd left all his official papers, including the gun permit, on the dead man at the train bombing.

As Taylor stalled with his wallet, Rantanbir stepped forward and took it from his hands. It was all Taylor could do to keep himself from slapping the man for his impertinence. The captain opened the wallet and thumbed through the large amount of cash inside, then took out the I.D. and read it. He looked at Taylor. "Jonathan Edmonds? Mr. Taylor, who are you really?"

Taylor took a deep breath—if he'd only left India in December. "Let me make one phone call. I can get all this straightened out very quickly." Even as he said the words, he remembered Mountbatten's warning—*if you get into any trouble, you're on your own. I don't know you exist.*

"We're headed to the station, Mr. Taylor, Mr. Edmonds, whoever you are. You can make your call from there."

And that was it. With a turbaned Sikh on each side, a handcuffed Roger Taylor was marched out of his room and down through the lobby. As he was pushed into the back seat of the waiting patrol car, Taylor spotted Chuluun coming down the street toward the hotel. He yelled out to him as the door was slammed shut. Chuluun walked past the car and into the hotel without even looking back.

CHAPTER 14

The questioning at the police station that evening went nowhere. Roger Taylor was essentially stuck in his own web. He had no identification papers because of his attempt to fake his own death, and he couldn't call Mountbatten or say anything more than that he was there to observe the fast. He could call his boss in Bombay at the C.I.D. office, but he'd been requested by New Delhi not to inform him of the mission, so that would open yet another can of worms. There was really nothing he could say that wouldn't make matters worse. He just clammed up and steamed.

Frustrated by Taylor's belligerent silence, Captain Rantanbir decided to hold him overnight on the alcohol charge. The cell was small and filthy. Taylor shared it with two common street thieves and slept not one moment during the night.

Midmorning the next day, Captain Rantanbir brought a turbaned man with a bandaged nose into the jail. It was one of the men Taylor had punched the day before, and he quickly identified Taylor as the perpetrator. The stress and strain of the circumstances, plus the night without sleep, pushed Taylor over the edge. He screamed at Rantanbir that it was he who was attacked and that he had fought back only in self-defense. The man with the broken nose countered by saying he and the other man were protecting the woman who was fasting and her mother. This man, Taylor, he said, was disturbing the fast and the pilgrims there to pay homage.

Again Taylor's best defense, having Rantanbir question Pipal or Areena, was off limits. His ensuing silence did nothing for his argument.

After the man who had identified him left, Rantanbir told Taylor he was dropping the alcohol charge, but that he would be tried in two weeks for assault, and because he couldn't be trusted to stay in Haridwar, he would have to remain in his cell without bail until the trial. Taylor demanded a lawyer, then told Rantanbir to forget it, knowing his entire case hinged on revealing who he was working for and that he was trying to stop the fast—which for now he felt had to be kept secret.

He stewed the rest of the day in his cell, wondering how the hell he would get out of this mess and see Pipal again. Beyond all reason, that was foremost in his mind. He wanted to ask her outright if she remembered her previous life. Even incarcerated, this made Taylor smile. Maybe here was proof he did, in fact, need to be locked up. He'd lost his mind. That seemed to make more sense than what he was thinking.

Shortly after Taylor rejected what was given to him as his evening meal, Captain Rantanbir came to his cell and asked him if he would receive a visitor. Having no idea who could possibly want to visit him, Taylor said yes. Rantanbir returned with Chuluun, who immediately identified Taylor as a C.I.D. officer. From the ensuing exchange between Rantanbir and Chuluun, Taylor understood that they knew each other. It was almost humorous now as Taylor looked out from the cell at these two men—one big and stout with a patch over one eye, the other short and thin with wire rimmed glasses and surely weighing no more than one hundred and thirty pounds. Whether for show or by happenstance, they'd just let him know who controlled security in the streets of Haridwar. He, Taylor, was the stranger in this city and he was to abide by their rules. At this point, Taylor figured he had nothing to hide but Mountbatten's involvement in the mission, so he told Rantanbir he was there to observe the fast for security reasons, concluding with, "How did you find me so quickly last night?"

"A boy in the street told us right away. He even knew your name, hotel, and room number."

Ah, yes, thought Taylor, he'd been played for a dupe from the beginning, even Chadi was likely part of the inside game.

"In light of this information, Mr. Taylor," said Captain Rantanbir, unlocking the cell door. "I believe I owe you an apology." Taylor, ever arrogant, especially when upset, reluctantly accepted a handshake from the wiry police captain. "You are a free man. I'll see what I can do about getting the assault charges dropped, but I would still like you to remain in Haridwar until the trail date—in case I can't get things settled by then. I believe I can trust you for that?" said the captain with just enough doubt to irritate Taylor.

"I'm already booked for two weeks at the Queen's Imperial, Captain. I'll be in town and available."

"You'd also be well advised to stay out of that neighborhood where the fight broke out." Rantanbir led Taylor and Chuluun into the front office and retrieved Taylor's now empty flask and his handgun from a desk drawer and handed them to him. "Good day, Mr. Taylor. You are free to go."

Taylor said nothing and walked out. Chuluun followed.

Taylor was relieved but still angry and somewhat humbled by the fact that it had been Chuluun who had rescued him. Once they had walked some distance from the station, Taylor addressed the bartender, still uncertain if he'd been set up or if the Mongolian had sincerely come to his aid. "Chuluun, I owe you my deepest thanks for coming to get me today. I was the victim of some very difficult circumstances."

The burly Mongolian merely nodded. "I saw you taken last night. I decided not to interfere until I checked with my contact in New Delhi. I got a hold of him this afternoon and he gave me permission to come get you."

"Well, I owe you one."

Chuluun stroked his chin hairs. "No, you owe me nothing. I only did what needed to be done." He motioned to a street on their left. "I go off this way, Mr. Taylor. Can you find your way to the hotel?"

Taylor said he could and extended his hand. Chuluun accepted the handshake, then said, "I was told to tell you to contact your superior." Taylor nodded, not eager at all to call Mountbatten. With that the two men went their separate ways.

CHAPTER 15

Night had fallen by the time Roger Taylor reached the Queen's Imperial. He stopped at the desk on his way through the lobby and asked for a phone connection to New Delhi. The phone was ringing when he entered his room. He reached into the shadows for the phone instead of the light switch. It was Mountbatten and he was furious. Why hadn't he called sooner? Why was he in jail? Taylor steeled himself through Mountbatten's fury, then tried to explain. When he told the Governor-General what happened the day before, Mountbatten pulled him off the job.

"Taylor, when I called on you, I assumed you were the only one that could get in and out of there without a mess. There was no one else who I thought was capable. And now even you have stirred things up. Maybe it's nothing as you say. But I want you out of Haridwar now. Come back to New Delhi and we'll talk about where you go next."

Taylor told him the police captain had asked him to stay in town until the assault charges had been settled. It might take two weeks.

This sent Mountbatten into another tirade, finally saying, "Alright, fine. If you must stay, at least keep an eye on the fast from a distance. And, for God's sake, don't visit the woman again or be seen—and don't do a damn thing until you've checked with me."

Taylor hated being talked to like this. He hung up even more upset than before the call. He flipped on the light by the bed and cursed at full volume. Three large swastikas were painted on the walls of the room in orange paint and the bedspread had been sliced diagonally in an "x" all the way down to the mattress.

The night in the jail cell had left Taylor exhausted and exasperated. This didn't help. He dialed down to the desk and asked for a new room. Once the change had been made, he bathed and had a late dinner. After the meal, he retired to the basement. Chuluun was tending bar, and for the first time, there were more than just a handful of customers. Taylor bought a drink and thanked the Mongolian again for coming to get him. Chuluun played it down, but clearly their relationship had changed. Though they weren't exactly talking like old friends, Taylor had gained considerable respect for the bartender and the Mongolian clearly felt that.

Taylor told Chuluun about the swastikas in his room and the attempt on his life in January. "Consider yourself lucky that you spent last night in jail," replied Chuluun with no emotion.

"Yes, that was a wonderful stroke of luck," said Taylor dryly. "What do you think of it, though? The Rashtra Dal in Haridwar? Isn't that unlikely?"

Chuluun remained nonplussed. "Not so much. They have cells all over India. And if they have a mark on you—stay sharp."

Taylor took a sip from his drink. "Any suggestions? I'll be here another two weeks."

"Watch your back," said the bartender.

Taylor nodded. "Maybe you could keep an eye out too?"

"Sure," replied Chuluun unconvincingly. Taylor had to laugh. For all the Mongolian's seeming lack of interest, it was just his way, and he did feel that Chuluun would be on the lookout.

When he finished his drink, Taylor asked Chuluun to fill his flask with whiskey. He paid twice the bill and retired to his new room.

Despite being terribly tired, Taylor had been unnerved by the orange swastikas. Before he climbed into bed, he looked inside the closet, checked all the window locks, blocked the door with the dresser, and put his handgun beneath the pillow. It took him a while to fall asleep, but he did and he slept amazingly well. He had several dreams, as he had ever since that night of the murder attempt in January, but he remembered only the last dream which featured languid Naija Kocchar there in his bed in Haridwar. He woke erect and vastly distracted. He lay in bed unable to get the image of Naija's welcoming thighs out of his mind and finally masturbated to clear his head. He bathed and shaved and went down for breakfast with no plan as yet for the day.

Following the meal and two cups of tea, Taylor strapped on his shoulder holster and took to the streets just to get out. He walked as in a daydream, rethinking all that had happened in the last twenty-four hours and knowing what was foremost in his mind was off limits.

Still, when Taylor became cognizant of where he was, he realized he was very near Pipal's neighborhood and that the noon hour was approaching. Arguing with himself the entire way, he decided to venture a little closer—and then a little closer still—until he was walking down the street to Pipal's home. From a distance, he saw there was no group gathered beneath the neem tree and that the line outside Pipal's home was the longest he'd yet encountered. It didn't bode well for Pipal's health. Against all reason, he took a place at the end of the line, telling himself that he needed to apologize to Areena and Pipal for his actions two days earlier.

He immediately became aware of a growing uneasiness in those near him and in others further down the line. Apparently it had become generally known that he represented the British government, and many in the line felt he was a negative influence and had no right to be there. But it was Taylor's personal motives that were pressing him to remain. Against his orders and amid growing commotion in the line, he resolved to stay. That is, until he saw the old woman from Calcutta, far up in the line, leave her place and totter up to him wrapped in her *pallu*.

Taylor forced a smile as Sumitra approached. She didn't return it. "You may not heed the words of an old woman, sahib," she said in Bengali, "but you would be wise to go back to where you are staying. Many of these people are unhappy that you are here. Many more than before."

Taylor didn't want this kind of advice from the old woman and his determined eyes reflected it. She continued. "I'm not the one to judge who has the right to be here or not, but regardless of your intentions, you are doing a disservice to Pipal. I'm certain the aggravation your presence here is creating is being felt inside by her. She is already very weak. Leave for her sake, if not for these others who threaten violence."

"Is it the leper who is causing the trouble, Sumitra?"

"The leper is only part of it. But he is gone now. Pipal accepted him to the fast on the condition he would return to his colony. Lepers make us all uneasy, Mr. Taylor. All but Pipal, I suppose. Still, others are agitated you are here. Please leave."

Taylor tried to deny her truth. "I appreciate what you are saying, good woman, but I must see Pipal. I must apologize to her for the things that happened two days ago. Nothing more."

Sumitra shook her head. "No apology will help today, if the effort you make to deliver it causes more reasons for apologies tomorrow."

Taylor made no move to leave the line. Several of the others nearby began to talk loudly and with hostility. The old woman took a step closer to Taylor and spoke softly but with intensity. "I want no trouble, sahib. Let me take your apology to Pipal. She will understand. Maybe another day the pilgrims will not be so angry. But today is a bad day for you to be here. You said the first day you were here that you would cause no problems. Prove that now, please, and leave," she beseeched.

Taylor looked the woman in the eye. It was clear he was being foolish and self-centered. He was there to resolve personal issues and to do this was disobeying orders from New Delhi. He must let this go. "You're right, Sumitra," he reluctantly acquiesced. "You're right. I will leave, but please do take my apology to her. Tell her I have no right to be here unless it's to support her cause, and because I can't do that, I won't bother her again."

With that the woman nodded and said she would do as he requested. Taylor turned, and amid taunting and laughter, hurried the other way down the street, knowing he'd made a mistake going there in the first place—and also that the question he most dearly wanted to ask Pipal would not be part of the apology Sumitra would deliver.

CHAPTER 16

The next three days Roger Taylor laid low. He did very little venturing out into the city. He had all his meals and his after dinner drink at the Queen's Imperial, but he didn't sleep there. After his room was broken into, he had little faith in the hotel's security and would slip off late each evening to the Hotel Hari Ganga, the hotel down by the river where he'd first rented a room for just this—an emergency sanctuary—and, for now, a place to sleep at night.

On a handmade calendar, he marked off the days and kept track of the length of Pipal's fast. It was now over thirty days. From this point on, the precariousness of her health would rise asymptotically with each ensuing day. Another week and the end would be in sight—if not passed. This awareness tore at Taylor. He wanted to talk to Pipal at least once more, and several times he started out for her home only to turn around in confusion. Why was he going there? To seek out the answer to a fairy tale? It was a tough choice to defend after he'd told Sumitra he wouldn't return and Mountbatten had ordered him to stay away.

A man accustomed to success struggled badly with his frustrations. Drink seemed to be his only balm and a poor one at that. He drank in the basement lounge when he was at the Queen's Imperial, then would sip on his flask at night when he'd removed himself to the Hotel Hari Ganga. From his room on the second floor, he could see the river—not a wide view, just a sliver between two buildings—but enough to see the candles sliding down the river at night, prayers seeking answers.

A little alcohol might have helped Taylor sleep, but too much did the opposite. During his nights at the Hari Ganga, he tossed and turned, woke frequently and dreamed so vividly he hardly knew when he was awake or asleep. Of the myriad of dreams he had in this period of inner turmoil, two stood out because they repeated.

The dream of his being in Victoria Terminus during the war came back several times—being lost, seeing the Rinpoche, and asking him about James. Was he reborn? Where can I find him? These dreams were particularly disturbing because they were invariably lucid dreams.

He also dreamed many times of going to Pipal's house. In one instance he arrived to find the line gone and the fast forgotten. Pipal was there sitting in the shade of the neem tree, wearing a printed cotton dress, not looking very Indian at all. They walked hand-in-hand east of town to a little wooded knoll. She spoke of her days in England and the time she'd been to a performance of the London Philharmonic Orchestra. They ate a picnic lunch and James Nielsen sauntered up to join them. The dream ended with the three of them talking as friends.

In another, he entered Pipal's room but instead found himself in Carolyn Williamson's bedroom back in Connecticut. Carolyn was fasting as a way to get him to marry her, and the same black and white photograph of Gandhi, sitting cross-legged before his treadle, was on the wall. The eyes seemed alive and watching. Reluctantly Taylor allowed Carolyn to lure him into an intimate embrace. She eased her hand into his trousers, then suddenly took hold of his testicles and squeezed, saying, "I should have taken these when I had the chance." The picture of Gandhi spoke. "You did."

In the most recent of these dreams, he knelt at the side of Pipal's *charpoy*. Pipal showed no signs of the fast and her beauty was supernaturally radiant. Taylor could not help touching and caressing her. With her mother watching from the doorway, he slipped into the bed alongside Pipal. He kissed her on the neck. Then remembering the other dreams and how she had changed, he looked into her eyes for an extended moment before kissing her deeply and passionately. With one hand he pushed her gown up above her waist, revealing small, hairless male genitals, the penis uncircumcised and erect. Aghast he dared to look her in the eye and in James Nielsen's voice she spoke, "Tenzing Chogyam." He stood up in fear and turned to the door expecting to see Areena. Instead it was the leper there watching him.

These repeating dreams unnerved Taylor. Too many of them suggested the same thing—that Pipal was the reincarnation of James Nielsen. Fighting the irrationality of what he was clearly obsessing on, he felt he must go back to see her, ask her the obvious question, and finally put an end to this nonsense.

The morning of his fourth day at the Hari Ganga, Taylor, wearing his lightweight suntan suit and a red cricket club tie, set out for Pipal's home. It was the thirty-third day of her fast. He turned back before going five blocks. Cursing his foolishness, he retrieved his shoulder holster and hand gun from his room at the Hari Ganga and headed for the Queen's Imperial.

He drank his lunch in the lounge that afternoon. After three gin and tonics, he abruptly left his table and set to the streets of Haridwar in search of a brothel, believing much of his inner tension and the strange sexual nature of his dreams could be relieved in this base way.

In the larger cities of India, especially Bombay and Calcutta, prostitution was prevalent and red-light districts could be found almost anywhere. This was not the case in the sacred city of Haridwar, and Taylor walked for quite a while before he gave in to flagging down a taxi and asking outright. Five minutes later, he was dropped off on the far south side of Haridwar at a rundown hotel with a conch shell over the front door.

After the taxi sped away, Taylor immediately began having second thoughts. The alcohol that had fired his urge had burned off considerably, and the setting was nothing like the high-class places he'd visited in Bombay. Still he felt he needed to do this to relieve his strained psyche and he entered the brothel.

The interior of the place didn't help. A sign handwritten in Hindi directed him up a dark stairway to the second floor. The walls of the stairway and the second floor hall were painted red with black ceilings. Cheaply framed illustrations from the *Kama Sutra* were the prevailing decor. The only light came in through a dirty window at each end of the hallway.

Despite god Shiva's teachings of transcendence through sexual communion, the exchange of money for physical amours had nothing to do with those beliefs. Prostitution under any name or guise was a dark karmic sink in the eyes of the Hindus. Most of the prostitutes were widowed child brides, forbidden from remarrying and left as outcasts after their older husbands had died. It was something Gandhi had spoken out strongly against, but the tradition remained.

Taylor rarely thought about this archaic institution he was helping maintain and had enjoyed Indian brothels without a second thought many times in his ten years there, but on this afternoon, Taylor unexpectedly experienced a heavy sense of guilt as soon as the madam presented herself at the top of the stairs.

Struck by Taylor's good looks and expensive suit, the madam immediately offered him a drink, which he declined, then asked him a single question, "Woman or boy, sahib?" She led him down the hall, opening one door after another so he could view the women that were available.

At the fourth door, Taylor had seen enough and selected a particularly young prostitute because of her resemblance to Naija. She was introduced as Parvati and was probably no more than sixteen. It was obvious from the start that she was very pleased to be chosen by so handsome a man, and like a valet she helped him out of his clothes. He took one look at the bed, and knowing he would never get between those sheets, asked for oral sex, requesting she undress to perform the act. Parvati began to glide around him, touching his body lightly with her silken clothing as she dropped each piece to the floor.

Parvati had a beautiful body and under ordinary circumstances, Taylor would have been vastly pleased with so lovely a young woman, but today his mind wouldn't allow it. Instead of being captivated by Parvati's seductive dance, he found himself thinking of Pipal on the other side of town fasting to end her life.

Seeing that her dance was not arousing him, Parvati knelt before Taylor and took his genitals in her hands, caressing and kissing them. Still there was no physical response, and Taylor, struggling with the increasing awkwardness, tried to act his part by gently touching her cheek and stroking her long raven tresses—while his mind clung to images of Pipal.

When Parvati looked up questioningly from her knees, Taylor saw Pipal's face superimposed over hers and it struck him as a deep perversion to imagine Pipal in this setting. When she dipped her head and took his flaccid penis in her mouth, he pulled away from the confused girl and quickly dressed himself, scattering a handful of loose cash around the room in his hasty retreat.

Entirely distraught, his tie undone and his jacket slung over his right shoulder, Taylor set off on foot across Haridwar, squinting into the bright afternoon sun and feeling quite awful from the effects of his liquid lunch and his impotence at the whorehouse. He walked for some time head down, keeping to the back streets, hardly paying attention, as he sought to unscramble the emotions and feelings that were knotted within him. The connection of Pipal to James Nielsen might be all in his head. That he could accept. But he did feel something real for the young woman. That was undeniable. The sexual dreams about her and the recent occurrence in the house of ill repute, however, suggested there were deeper motives buried in his subconscious that he wasn't quite ready to face.

Fully distracted, walking up a narrow empty street, Taylor heard his name pronounced by a heavily accented voice behind him. He turned around. Two men in turbans came striding at him aggressively. Taylor began to run only to have another turbaned man step out from a side street right in front of him, wielding a long knife. Taylor reached for his handgun, quickly discovering he'd left his shoulder holster and gun behind at the brothel.

With little choice, he twirled his jacket around his left arm, wrapping his hand and forearm in the cloth—then ran at the man with the knife. Using the mass of his jacket as a shield, he deflected the knife with his left forearm and knocked the man flat with a right cross. He abruptly darted down an alley with all three men in hot pursuit. He took a turn to the right, then to the left, before tripping and falling flat on his face. The men were on him in a flash, a man on each arm and a third kneeling on his chest, pressing a knife up under his chin.

"This is for not minding your own business, Mr. Taylor," said the man with the knife in Hindi. With his free hand, the man drew a piece of orange chalk from his shirt pocket and was about to apply it to Taylor's forehead, when a single shot rang out. The man fell sideways off Taylor.

"Let him go or you'll get the same as your friend," commanded Captain Rantanbir running down the alley, a smoking carbine in his hand, and his two Sikh officers right behind. The two men let go of Taylor and stood back. Taylor, a large slice across his forearm and a smaller one on his neck, struggled up to his feet.

Rantanbir, his hat cocked jauntily on his head, grinned beneath his moustache. "I trust you're enjoying your stay in Haridwar, Mr. Taylor."

Taylor dusted himself off and offered the captain a reluctant thanks. "I guess I owe you one, Captain."

"Yes, I'd say that was quite close."

"Damn lucky you happened by."

"No luck at all."

"What do you mean?"

"I've had a man on your tail since the day we let you out of jail."

"You ass," snarled Taylor.

"Now, now, Mr. Taylor. I couldn't let a British intelligence officer wander around my town without a backup."

"Well, I thought I had Chuluun."

"He's done a few shifts."

Taylor shook his head.

"By the way, you left your handgun back at your last stop." Rantanbir winked. "It's in my car. My men will take care of the prisoners and the body. I'll give you a ride. Where do you want to go? The Queen's Imperial…or the Hotel Hari Ganga?"

It was a short ride back to the Queen's Imperial. When they reached the hotel, Taylor remained in the car and thanked the police captain again.

"I realize, Captain, that I can be quite a pompous ass. It's been said I don't care what others think, and I'm no good at offering thanks. But in the work I do—we do—there is a cold, mutual appreciation for the dangers we share that acts as a weak substitute for deeper feelings." He extended his hand.

Rantanbir took Taylor's hand. "From an intelligence officer for His Majesty—for whom I did fight in the war as part of the 1/13th Gurkha Rifles," he added proudly, "I accept that as a weak substitute for friendship."

This made Taylor smile openly and with real affection. "Then we understand each other."

"Mostly," replied the Gurkha in total seriousness. "I asked you not to go back to the fasting woman's neighborhood and you did five days ago. Please, heed my request. You are likely to get yourself and perhaps the young woman into more trouble than I can get you out of."

Taylor took his shoulder holster and handgun off the seat beside him and pushed open the car door. "It's in my orders to keep an eye on the fast, Captain."

"Perhaps, but it's also part of my duty to ask you to stay away," said Rantanbir. "Let's not ruin our new weak substitute for friendship. Good day, Mr. Taylor."

CHAPTER 17

Roger Taylor entered the Queen's Imperial and went directly to his room. He bathed and dressed his wounds, put on clean clothing, and sat down in the room's one armchair to rethink the last week and impossibly puzzle the pieces of his life back together. Sitting there in the room alone, very unsettled by the turn of events, especially this recent attack in the street, he found himself starring at the engraved flask sitting on the bedside table. Somehow he felt that all the trouble he was having now originated with the wager he'd made with Tenzing Chogyam, and that the wager had subtly changed his relationship with his friend James Nielsen and had served to shape his attitude about life from that point on. He recalled an exchange he'd had with James the day of the rugby match in Twickenham. It was right after he'd discovered James' flask contained water not scotch, and they were still sitting in the grass outside the stadium waiting for the return of the others with food.

"James, how's your work progressing with Tenzing Chogyam?"

James contained his smile. "Quite well."

"Does he mention our wager?"

"He hasn't yet. But I wonder if we might have pushed him into an agreement he doesn't really wish to honor."

"Ask him about it. It's just too perfect an opportunity."

"No, I don't want Tenzing to feel any pressure from me. Do you remember what he said that night? If there are black arts, misuse of the Tibetan art of dying would be included. There are karmic costs for improper use of the knowledge."

"But James, this isn't improper use. It's a chance for you to take on the question of the afterlife. We can't let you waste your life without using this opportunity to pursue a greater goal."

"You mean waste my death for a greater goal," he replied soberly.

"No, I mean your life, James," denied Roger not hearing all that was intimated in James' words and tone. "We are scientists. Scientists on the cusp of greatness.

112

Think of it. Finding me in twenty years and telling me you've experienced death."

James sighed, diverting his eyes to all that surrounded them, as though taking full appreciation of the beautiful day, the green grass, the blue sky, the brilliant sunshine.

"Don't you remember our talk that night?" asked Roger, trying to draw his friend into his enthusiasm. "What of our friend Elias Ashmole? Can you imagine your bust decorating the walls outside the Ashmolean?"

James looked his friend in the eye. "I'm not so sure a bust outside the Ashmolean means that much to me, Roger. Yes, there would be great emotion in our meeting again in some distant future. And I would prefer to give my life in a quest for something important. But I'm coming to the belief that no lives go for nothing. There is meaning in everything. Every breath of wind, every lost rugby match." He plucked at the grass beside his knee. "Every blade of grass." He selected one blade of grass from his fingers and stopped to study its detail. "With every advance I make into the study of the Buddhist doctrines, Roger, the less I feel the need to be reborn again."

"But there is no transcendence in seeking the void. It's a blank illusion. The real breakthrough is returning to the material world of crisp edges and mathematical certainty."

James' eyes dropped to his hands, where he held the blade of grass between his fingers. "Buddhist enlightenment is not an illusion. It's this materiality, this tiny piece of grass, this huge stadium behind us. All of this," he spread his arms wide, palms up, "all of this is the tempting illusion. We are consciousness, pure, clear, infinite."

"You're giving in to him, James. I can hear it. This kind of non-logic will allow Tenzing to slip out of the promise he made that night. You must not miss this opportunity—unless you are simply afraid it won't work."

This last comment struck James with a bite. "If there is to be any kind of transference or rebirth, you Roger, must also be part of it, fully onboard and not just going through the motions—as I say, even if it's only transference."

At this point, Harry, Todd, and Timmy came strolling up, merrily swinging big bags of groceries. "Food and drink to the rescue," announced Harry as he sat down alongside Roger and James, oblivious to the tension the moment had held.

"Yes," followed Timmy, "it's tough to take a loss to Cambridge on an empty stomach. I think we've come up with just what we need to save some flagging spirits."

Roger looked up still hanging on James' last comment. James smiled weakly, slowly gaining on his state of mind. "Spread it out, boys. I don't know about Roger, but I could sure use something." He picked up the flask that Roger had laid on the ground before him, took off the cap, and lifted it to his lips as though it contained the real thing.

Roger watched wordlessly as James took a long swallow, knowing what James had just demanded of him was necessary and true.

These many years later, Taylor knew deep down that he had never "been fully on board," as James had requested. If he were to go to Pipal and ask her straight out, did she remember her last incarnation? If she were James reborn, her answer would justifiably be, "What right do you have to know?"

Taylor went down to the hotel dining room for dinner that evening. For the first time since he'd been there, he had to wait for a table. The festival of Kumbh Mela was a week away, and the influx of pilgrims and tourists was beginning. After his meal, he descended to the lounge. A light haze of cigarette smoke was apparent beneath the lights in the otherwise dark little speakeasy. It wasn't just five or ten people in the lounge; there were fifteen or twenty westerners there to observe the festival. But Taylor knew this was nothing. The real surge would be devoted pilgrims, and they would be increasingly evident in the streets of Haridwar over the next few days.

After a couple of stiff drinks in the back corner of the lounge, Taylor got up with a nearly empty glass and sidled up to the end of the bar where Chuluun mixed the drinks. The Mongolian went about his business, a cigarette hanging from his mouth, and Taylor just sat there watching him until he'd finished his drink. He asked Chuluun for another. When the bartender delivered the drink, Taylor asked him the same question he'd asked him the first time they'd spoken. "What do you know about this fasting woman?"

Chuluun looked Taylor in the eye, then lowered his gaze to take a drag off his cigarette. Chuluun rarely showed emotion one way or the other. A smile, a laugh, a grimace were seldom seen. He evinced more feeling in the way he smoked his cigarette than he did with his eyes or his facial expressions. He exhaled thoughtfully and gazed out across the lounge watching the smoke disperse. "I think she's a holy woman."

"You've seen her?"

"Early on in the fast." He took another pull on his smoke. "I went by her home and saw her talking to a group of visitors on the doorstep."

"You told me you didn't know where she lived?"

Chuluun exhaled the smoke under his breath as he spoke. "Shortly after I made my report to New Delhi, I heard the C.I.D. would be coming. I felt the reaction was excessive and wished I'd said nothing." A man in evening clothes stood up to the bar and waved an empty glass at

Chuluun. "When I heard you'd been killed by a bomb on the train, I was glad." He moved down the bar to take the customer's order.

When Chuluun came back to mix the drink, Taylor continued to pursue the question. "So when I got here, you decided to make it as difficult as possible for me."

The Mongolian looked up from his work and nodded ever so slightly. "Something like that." Chuluun delivered the drink to the customer, then took his time wiping down the bar and collecting empties before returning to the end of the bar where Taylor sat.

"What makes you think Pipal isn't just a high strung young woman with misplaced intentions?"

Chuluun took another drag from his smoke. "Mr. Taylor, clearly I'm not a religious person. I'm here in the sacred city of Haridwar serving prohibited alcohol. To many what I do is considered a sacrilege. Maybe it is. I don't know." He paused to exhale. "I grew up in Tibet. I saw many lamas and other purported holy men throughout my youth. Though I do not live by the ideals these people teach, I do recognize their commitment and I'm respectful. In this woman, Pipal, I felt something special right away—in a single short appraisal. She is a holy person. I don't really know what that means exactly. But that's what I think."

"I've felt the same thing." Taylor took a sip from his drink. "And I don't believe any one thing is more holy than anything else."

Neither man spoke for a while. It was as though they had both agreed on something that neither could quite understand. Chuluun returned to his chores. Taylor remained at the bar nursing his gin and tonic.

Sometime later, when Chuluun was putting together a tray of drinks, Taylor addressed him again. "Chuluun, what do you know of these holy people?"

"They make me feel guilty. I stay away from them," answered the bartender without looking up from his work.

"Can they work miracles? Can they heal people? That's been said of this woman. Have you ever seen such a thing?"

Chuluun gave Taylor a quizzical look and shrugged his shoulders.

"I've heard that some claim to have been reincarnated." Taylor's third drink was taking him into the gray zone. "And that they know their past lives. What do you make of that?"

Chuluun glanced up at Taylor. "Perhaps you've had too much to drink."

Taylor had to chuckle at this, but then shook his head. "No, I'm serious. I saw Pipal fix a child's badly dislocated elbow last week. It seemed like nothing to her. If she is one of these holy people as you say, I want to ask her about her past lives."

"You're getting stupid, Mr. Taylor. Rantanbir told you to stay away. Go to bed. Sleep it off. Maybe you will get your answer in your dreams." Chuluun took the tray of drinks and headed off to a table of customers

Taylor stood from the bar, left a large tip, and went off to his room. As he did the last time he'd slept at the Queen's Imperial, he opened the closet to ensure that no one was inside. He checked to see that the windows were locked, and he pushed the dresser in front of the door. When he finally lay down in the bed to sleep, his Beretta beneath the pillow, he wondered if he would get out of India alive. He'd been within a whisker of having his throat slit that afternoon, and mostly it was because, as Chuluun had said that evening, he was getting stupid.

CHAPTER 18

The Queen's Imperial Hotel compared favorably to any building in Haridwar for sheer opulence. The two-story lobby, in particular, was extreme. Two wide staircases curled into the expansive room from the second floor and opened onto the first floor on either side of a long mahogany reception desk. The floors were tiled in black marble. Six matching marble columns were spaced evenly across the foyer. Four crystal chandeliers hung like giant tiaras from the second-story ceiling. Expensive furniture ensembles were situated throughout for people to sit and talk. The most exquisite in English taste was now but a leftover from two hundred years of colonialism finally come to an end.

Roger Taylor, dressed for breakfast in black slacks and a white jacket, descended from the second floor on the west staircase the morning of Pipal's thirty-fourth day of fasting. Halfway down, he saw Captain Rantanbir sitting at a table in a corner of the lobby, sipping from a tea cup and reading the *London Times*. The Gurkha looked up from his paper just as Taylor spotted him. Taylor had no choice but to go over and say good morning.

Rantanbir stood as he approached. He wore his standard uniform, a short-sleeved khaki shirt and matching shorts with his wide-brimmed hat, as was the style, tilted off to one side of his head. The insignia of the 1/13 Gurkha Rifles was pinned prominently to the hat band. It was one of the most highly regarded of all the Indian units during the Second World War and a badge of tremendous honor.

"Captain Rantanbir, I trust you're not here this morning to arrest me." Taylor smiled and extended his hand. He had a bandage on his neck from the close call the day before.

Rantanbir took his hand. "Maybe another day," he quipped with a tight little smile that was both charming and mischievous.

Taylor laughed at this, but Rantanbir wasn't laughing. "Sit down, Mr. Taylor," he said. There were several large arm chairs arranged around the coffee table. "Have a cup of tea with me." There was a tea pot, cream, and an extra cup on the table. "You'll be happy to know I got the assault charge against you dropped. The trial is off."

Taylor took a seat. As he reached across the table and poured himself a cup of tea, he looked up at Rantanbir. "Thank you for taking care of that, Captain. Does that mean I'm free to go?"

"The sooner the better would be my suggestion."

Taylor stirred some cream into his tea. "You enjoy my presence that much?"

"It has nothing to do with my personal feelings," said the policeman. He took a studied sip of tea, then sat back and held the little cup and saucer on his lap. A 9mm Glock hung in a holster at his hip. "I spent a little time questioning those two thugs we arrested yesterday."

Taylor's left eye brow lifted with interest. "The RSSS?"

"No, they had nothing to do with the Hindu Rashtra Dal or any other extremist group."

"They were just out there to kill me and draw orange designs on my forehead?"

"That was to throw you off."

"What about the train bombing and my room?"

"The train I know nothing about, but your room was broken into by those men I arrested."

"What are you telling me, Captain? Who were they?"

"Do you know a Hindu princess from Gwalior with a jealous husband, Mr. Taylor?"

Taylor felt his mouth fall open. The only civilian who knew he'd come to Haridwar was Naija. He didn't want to believe this.

"I take that silence as a yes." Rantanbir stroked his mustache out to the sides. "Even worse, Mr. Taylor, just to help cloud the waters, those men told the RSSS cell in Haridwar that you're here and what you're doing. Apparently their people have been watching the fasting woman's house since your third day in Haridwar. That's part of what I'm here to tell you—there are two sets of assassins on your trail. The arrest yesterday may have eliminated one set for now, but the RSSS is still out there following your every move."

"Is the woman who's fasting in any danger?"

"That's the other reason I'm here." Rantanbir looked down at the cup and saucer in his lap. "One of the men we arrested yesterday told us the RSSS spoke of kidnapping the young woman as a trap for you."

"Damn," cursed Taylor under his breath. He placed his cup of tea on the table. "We need to have someone there. All the time. And immediately!"

"I have two men there now working undercover."

"I should be there too. But there can be no word of this. It will only make things worse. The woman is already too weak to deal with any kind of disturbance."

Rantanbir was staring at Taylor. "I knew I was taking a chance telling you this, but I want you to stay away, Mr. Taylor. I will take care of it. Your being there will only make matters worse."

"No, Captain, this is my mission. You're to put your men under my directive."

Rantanbir wagged his head, not surprised by Taylor's call for the command, but surprised by the intensity of his emotion. "What exactly is this to you? The safety of a woman intent on her own death? I don't get it."

Taylor thought of the story he would have to tell. Were it not for a wager he'd made with a Tibetan lama years ago, he would be glad to leave this damn place—and India for that matter—immediately. Instead he gave an easier answer. "I'm here to prevent any kind of disturbance. Who knows what a kidnapping would prompt with Kumbh Mela just a week away. We could have ten thousand dead in a matter of hours."

The violence of partition had been going on for almost nine months. Nearly a million people had lost their lives. Like every law officer in India or Pakistan, Rantanbir knew it was a situation ever teetering on further catastrophe. "That's my problem not yours," he replied calmly. "I've been preparing my officers for the festival for more than a month. The best thing for you to do is leave." He reached into the pocket of his shirt and withdrew a train ticket. "I've purchased a ticket back to New Delhi for you, Mr. Taylor. The train leaves today at four p.m. Be on that train or I will put you back in a cell for your own protection."

"I'm sorry, Captain. I'm here on higher authority than yours. Until my orders change, I'm in charge. If you choose to arrest me, it will cost you your job." Taylor stood to leave. Rantanbir also stood.

"You're not on higher authority, Mr. Taylor. Prior to India's independence, yes, the C.I.D. did have jurisdiction over local police services, but not any longer. Two of my men are waiting outside." He extended the train ticket to Taylor. "Your choice. The train or a cell?"

Taylor put a hand to his brow and swept it back through his hair in frustration. "Alright, Captain. Give me a third choice. Let me stay and help with the protection of this woman. I'll do whatever you ask."

This gave Rantanbir pause. "Including staying away."

"No, damn it," spat Taylor, attracting the attention of several bystanders and the clerk at the reception desk. "This was my charge from the beginning. Allow me to save face and help bring resolution to this insanity."

Rantanbir bowed his head, clearly troubled by the arrogance of this man he had to deal with in some way or another. "Taylor, you are an ass. But I have no time for fighting with you. I'm short on men and that will only get worse as the city fills with pilgrims. Come let's go. More talk is only wasting time."

CHAPTER 19

It was noon when Captain Rantanbir and Roger Taylor left the Queen's Imperial Hotel. The streets of downtown Haridwar were noticeably more active than the previous week. The entire city was gearing up for the festival of Kumbh Mela. The ordinary excess of Hindu art work and commerce had tripled. Vendors and religious art peddlers were everywhere, hanging their colorful festival banners, laying out their trinkets, and preparing for a big week of sales. Taylor found the entire scene repugnant.

An hour later, Rantanbir, six of his officers, and Chuluun, all in some form of undercover, were planted throughout the neighborhood around the home of Areena Kaur. Taylor, because of his height, was more difficult to camouflage. With Rantanbir's help, he was disguised as a legless beggar. He knelt on an elaborate wooden platform mounted on little caster-like wheels that Taylor could move by pushing himself along with his hands. To hide his legs, he was wrapped in several old blankets that completely covered him and most of his face. It was an extremely uncomfortable contraption, but it allowed Taylor to be on the street, mixing with the pilgrims camped outside Pipal's home or waiting in the line that had grown to several hundred people.

The surveillance operation was put in place without any notification to those in the neighborhood, in the line, or to Pipal or her mother. And for one entire day, this protective force watched the neighborhood and the progress of the line without incident. For Taylor, the situation was a horrible temptation. Despite a strong desire to talk to Pipal, he pushed himself up and down the street like an itinerant beggar, collecting alms from the few tourists passing through or those people in the line. He kept tucked within his cloaking blankets, sweating profusely and saying nothing, but learning in bits and pieces of overheard conversation that Pipal was extremely weak and confined to her bed. Areena was trying to stop the visits entirely, but Pipal wouldn't allow it, and the process had slowed down considerably. Only a handful of visitors were getting the chance to talk to Pipal each day.

When dark fell, the line did not disperse as it had before. The pilgrims simply remained in line, staying there through the night, sleeping on the ground so not to loose their place. A second shift of undercover officers came in at eight that evening, beginning a series of eight-hour rotations. Taylor could remain on his platform for only an hour or two at a time. At intervals he would push himself out of the neighborhood to a nearby safe house to stand and stretch his legs and, at night, sleep.

This level of surveillance, however, could only continue so long. Once the festival got fully underway, the number of pilgrims in Haridwar would be in the hundreds of thousands, and Rantanbir would simply not have enough men to cover this situation. If Pipal's fast were to last another week, which would put it past forty days, watching this neighborhood would be an impossible luxury and, unfortunately, a welcoming keg of dynamite to anyone bent on creating a disturbance.

The second day of the stakeout was like the first. Nothing happened and there was no further evidence that anything would happen. The third day was quiet also. At the same time, the influx of pilgrims to Haridwar was steadily building, causing Captain Rantanbir to question a surveillance strategy based on what might only be a false lead from an untrustworthy source.

The situation was even more stressful for Taylor. The fast had reached its thirty-sixth day, and from what little he could gain from the people in line, it seemed that Pipal was under considerable physical duress. She could die before he got a chance—if he ever got a chance—to ask her the one question that was ticking in the back of his mind like an emotional time bomb.

On the morning of the fourth day, the thirty-seventh of fasting, Rantanbir told Taylor the stakeout would last only until the next day. If nothing occurred and no other information came in, he would pull his men, and only Chuluun and Taylor would be available to stay.

By this time even Pipal's east side neighborhood was feeling the effects of the approaching festival. The usually quiet streets were alive with walking traffic, tourists, pilgrims, and vendors, and the line to Pipal's house stretched out farther than one could see. The majority of those in the line were destitute, elderly, or sick; those come to Haridwar to die and in their last days bask in the *darshan* of a woman they were now calling Gandhi's disciple or the woman Jesus. But the line moved almost not at all, while the street carried a steady flow of strangers and new faces. It was difficult enough for six men, Taylor, Rantanbir, and Chuluun to keep track of all that was going on. Should that group be reduced to Taylor and Chuluun the task would be next to impossible.

Just after three o'clock the afternoon of this fourth day, Taylor saw Sumitra walking up the length of the line, coming his way. He had seen her progressing through the line each day, and it seemed she'd finally gotten in. As much as he wanted to ask Sumitra about Pipal, Taylor made no effort to make contact with her as she approached the spot where he was temporarily parked and seeking alms. He felt that his disguise was working and that he had created an accepted presence in the neighborhood. He didn't want to risk that by talking to Sumitra.

Just as she was about to walk by, Sumitra suddenly stopped and dropped a coin on Taylor's wooden platform. He looked up at her through the rags wrapped around his head and face. She surprised him by looking right into his eyes and whispering, "There is a man who barged into the line during the night, then let two of his friends in this morning. None of them belong here." Then she continued on her way,

As soon as she'd said this, Taylor saw it. It was as though six sets of Hindu eyes in the immediate vicinity suddenly swung furtively from side to side at the same time. The RSSS was there. Taylor put his palms together and bowed his head as though acknowledging the coin he'd just received. It was a signal to Chuluun on the rooftop across the street that he'd seen something. When Taylor lifted his head, Chuluun was gone to pass the word.

At the same time, the RSSS was preparing to make their move unaware that they'd been spotted. Taylor saw the rifle barrels slowly peek from beneath their robes. He loosened his Beretta from its holster. He could see Rantanbir on a rooftop opposite Pipal's home. Coming up the street were Chadi and a friend chasing another boy on a bicycle. A woman in a yellow *sari* walked by Taylor with a crying baby wrapped in her *pallu*. The street traffic flowed by like water. Several hundred people were within a three block area going about their business. The entire scene could erupt with rifle fire at any moment. This was Taylor's greatest fear. If they came for Pipal in number, as they had, they couldn't be stopped without force and vast danger to anyone nearby—and, perhaps, a cascading effect that would erupt throughout the city.

A man in a white turban and a long brown robe suddenly stepped out of the line and commanded in Hindi. "Everyone leave. We want you all out of here." Three men stood up across the street with automatic rifles. Two more came out of the line. They split into two groups, waving their rifles, moving the people down the street in both directions. The walking traffic hurried into a run to get away, but the majority of those in line, fearing for Pipal's safety, refused to leave. Two of the men with rifles stood before these pilgrims and told them to go or they would be shot. No one moved. The men leveled their rifles and prepared to open fire.

Captain Rantanbir suddenly stood up from his roof top position and called out, "You men, all of you, put down your rifles." Six more police officers stepped out into sight on roof tops or from doorways. Their numbers and advantage were clear. Taylor, still undercover, his Beretta at the ready, was among the cluster of pilgrims that refused to leave.

All of the gunmen froze, but their leader in the center of the road, unconcerned by the prospect of death, simply grabbed the nearest child as a shield. It was the girl who had dislocated her elbow in the bicycle accident. Then he shouted out, "I have a grenade held in one hand and the pin held by the other." With his arms around the girl, the grenade was in the center of her chest. "I want all of you out of here now or I pull the pin." Without letting go of the girl, he took three steps to the left and kicked open the door to Areena Kaur's house. "Leave or this grenade goes into the house. Now! Everyone! Out of here!"

Still no one moved. Taylor, about thirty yards away, wanted to simply shoot the man, but he couldn't take the chance with the little girl right there. He glanced up to the roof across the street. Chuluun had his rifle aimed at the man with the grenade. Chuluun caught Taylor's eyes. It was clear he also would not risk a shot. A child down the street began to cry. A woman wailed. Taylor was all set to stand up, announce who he was, and give himself up when everything suddenly went still. All eyes turned to the kicked open doorway.

Pipal, barefoot and wearing a simple white homespun dress, was there on the doorstep. Taylor wanted to cry out *get back inside,* but the sight stopped him as surely as it had everyone else. Pipal, thin and frail, thirty-seven days into her fast, floated like a ghost out into the street, so quiet, so stunning in her mystery that everyone was transfixed— everyone, on both sides, lowered their guns. The man with the grenade, however, who stood just a few feet from Pipal, his eyes fiercely ablaze, was unfazed.

Pipal extended her hand. "Please, Hindu brother, let go of the child," she said softly. "Give me that grenade and take your men away from here. There is no need for violence. These people honor your beliefs—as do I."

With all watching and spellbound, the man cursed her as a follower of the traitor Gandhi. Her hand still extended, Pipal replied, "Gandhi was a devout Hindu like you. He did all he could to prevent partition."

The man spat on the ground at her feet.

"Please, brother, give me the grenade."

The man simply glared at her and pulled the pin from the grenade. "Join Gandhi in hell," he said, placing the device in her hand, clearly prepared to go there with her and still gripping the child.

Everyone nearby dove to the ground, scrambling for any kind of cover they could find. Taylor could only watch in horror as Pipal pressed the grenade to her breast, knelt to her knees, then bowed all the way to the ground, using her body to shield the explosion from the others. He remembered what he'd felt covering the bomb in Karachi. It was as though he was there with her waiting for the end.

Five seconds, ten seconds, twenty seconds passed with no explosion. People began to lift their heads to see what was happening. A minute passed. Nothing. Finally Pipal stood and extended her hand to give the grenade back to the man who had given it to her. He stared wildly at her in disbelief, then let go of the child and dropped to his knees, touching his head to the ground in homage. Up and down the street people began to whisper. "A miracle," one woman shouted. "The woman Jesus," called out another

Pipal placed the grenade on the ground, then speaking softly, but in a voice all could hear, said, "Those of you with weapons, please leave. This is not the place for you." As she spoke, her eyes surveyed the street, clearly noting the legless beggar on the wooden platform, even holding a moment on Taylor as though to say she had seen right through his disguise. Then she turned and floated into the house.

The man who had threatened the crowd with the grenade stood. He motioned to his men, and the entire group of them walked away without a word. The neighborhood began to flow with traffic again, everyone talking madly about what had just happened.

Taylor used his hands to push himself down the street and back to the safe house. Within minutes, Rantanbir, who had retrieved the grenade, and his officers and Chuluun were gathered there with him. For quite a while no one said a word. Finally Rantanbir broke the silence, holding the grenade out for all to see. "Thank God this was a dud." Several of his officers nodded in agreement. Taylor looked straight at Chuluun. They were thinking something entirely different.

CHAPTER 20

Roger Taylor returned to the Queen's Imperial Hotel after dark that night. His knees and back ached from four days on the wooden platform and he needed a drink and some time to think. He bathed and put on clean clothes and went down to dinner. He waited forty-five minutes for a table, ate, then descended to the basement lounge.

The lounge was packed. Chuluun was behind the bar with a second bartender, working with the speed and dexterity of sushi chefs to keep up with the orders. Taylor sat down at the bar and ordered a gin and tonic. It was five minutes before he got it. He took the first sip with a flood of relief, then sat there pondering the occurrences of the day and watching Chuluun take orders and mix drinks.

After a while there was a lull in business. Chuluun lit up a smoke and wandered down the bar to where Taylor was sitting. Taylor spoke first. "Well, what was that we witnessed today?"

Chuluun took a drag from his smoke and exhaled off to one side. "I read somewhere that one in twenty of those old British grenades don't explode. What we saw was either plain luck or—something else."

"What does your gut say, Chuluun? I've never seen anything quite like that before. Those RSSS boys, I think they believe Pipal's something special and are scared to do anything but pray for her now. What do you say? Did she defuse that grenade with the purity of her soul?"

Chuluun stared momentarily at the wisp of smoke curling upward from the end of his cigarette. "As I said before, I am not a religious person—Hindu, Christian, or otherwise, Mr. Taylor, but if you want to press me and know what I felt at that moment she covered the grenade." A man stood up to the bar next to Taylor and asked Chuluun for a drink. Chuluun ignored the man long enough to answer. "It was like I'd just seen Jesus Christ here in the streets of Haridwar." Then he moved down the bar to fix the man's drink.

Taylor felt the same way. The earth had moved.

And it underscored Taylor's deepest desire—to ask Pipal one last question. And it was something that might never happen. The line of pilgrims outside Pipal's home was so long now that those at the end would never go through the door while she was still living, and there was no way he could simply go there and take a spot at the front of the line—or even expect to be allowed into the house. Pipal, like Sumitra, had seen through his disguise and must surely connect him to the intruding presence of weapons in her neighborhood. He would not be welcome in the neighborhood, in the line, or in her house. As Sumitra and Areena had warned, he had become a source of trouble—the very thing he was there to prevent. He simply couldn't go there again.

The next two days Taylor remained at the hotel without going out at all. The evening of the second day he put through a call to New Delhi from his room. An hour later, he had Mountbatten on the line. He told the Governor-General the entire story.

"We have been quite lucky," replied Mountbatten. "Had that woman been killed by the grenade, you'd still be collecting corpses from the streets of Haridwar."

"Yes, your lordship," said Taylor, just wanting to be done with the conversation, certainly not daring to ask the Governor-General the same nagging questions he'd asked Chuluun.

"How much longer do you expect this woman to last?" asked Mountbatten.

Taylor felt a surge of emotion. It was all he could do to keep his voice from breaking when he answered. "Today completes her thirty-ninth day of fasting. I doubt she can last another week."

"But the crowds have already begun to gather and the festival begins quite soon."

"In two days, sir. I can barely imagine what it will be like once things really get going."

"Then your orders remain the same, Taylor. Watch from a distance, monitor the situation, and remain only until this woman has died and you can determine if the chain of fasts is actually going to continue."

After Taylor hung up the phone, he fell face down on the bed and sobbed uncontrollably. When all the emotion and strain had finally been exhausted, he went into the bathroom and splashed cold water on his face. He stared into the mirror over the sink wondering what had come over him. Never had he broken down as he just did. For untold minutes he remained at the sink lost in what seemed a deep hole in his being.

Later that night, well after midnight, Taylor was camped in a corner of the basement lounge. The place was mostly empty. A layer of cigarette smoke hung motionless and stale over the room. Chuluun was gone and the other bartender was cleaning up the bar, preparing to close. The only sound was the periodic clink of glasses as they were put away.

A woman appeared in the entrance to the lounge. She walked directly to Taylor's table. In the dim light, she was only a silhouette until she was just a few feet away. It was Carolyn Williamson. She was wearing a sheer nightgown. Through the thin cloth, Taylor could see the shape of her breasts and the dark circles of her nipples, also huge welts and bruises on her arms and torso, karmic tattoos from the car accident that killed her. A vicious-looking, purple lump wept below her left eye. She sat down next to him at the table.

"It's good to see you, Roger," she slurred, obviously a little drunk.

This startled Taylor. He was becoming accustomed to these visitations, but never had an apparition spoken to him. He looked around anxiously. The bartender was absorbed in his work. "Yes, it's good to see you also," he said as quietly as he could.

She smiled a wicked smile. Two of her teeth were chipped; one was missing. "I'll bet," she leered sarcastically, moving up into his face and sliding a hand onto his leg.

He pushed her hand away.

"What's the matter, Rog? Am I being too aggressive for you?" Again she placed her hand on his leg, but higher this time.

"Yes," he replied stiffly. Her hand moved to the center of his crotch and he forcefully shoved it aside.

This sent her reeling with a hideous high-pitched laugh. She leaned over and wrapped her arms around him. "You're really something, Roger." She kissed him on the mouth. It repulsed him and he wiped his mouth with his sleeve.

Just as he did this, another woman appeared at the entrance to the lounge. It was his mother holding a Bible and peering into the darkness this way and that until she spotted him catching sight of her.

"God, Carolyn, stop. My mother's here," he moaned. "Please."

Then his mother was there, seated beside him, taking no heed of Carolyn's provocative attire and placing her Bible down on the table. "I knew all of this would catch up with you eventually, Roger," she said looking him in the eye.

Taylor just bowed his head.

"Do you think you'll ever marry Carolyn?" his mother continued.

Carolyn squeezed herself up closer to Taylor, forcing him to lift his head. "Yes, Roger, do you think you'll ever marry me?" she chortled.

Taylor had become extremely uneasy. He wasn't certain where reality left off and his hallucinations began. As far as he knew he was dreaming. Finally, in frustration, he just blurted it out. "What is it you want from me?" The bartender looked up from his work. Carolyn broke into a loud horsey laugh, and his mother gave him a blank stare.

Taylor was at his wits end. He threw down the last of his drink, all set to leave, when a scream exploded in the lounge. Gopal Dutta came running straight for the table and leapt into the air, hands outstretched for Taylor's throat. Taylor caught him in mid-air, but Dutta arrived with so much force Taylor went over backwards in his chair, knocking his empty glass to the floor. Dutta grabbed a piece of the broken glass and dove at Taylor with it. Once, twice, three times he struck at Taylor with the shard. Then a gunshot rang out. Dutta suddenly went still and dropped to the floor. Edwin Taylor, wearing the Union officer's uniform he'd been buried in, a smoking revolver in his hand, and a saber at his hip, strode over and helped his grandson to his feet.

"Sit down, son. You don't look so good."

With the bartender staring at him, Taylor righted his chair, picked up the broken glass, and sat down at the table. To his left was Carolyn. To his right was his mother, sitting well away from the table, reading from her Bible. Gopal Dutta lay on the floor in a pool of blood, and his grandfather sat across from him. Nothing more was said. A spidery gauze blanketed them all, stretching and pulling with the slightest motion, each movement of a head or a hand, each page turned in the Bible.

After a few minutes, a distraught Taylor, now closely watched by the bartender, pushed away from the table prepared to leave, but it wasn't soon enough. A figure appeared in silhouette at the entry to the lounge and glided up to the table. James Nielsen parted the gauzy web and joined the ghastly quartet. James was as Taylor had last seen him, a skin draped skeleton, wasted by leukemia. There was a deep sadness in his eyes, but he said nothing, simply stared downward at the table.

Visibly shaken and trembling, Taylor looked from James to the others around the table, and then to the lounge entry, suddenly wondering in a surge of anxiety if Pipal's appearance wouldn't be the final capper to this gay party. He stood and walked unsteadily from the lounge, knowing he needed a good night of sleep.

CHAPTER 21

Roger Taylor woke in the middle of the night to the sound of someone beating on his door. Still groggy from alcohol, he pushed himself up out of bed, turned on the bedside lamp, and stumbled across the room. "Who is it?" he called out. No one answered, but the knocking came again, louder, more insistent. An infuriated Taylor pushed the dresser away from the door and brusquely pulled the door open. Chadi stood there alone, wide-eyed and out of breath. He chattered out something in Nepalese. Taylor didn't catch all of it, but he got the message. Pipal was very sick and she'd asked to see him.

Taylor took a quick look at the clock. It was after two. He told Chadi to hurry back and tell Areena that he'd be there as soon as he could. He went straight to the bathroom and splashed water on his face and pushed his hair in place with his hands. Five minutes later, he was dressed and rushing through the lobby. When he hit the street, he took off at a slow jog with no thought of the greeting he'd receive from those in the line when he reached Pipal's home.

Walking it usually took forty-five minutes to get there. He made it in twenty. The line stretched out for many blocks. The pilgrims were huddled up against the buildings in their blankets asleep. No one looked up as he ran down the length of the line to the house. Chadi was sitting on the doorstep. He pointed inside. Gasping and sweating, Taylor entered without knocking.

A Buddhist priest sat in the front room chanting. Areena came out of Pipal's room as Taylor walked in. She took his hand like a friend and spoke hurriedly in English. "Pipal's kidneys are not functioning properly. If she doesn't take some fruit juice soon—and maybe even if she does, her kidneys will fail—that will be the end." As she talked, she led him through the curtain to Pipal's room. "She'd been sleeping for several hours, but woke a little while ago asking for you, so I sent the boy."

The room was dark except for a single candle on the table by the pitcher of water. It cast a small yellow ball of light on Pipal and the wall behind. Her hair was pulled back in a braid as it had been before, and she had become so pale and thin that with all the flowers on her bed her body was barely visible beneath the covers. The candlelight flickered obliquely across her face, accentuating the circles under her eyes and the shape of her skull. It reminded Taylor of James Nielsen's face five days dead. Unnerved by the sight, he knelt almost in a faint at the side of her bed. She looked at him through half open eyes. A faint smile creased her death mask.

"Mr. Taylor, I was afraid you weren't coming back," she said with much effort.

"After the other day," he stammered, "I was afraid to come again for fear of more turmoil. I haven't lived up to my promise. I have brought what I sought to prevent. I'm not even sure if I should be here now." He turned and looked over his shoulder. Areena was standing in the doorway. "Did the woman from Calcutta tell you that she spoke to me last week? Did she express my apology for the rudeness of my last visit and for the disturbance I created?"

"Yes, but there was no need for apology. I should have spoken to the pilgrims. They needed to know I want you here. They needed to know I wanted a westerner to witness the conviction of my actions and take my story to the rest of the world. I know you will do this now because you have come when I requested, and you will not be able to deny my courage."

"I never once doubted your courage, Pipal, and certainly you proved that the other day when you covered the grenade, but I'm not a journalist. That's not why I'm here."

"My message is simple, Mr. Taylor," she continued, ignoring what he'd said. "The partition of India was a slap in the face to the greatest man of this century. India has effectively crucified its one truly transcendent soul. Gandhi is the Christ of the East and this series of fasts is in his honor for perpetuity."

"Pipal, Pipal," said Taylor, fighting his emotions. "Couldn't you spread this message better alive than as a memory?" Tears welled in his eyes and he thought again of his last days with James Nielsen. He wanted to ask Pipal straight out if she were James reborn. But it just seemed so inappropriate now. Then her eyes closed. Thinking that perhaps she had died, he took her wrist and found a slow, weak pulse.

Areena stepped up next to him, her thoughts the same as his.

"No, she's sleeping," he comforted.

Areena knelt beside him and put a hand on her daughter's forehead. "She has spoken more now than in one whole day. She slept almost all of the last forty-eight hours because of the fever. Come, let her sleep."

The front room was dimly lit by two oil lamps. Taylor took a seat at the table. Areena sat across from him. Neither said a word for quite a while. In the background, the Buddhist priest maintained a low, steady chant. Every now and then his finger cymbals sounded. Areena finally spoke.

"Mr. Taylor, you don't seem like the usual Englishman."

"I was born in the United States, Areena. I'm an American, but that's not it." Taylor looked down at the table and spoke without lifting his eyes. "Your daughter reminds me of someone who was once very close to me. And it has affected me in a way that I can't explain."

"Was that someone your wife?"

"No." He shook his head. "I have no wife or family." He looked up at Areena, fixing on the cross hanging from her neck and thinking of his mother. "It was a friend I had at Oxford. A disease took him before he really had a chance to get started in his life—much like Pipal."

Areena nodded.

Taylor stumbled through his thoughts. The reincarnation question was nagging at him, and he wanted to ask Areena the date of Pipal's birth, hoping for a fact or anything that might break this peculiar spell.

"Forgive me," he said, "but I'm at a loss. My friend, though English, was a Buddhist. I have assumed the same for Pipal."

Areena looked at him through sad eyes. "Pipal would say, as Gandhi would have said, she is a Hindu, a Muslim, a Christian, and a Jew. But she is prepared to die as a Buddhist." Areena motioned to the chanting priest. "He'll conduct the funeral. And do the recitations and take her through the *Bardo Thödol* ceremony."

"Then you believe in the Buddhist concepts also?" he asked, inching closer to the question he was afraid to ask.

"No. I'm a Christian." Areena smiled despite her despair. "I was born a Hindu, Mr. Taylor. My father was a farmer, a member of the vaisya caste. I was married at the age of ten to a man of thirty-five because of a promise my father made on the day I was born."

She paused as though caught in the matrix of those memories. "You might imagine what horrors are perpetrated in the name of honor by the child marriage. That husband died of tuberculosis four years after we were wed. I've spent much of my life trying to recover from that first marriage."

The conversation was not going in the direction Taylor had hoped, but he understood Areena was opening up to him as a way to cope with her emotions. "I didn't think the Hindu religion allowed a widow to marry again?"

"It doesn't. But I'm also not a Hindu precisely because of this kind of ignorance. The Hindu widow may as well be an untouchable for her rights. After the death of my first husband, I returned to my family, but even there I was an outcast.

"I was no longer a virgin, but I was really too young to be a woman. The confusion increased as I got older. I became more and more a piece of awkward furniture in the home of my parents.

"I succumbed to the temptations many of the young widows are drawn to. I began to see single men. This led to my being cast out of my family's home.

"The next temptation was prostitution. Almost all the prostitutes in India were victims of the child marriage, trying to make do in a society set against them. It's one of the few ways a Hindu widow can survive on her own. The woman from Calcutta—who you have seen in the line— Sumitra. She suffered this same fate and was a prostitute for more years than she would tell me. That's why she's so eager to join the fast—to repent and purify her soul."

Taylor couldn't help thinking of his ugly trip to the brothel the week before.

"I'd begun down this sad path when I first heard of Gandhi. This was in the late 1920s. As he took the untouchables under his wing, he also spoke out against the child marriage and the frightening number of child widows. I never became the kind of disciple to Gandhi that Pipal did. I admired the man more for what he did for the nameless majority of India than his push for independence. This man, seemingly of another world, like another Christ, another Buddha, another Mohammed, considered the homeless, the poverty stricken, the ill, his children. He seemed to draw more from the comforting of the needy than anything else he did but fast. Teaching them how to eat and how to live in a sanitary way was as important to him as their learning nonviolent resistance. I suspect Gandhi did more than any man in history for the causes of sanitation and nutrition."

Areena suddenly became aware of how much of herself she was

revealing. Self-consciously she got up and went into Pipal's room. A moment later she came out. "She's still sleeping. The fever has abated somewhat, but it matters little if she won't take sustenance. She is no longer relieving herself of fluids. The end is near." She sat down at the table and hung her head.

Taylor had been touched by Areena's story. Not once had he considered what tortuous path she had followed to this crossroad where they now met. Still he was preoccupied with the James Nielsen connection. "How did you meet your second husband?"

Under other circumstances, Areena might have avoided these questions, but tonight it was obvious; she needed to talk to someone. She was about to be alone again. She'd already spent much of her life alone. She could feel the wheel of her life completing another revolution—as it was for Taylor also.

"It was in the spring of 1930," began Areena wistfully. "All of India was in anticipation of Gandhi's next move. If you recall, Gandhi had promised England some kind of civil disturbance in 1930 if no progress was made toward India's independence during 1929. The New Year came with no sign of conciliation from England. January and February passed without action from Gandhi. Then word came in early March. Gandhi and seventy of his disciples were headed by foot directly south from his ashram in Sabarmati to the coastal town of Dandi on the Gulf of Cambay to extract salt from the ocean, a crime against the English monopoly in salt production."

"Yes," said Taylor. "I remember the times well. I was still at Oxford. As a matter of fact, Gandhi would come to Oxford later that year as part of a trip to England and the business of the Round Table Conference. I saw him speak when he was there. The march to Dandi was still a fresh topic."

"I lived in Cambay then," said Areena. "And wasn't far from the route Gandhi was taking to Dandi. My own life was in shambles. I was living alone in the city. I'd just given in to the necessity of prostitution when I got word of his march. I heard that other widowed women had gone to Gandhi's ashram to escape the horror of their lost lives. I recall thinking that maybe there was something left in my life and that maybe there was hope for me. I was twenty-two years old with nothing to lose when I headed off to see this man Gandhi for the first time.

"I reached the road that Gandhi would take on his way to the shore the day before he arrived. Peasants lined the road, sprinkling handfuls of leaves and flowers over the hard dirt to make the walk easier for the Mahatma. By the time his entourage reached our position, just a day or so from Dandi, the seventy had grown to several thousand. I couldn't resist and joined in as they triumphantly headed to the sea, led by this frail bespectacled man with a walking stick and the flag of India flying before them.

"I stayed with the pilgrims the next few days. I was there when Gandhi took a few grains of salt from the sea. I was eventually arrested for using a pan to evaporate salt from sea water. It was a fateful arrest. I was among many violators of the salt law and like everyone else was treated roughly. We were forced to walk many miles to be confined. During the walk I received a blow to the head by one of the guards for dawdling. It knocked me unconscious. I was left for dead by the side of the road. I woke to the voice of a major in the British Army. He was coming down the road alone in a jeep when he spotted me. He administered first aid and fed me there by the roadside. He was a kind and soft-spoken man. He told me that as far as he was concerned I was free, and he offered me a ride back to Dandi. Embarrassed by my life and my predicament, I told him I had no home and no where to go. He took me to town and got me a room. Though he made no advances, I repaid him in the only way I knew how.

"I was young. I didn't know what to expect from this man. As it turned out, he put me up in that room in Dandi for several months. During that time, possibly even the first day, Pipal was conceived. Four months later, Major Thomas E. McElwee suggested that we should be married. If I hadn't been so desperate, I would have told him it wasn't necessary, but I hadn't the courage to go on alone. This second chance at life, his Christian morality, and my hatred for the hypocrisy of the Hindu traditions caused me to take Jesus Christ into my heart."

Not only did the story touch Taylor, but the suggested timing of Pipal's birth was too close to ignore. "What happened to Major McElwee?" he asked, still puzzling with the dates in his head.

"Thomas spent the next ten years of his life paying for his marriage to me. He received criticism from his parents in England and his peers in the military here. He was under constant pressure the rest of his life for marrying a brown-skinned woman. He was a good man, and he never backed off from his promise of love to me and his half-breed daughter. The constant stress, the treatment by his superiors, always moving him from one trouble spot in India to another, worked against his health. In 1940, we were living in Dacca and he caught malaria. He never recovered. And so it was, that which meant the most to me was taken away. His last wish was that Pipal should be educated in England. It took everything I had to make that happen, and now she will be leaving me. One must have tremendous faith to believe that all of this is God's plan."

With that Areena got up again and checked Pipal. Taylor looked at his watch. It was half-past three. He considered asking Areena if he could stay through the night, but he decided against it. When she came from Pipal's room saying her daughter was still asleep, he told Areena that he would be leaving. "I would be honored, however, if you would grant me permission to return tomorrow."

"It could become difficult if you are seen," said Areena. "But there's a back door that is never used. It leads to a cluttered alley behind the house. It's very narrow and has little if any traffic. No one would see you if you were careful."

"Then I will come to the back door sometime in the morning."

Taylor left through the back of the house and picked his way through the narrow alley out to the street. The streets that had been full all day were almost entirely deserted at this hour of the morning. Head down, dwelling on the fact that Pipal wouldn't last more than a few more days, he walked dejectedly back to the Queen's Imperial.

He hadn't gone more than five or six blocks when he became aware of a car on the road behind him. He continued on his way another block gradually realizing that the car was traveling very slowly and seemed to be following him. Out of courtesy for Pipal, he was not carrying his handgun. He moved far over to the right of the street, hoping the car would simply go by. It didn't.

Taylor abruptly turned down an alley. The car came to a stop at the end of the alley, and he heard the car door open and close. Just as he broke into a run, a familiar voice called his name. "Taylor, stop. It's Rantanbir."

Taylor turned around and saw the unmistakable silhouette of the wiry Gurkha with his terai hat cocked to one side at the end of the alley. He took a deep breath and walked back the way he'd come in.

"Just making sure I get home all right?" he asked sarcastically as he approached the police officer.

"Not exactly. One of my watchers saw you leave the hotel just a while ago. He followed you until it was clear where you were headed, then he called me. You almost lost me coming out of that alley. Would you like a ride?"

"You're not arresting me are you?"

Rantanbir laughed. "No. I learned days ago that you wouldn't listen to me no matter how I threatened you."

The two men climbed into the car, and Rantanbir drove them back across town toward the river and the Queen's Imperial Hotel. Neither man said anything for the first few minutes, then Rantanbir asked the obvious question. "So, Taylor, what exactly were you doing there tonight?"

Taylor gazed for a moment out the patrol car's side window at the dark, quiet streets, wondering how far he might go with his explanation. "The mother sent for me. Pipal is near the end. She requested to see me."

"She asked to see you? What are you to her?"

"She wants me to write her story. She wants the world to know of this fast, this chain of souls as it's called."

"But that's the exact opposite of why you're here. I don't get it."

"Captain, I'm not a journalist. I have no intention of writing anything. It's just that I'm the only non-Indian to seek her audience. I mean importance and recognition. That the world is watching. She's grasping at straws."

"But you came to see her. You answered her request. There must be more."

Taylor lifted his eyes in exasperation. He didn't like being questioned. "I came because I was asked. That's it."

Rantanbir let it go at that, but Taylor followed with his own question.

"What did you make of what happened the other day—with the hand grenade?"

They were just pulling up in front of the hotel. Rantanbir cut the engine and turned to Taylor. Light from the hotel entrance illuminated half his face; the brim of his hat shadowed the other half. "Something very ugly was narrowly averted."

"Nothing more? What of the woman herself, Pipal?"

"Now I see what's eating at you, Taylor," replied Rantanbir with a grin. "You're wondering if this woman you came here to stop is a real bodhisattva."

"Is she?"

"I am a Hindu, Taylor. I try not to bring my religion to work, and I deliberately said nothing to my men afterward that day." He took a glance at his watch. "But I'm off duty now, and my personal opinion is that she is a transcendent being and a holy woman of the first order."

"And she defused the grenade with her goodness?"

"Yes," said the Gurkha solemnly.

Taylor nodded, impressed by the man's answer. Taylor pushed open the door and climbed from the car. Before closing the door, he leaned back in. "Maybe I should write her story."

"That's for you to decide."

CHAPTER 22

The basement lounge was closed by the time Roger Taylor entered the hotel lobby. He went to his room, took a soothing sip from the engraved flask, and went to bed, but it took him a long time to fall asleep. Pipal would soon die. He had not asked the question yet. He might get another chance to speak with her the next day; he might not. In some ways, it was almost too much to know—either way. But Pipal had been conceived in the spring of 1930, very near the time that James had died. That much he had ascertained from Areena's story.

Lying there in bed, Taylor recalled James Nielsen's last few weeks and how the end came so quickly. James wasn't able to complete his final term. He was awarded an honorary degree, but it was still a major disappointment to James not to finish the work. Then there was the unpleasantness of the funeral. Memories of those difficult days began to roll like thunderheads through Taylor's mind—a vivid revisiting of the Buddhist rituals that Pipal's corpse would surely also have to endure.

If ever there was a scene of courage, it was in James Nielsen's final hours. He had moved into a private cottage in the last month. It was a small, cozy place just off campus with a fireplace, its own kitchen, and two small bedrooms. James was given one room. Tenzing and Roger took turns using the other room so that someone was always there with James. Though his last days were filled with pain, James denied himself the morphine that the doctor prescribed, because he wanted to be alert to the instructions of his guru Tenzing Chogyam.

Roger on the other hand could not come to grips with the process. He participated but it was at a studied distance. The meditations, the Buddhist prayers, the guru's continual chanting, all served to push him to the edge with frustration and sadness for his dying friend; and yet these same rituals served to focus James, centering him for the most difficult test of concentration a mind can ever know.

Over and over in the days before his death, James and Tenzing went through the recitations of the **Bardo Thödol***, reading and rereading aloud, together and* *separately, the instructions that the Rinpoche would eventually be pronouncing over James' dead body as though he could still hear.*

"Remember," said Tenzing for the thousandth time, "the hardest thing for you to understand when your body has been left behind is that you—as James Nielsen—are dead, because in your astral body, you will still possess the five senses that you had while living. You will hear and see those of us you have left behind. You will feel temperature changes in the room. You will even smell the food that we cook and taste it as we eat in your presence, but you will be frustrated by any attempt to communicate with us. Calm yourself before this panic. Listen to what you will hear me saying. Allow what I say to reassure you that everything is progressing as it should. Know that the visions you see are simply the release of the karma you have gathered all your life. And remember that these sometimes frightening images are creations of your mind and as such can do you no harm. Accept them. Conjoin with them. They are simply a product of your imagination."

James had been raised as an Episcopalian and the idea of a Tibetan funeral caused much distress to his family. Roger was good with this issue and helped them come to terms with James' last request. When it came down to the final hour, James and his parents spent all but the last few minutes alone together. Then as the end could not be denied, Roger and Tenzing Chogyam joined the family. With James' mother giving in to tears and uncontained grieving, James' father escorted her from the room. As had been previously discussed, open lamenting and grief would tend to divert James' concentration when he would need it most. Roger, determined to make a pleasant farewell, despite deeper resignation, was the last to speak with James before the guru took over.

Roger sat down in a chair beside James' bed. "Can I make you more comfortable, James?"

"If you could prop my head up, please, Roger. Maybe pull back the covers a bit. They're awfully heavy on my chest."

Roger preformed these modest requests, then took hold of his dear friend's hand as the disease tightened its grip. "Are you in much pain, James?"

James' eyes closed and his pulse weakened. Roger was sure it was over, then James' eyes opened once again. He smiled dimly at his friend. "It will be all right, Roger. It will be all right. I have seen through to the other side. The pain is gone now." James' eyes moved while his head lay still on the pillow. "Make my parents understand that death is not the end."

Roger nodded, awash in tears.

"Don't be sad for me, Roger." James reached unsteadily for his engraved flask on the bedside table and handed it to Roger, saying he'd had full use of it. "Think only

your happiest thoughts of me when you drink from this flask. Remember me as one bloody good rugger and to always keep the flask topped off." Then quoting the **Bhagavad Gita**, *a book he had read from every day in the last month, he spoke his final words. "Many lives you and I have lived, my friend. I remember them all, but thou dost not."* He closed his eyes. Roger motioned to the lama. Tenzing took Roger's seat beside James.

James was not quite gone but he was beyond speaking. There was a light sweat building at his temples. His nose was running and a milky discharge had begun to accumulate in the corners of his eyes. After delicately wiping away these bodily secretions, the guru put an ear to James' chest to assess his breathing and his heart-beat. Roger, overcome with emotion, backed into a corner of the room to watch.

Tenzing spoke a few words softly to James to make sure he could still hear and to make sure he knew who he was and what they were about to do. Thus Tenzing began the delicate metaphysical work of the hpho-bo, literally, the extractor of the consciousness principle.

From the effort behind his faint breathing, it was clear that James was very near the end. Tenzing leaned over him, putting his lips near the dying man's ear, and began the initial recitation from the **Bardo Thödol** *"O nobly-born, James Nielsen, the time hath come now for thee to seek the Path. Thy breathing is about to cease. Thy guru hath set thee face to face before the Clear Light; and now thou art about to experience it in its reality in the Bardo state, wherein all things are like the void and cloudless sky, and the naked, spotless intellect is like unto a transparent vacuum without circumference or center. At this moment, know thou thyself; and abide in that state. I, too, at this time, am setting thee face to face."*

Tenzing repeated this recitation slowly, over and over again, trying to help James focus on the urgency of the moment and their purpose. Ever mindful of James' precarious state, he continued this repetition until he felt the presage of the final moments of life.

Tenzing placed a hand on James' forehead. It was dry and his nose no longer ran. His breathing lost its rhythm, and he began to rasp and pant. His in-breaths became short and his out-breaths long and wheezing. He was losing focus. It seemed he might lose consciousness before he expired. This was at cross purposes to their work. It was important to keep James keenly aware of every critical instant of his dying, so Tenzing kept whispering in his ear, helping James fight off his drowsiness, quietly reminding James that both he and Roger were there and that he should focus on the sound and rhythm of his words.

At the instant James' heart stopped, Roger could read it in the lama's eyes. Shuddering with the unpleasant memory of that morning he found his grandfather dead, he watched Tenzing carefully turn James over on his right side and lay a white *cloth over James' face. Then the guru placed a finger on the arteries on the either side of James' throat. This was to ensure that when the vital spirit left the body it would be trapped in the head and forced to exit out the "Aperture of Brahma" at the crown of the skull.*

Tenzing then returned to the recitations, speaking softly into James' ear just as he had before, as though James could hear—though dead. "O nobly-born, James Nielsen, let not thy mind be distracted. That which is called death being come to thee now, resolve thus: O this now is the hour of death. By taking advantage of this death, I will so act for the good of all sentient beings, peopling the illimitable expanse of the heavens, as to obtain the perfect Buddhahood, by resolving on love and compassion towards them, and by directing my entire effort to that sole perfection."

*Roger was familiar enough with the **Bardol Thödol** philosophy to know that the height of the dying experience occurred immediately upon death. It is the moment of the first and most stunning glimpse of the Clear Light of reality. Only the most adept yogin would be capable of conjoining with this first light and taking the opportunity for immediate transference and passage to Nirvana. According to Tenzing, James would have no chance of responding properly to this first appearance of the primary light, occurring in the first of three Bardo states called the Chikai Bardo. "Besides," warned the guru, "if our purpose is directed rebirth, James must resist the Clear Light in its every appearance, while holding himself together in the abstraction of a fuller reality. Then he must withstand the unfolding of his karmic record and accept the consequences of all the actions, good or bad, in his life, which he will review as illusory hallucinations throughout the fourteen days of the second Bardo state, the Chonyid Bardo. Following this, he will enter the Bardo of rebirth, the Sidpa Bardo, where he must select the proper womb in which to be reborn."*

Roger struggled with the impossibilities this kind of thinking held for him. He did know the story but he didn't believe in it. Meanwhile, Tenzing Chogyam continued his recitation to what Roger could only see now as his best friend's corpse.

"O nobly born, James Nielsen, listen. Now thou art experiencing the radiance of the Clear Light of pure reality. Recognize it. O nobly born, thy present intellect, in real nature void, not formed into anything as regards to characteristics or color, naturally void, is the very reality of the all good. Thine own consciousness, shining, void, and inseparable from the Great Body of Radiance, hath no birth, nor death, and is the Immutable Light."

Tenzing repeated these recitations, slowly and with feeling, for what seemed an eternity to Roger. All the while, the guru maintained pressure on the arteries on either side of the corpse's throat. It was during this period that James' consciousness principle was said to be in a state called the swoon, still within the body and not free to understand its own cognizance, which would not occur until it had left the body. This period could last but an instant or four days. With the assistance of a practiced hpho-bo, it should take less than an hour.

After three-quarters of an hour, Tenzing raised James' head and inspected the crown closely, even pulling out a few hairs, then announced quietly to Roger, laboring beneath encumbering suspicions, that the principle of consciousness had departed from the physical being.

"From now until we feel that he has been reborn," said Tenzing, surely feeling the doubt across the room, "we must assume that the spirit of James is with us, hearing all we say, watching all we do."

Roger made no utterance. The grim death of his friend had numbed him. The reality for Roger was that this was the undeniable end. He couldn't even consider the hope of reincarnation. He became as a zombie for the depression settling down upon him. He, too, may as well have died.

With Roger's emotionless assistance, Tenzing removed James' night shirt and wrapped his entire body in a cotton sheet like an Egyptian mummy. They placed the body in a chair beside a table as though it were actually sitting there sharing their company. After this was completed, Tenzing did an astrological reading for James' spirit. All he would tell Roger was that it was favorable to their deepest purpose.

The guru sat down beside the wrapped corpse and speaking into its right ear returned to the Bardo recitations. "O nobly born, James Nielsen, listen with thy full attention, without being distracted." Nearby, it was all Roger could do to bear the manifest absurdity of the guru's words to a dead body. He knew not whether to break into tears, laughter, or just let go with a horrible scream of agony at the irony of it all. He did none of these and the recitations pressed on.

"O nobly born, in death thou wilt experience three Bardos, the Bardo of the moment of death, the facing of the Clear Light of reality; the Bardo of sangsaric wandering, facing thy karmic judgment; and the Bardo of seeking rebirth. The first, you have already experienced. The second, called the Chonyid Bardo, is upon you now and will last many days. Thou wilt pay undistracted attention to that which I am about to set thee face to face, and hold on.

"O nobly born, whatever fear and terror may come to thee in the Chonyid Bardo, forget not these words; and, bearing their meaning at heart, go forwards: in them lieth the vital secret of recognition." And so Tenzing continued, reciting to the spirit of James Nielsen lines that James had memorized before his death, so they would be so familiar to him, even in the tortuous unwinding of his own karma, he would not forget them.

"When the uncertain experiencing of reality is dawning upon you, recognize that whatever visions appear, they are the reflections of thy own consciousness; know them

to be of the nature of apparitions in the Bardo: When at this all-important moment of opportunity for achieving a great end, do not fear the bands of peaceful and wrathful deities, for they are thy own thought forms."

*This was the beginning of forty-nine days of ceremony. It was mostly recitations from the **Bardo Thödol** and chanting and proceeded at a nerve-racking, tedious pace for the distraught Roger Taylor. He often found it difficult to watch the lama, who took so naturally to the work, whispering constantly into the ear of the corpse as though it heard every word. Roger tried to stay positive, but deep down he knew he did not believe.*

The ceremony was not widely announced and was mostly misunderstood by those who were told. Only James' parents and a few of Tenzing's seminar students came by to witness the ritualistic funeral and pray or chant. None stayed long. This was for the better. The procedures could seem quite gruesome to one raised in the West, and as far as anyone but Tenzing and Roger knew, the funeral was a traditional Buddhist ceremony designed for the express purpose of facilitating the liberation of James' consciousness—nothing more.

From the beginning, Tenzing and Roger treated the mummy as though it were James alive. Tenzing did it gracefully. Roger with great effort. Whenever they ate, they filled a plate for James and sat it before his wrapped body. As with the periodic recitations from the book, when they spoke it was as though James were included. More than once these procedures undid Roger and he would have to leave.

After five days, the corpse was removed and cremated. In this case, it satisfied both the Buddhist tradition and the wishes of James' parents. An effigy was made by stuffing some of James' clothing. A photograph of his face was enlarged and attached to the pillow that was the effigy's head. This effigy was then placed in the chair where the corpse had been. To heighten the experience of the effigy, Tenzing placed various symbolic objects around it: a mirror for reflection and the sense of sight, a lyre for the sense of sound, a vase of daffodils for the sense of smell, some holy rice cakes for the sense of taste, and a silk shirt for the sense of touch. Then it was back to the recitations and chanting which would continue for the remaining forty-four days of the ceremony.

These long days with the effigy of James wore on Roger. It was during this time—specifically during the eighth to fourteenth day, when what are called the "wrathful deities" descend upon the spirit of the deceased—that Roger finally closed himself off completely to the Tibetan beliefs.

"O nobly born, James Nielsen, prepare thyself," read Tenzing to the effigy on the morning of the eighth day, "for the Lord of Death will place round thy neck a rope

and drag thee along; he will cut off thy head, tear out thy heart, pull out thy intestines, lick up thy brain, drink thy blood, eat thy flesh, and gnaw thy bones; but thou will be incapable of dying. Even when thy body is hacked to pieces, it will revive again. Though these repeated hackings will cause intense pain and torture, fear them not. Be not awed. Know it to be the embodiment of thine own intellect."

Roger found himself closing his ears to these particularly primitive and savage sections of the recitations. They seemed far too barbaric and antiquated to take seriously. Though he would continue to study eastern culture in the years to come, it would always be with an academic distance. He retained the scholar's interest, but lost what little of the initiate's faith he might have had.

As to the actual process of the hpho-bo escorting James' vital spirit through the transitional stages of death as described by the **Bardo Thödol**, *Roger could not follow it because of his diminishing belief. He had studied the ancient text as closely as any student at Oxford except James, and in his opinion, it did offer a unique psychological perspective on death. But the story book imagery of the wandering soul in the psychic sea of karmic images read like a fairy tale to him. And the recitations seemed little more than reading instructions and fanciful poetry to a corpse and then an effigy. While the* **Bardo Thödol** *presented ideas that had once intrigued him, in its implementation, it seemed slow moving, overly drawn out, and dull—even absurd. How could anyone spend six weeks with the effigy of a recently departed friend, much less talk to it and feed it like it was alive?*

Though most of the recitations, reminder after reminder that the source of all karmic hallucination was the self, passed through Roger's head like wind through a tunnel, one particular recitation did gather Roger's interest. It was during the morning of the fifteenth day when Tenzing began the recitations concerned with selection of a womb for rebirth.

Without any announcement as to what the subject of the recitations would be that morning, Tenzing approached the effigy and began, as he had every day, speaking softly into the ear of James Nielsen's mock up. "O nobly born, James Nielsen, you are entering into the third and final Bardo, that of rebirth. Thou hast, because of the influence of karma, to enter into a womb; the teaching for the selection of the womb door will be explained now. Listen."

Roger, who had been growing more and more absent with each day, suddenly sat up attentive with these last words as the guru continued with his message.

"Do not enter into any sort of womb which may come by. Since thou now possessest a slender supernormal power of foreknowledge in the state thou art now in, all the places of birth will be known to thee one after another. Choose accordingly.

"There are two alternatives: the transference of the consciousness principle to a pure Buddha realm or the selection of the impure sangsaric womb door, whichever

your karmic path dictates.

"If, however, the transference to the Buddha realm be not possible, and one delighteth in entering a womb or hath to enter one, look with thy supernormal power of foresight over the continents, as from above, choose that in which religion prevaileth and enter therein.

"If birth is to be obtained over a heap of impurities, a sensation that is sweet-smelling will attract one towards that impure mass, and birth will be obtained thereby. Whatsoever the wombs or visions may appear to be, do not regard them as they are or seem, and by not being attracted or repelled a good womb should be chosen. In this, too, since it is important to direct thy wish, direct it thus: I ought to take birth as a universal emperor, or as the son of an adept in siddhic powers, or in a spotless hierarchical line, or in the caste of a man who is filled with religious faith, or as a Brahmin, like a great sal tree; and being born so, be endowed with great merit so as to be able to serve all sentient beings.

"Thinking thus, direct thy wish, and enter the womb. Even though a womb may appear good, do not be attracted; if it appear bad, have no repulsion towards it. To be free from repulsion and attraction, or from the wish to take or to avoid—to enter in the mood of complete impartiality—is the most profound of arts."

This particular recitation Tenzing repeated seven times a day for the course of the rest of the ceremony, some thirty-four more days. After the third day, Roger, despite his disbelief in the outlandish tradition, could not resist asking Tenzing what James in the spirit state might see to repulse or attract him to a womb.

Tenzing, too aware of Roger's failed faith, answered with remarkable sincerity, full knowing these lessons might take the entire course of Roger's life to learn. "In the Chonyid Bardo of wandering, James is bodiless mind. He floats through changing panoramas of his own memories from this life and others, colored by the varied karma associated with those memories and lives. With the transition to the Sidpa Bardo, the kaleidoscopic dreams will continue, but he will encounter holes or tubes within that dreamscape that seem to lead out of this private realm of self. When he looks down these tubes, he will see couples making love, either pleasantly or violently or with sweet smells or sour. These scenes of love-making will draw him to the holes. Should he be so attracted that he gets too close to a hole, and it is the moment of conception, like water down a drain, he will flow into a new being."

Roger nodded that he understood—though feeling it was yet another chapter in the perverse Tibetan fairy tale.

When, at last, the forty-nine days had passed and Tenzing Chogyam was preparing to burn the "spyang-pu," as the effigy's paper face is called, Roger asked the Rinpoche if he thought his efforts to lead James to a womb had been successful.

Tenzing Chogyam held the spyang-pu in one hand and lit a small butter lamp. "Roger," began the lama in extreme seriousness, "to take a directed path to a womb requires the utmost yogic strength. It means passing up the Clear Light of liberation that all yogin are taught to seek in death. Fourteen times the temptation of the Clear Light must be faced. Fourteen times it must be resisted. Then there is a harrowing flight on the turbulent and hallucination filled karmic winds, which to our minds is long at forty-nine days, but seems forty-nine eternities to the astral traveler." He placed the paper face in the flame of the butter lamp.

"It is said," he continued with utmost sobriety, "that the flame of the spyang-pu as it burns reveals to us the nature of the spirit's voyage." As he said these words, the piece of paper flared up and Tenzing dropped it into the ceremonial dish. The flames rose high and clear without a ruffle or a twist.

Roger and Tenzing watched the flame as though it would tell both their futures. Roger could see nothing. The lama shed a tear.

"Rinpoche, what is it?" plied Roger like a pagan at communion.

"James Nielsen was not meant to be reborn. His next incarnation must be in the most pure of heart—a priest or yogin or something more," was Tenzing's somber reply.

Roger was not satisfied with this answer; more than that, he felt a trace of reproach within the lama's comment, but he left it at that.

These were bitter memories for Roger Taylor from the perspective of the Queen's Imperial lounge in Haridwar eighteen years later. He felt as though he'd made many mistakes in his life, but realization of his gravest was waking in him now. He'd learned the Great Knowledge for the wrong reason. He'd studied it and intellectualized it. But he'd never believed it. He'd never taken it to heart. And now his recent acquaintance with Pipal was causing him, again, to confront something he had tried all his life to disavow—*that there was a greater truth.*

CHAPTER 23

Victoria Terminus was jammed with people of all colors and stripes. Many were in uniform. Many were wounded and bandaged. Many were simply refugees moving from one part of India to another. The war had been going on for some time and the entire subcontinent was roiling with activity and the call to duty.

Roger Taylor stood in the middle of this amorphous, ever-moving crowd with no clue why he was there or where he was supposed to go. He stared up at the train schedules posted overhead. The words were written in a script he couldn't decipher. As confusion turned to panic, he suddenly realized that he was dreaming and that he'd had this dream before, several times. Knowing the dream could end at any moment, he immediately began to scan the surging crowd for Tenzing Chogyam.

In the distance, he saw his mother with Carolyn trailing behind. Then he spotted his grandfather in uniform and Gopal Dutta wrapped in bandages. Finally, there was Tenzing walking calmly through the crowd. Struggling against the tide, everyone seemingly going in the opposite direction, Taylor managed to reach through two intervening soldiers and touch the guru's shoulder. The Tibetan turned and smiled. Taylor told him he was lost and needed help.

"Then it's time," said the guru. "Follow me. We need to catch a train." He pointed to a tunnel at the far end of the station.

Tenzing took his hand and led him through the push and pull of the teeming masses. When they neared the long row of tunnel entrances, a powerful wind began to blow, building with snow and hail each step of the way. Throughout this ordeal, the beasts sculpted or painted into the railway station decor became animated, growling, snarling, even jumping off the walls or ceilings as they passed. Tenzing reminded Taylor to ignore the creatures. "They are only figments of your imagination."

As they approached the first of the tunnels, gusts of wind threatened to sweep them in if they got too near. Taylor managed to get a peek

150

within. He saw a nude couple making love. He tried to get a closer look, but Tenzing grabbed him by the arm. "This way, Roger, we're not looking for a womb. We're trying to get to Haridwar."

After what seemed hours of struggle and hallucination, peering into one tunnel after another, Tenzing and Taylor arrived at the proper tunnel. The train was there waiting and Taylor rushed ahead to board, but Tenzing called out to him. "Slow down, Roger. We must wait for the others."

Taylor shouted back over the howling wind. "What do you mean, others?" But as soon as the words were out of his mouth, his mother, towing Carolyn by the hand, stumbled into view at the tunnel entrance. While Tenzing remained at the gate, the two women ran down the tunnel and climbed aboard, leaving Taylor standing outside the train. He looked back to Tenzing and there was his grandfather and following him Gopal Dutta. They also came running down the tunnel and climbed aboard the train. Tenzing was the last to get there. He was carrying the mongrel dog-half under his arm. "Are you ready, Roger?" he asked.

Taylor took a deep breath, his eyes momentarily averting to the dog, still oozing internal fluids from its open end. "Yes," he affirmed. And they stepped onto the train just as the whistle blew and the train lurched into motion.

Within the train, the wind was gone, and Taylor finally got a chance to ask what he'd wanted to ask all along. "Rinpoche, why are we going to Haridwar?"

"I thought maybe the two of us should talk to Pipal."

"How do you know Pipal?"

The guru smiled his widest cheshire grin.

"You mean?"

"Yes, and between the two of us maybe we can do something about this chain of souls that's troubling you." The dog beneath the lama's arm seemed to nod in agreement.

"Do you think there's a way to make her stop the fast?"

Tenzing stroked his chin hairs. "I don't know about that, but we might be able break the chain."

When the train arrived in Haridwar, the entire group, led by Taylor and Tenzing, the dog under his arm, walked the rest of the way to Pipal's home. The streets were empty. No pilgrims. No walking traffic. And soon they were on the doorstep. Tenzing put the dog down in the street. Taylor knocked lightly on the door. Behind him stood Tenzing,

Mary, Carolyn, Edwin, and Gopal. Areena Kaur came to the door. "I'm afraid you may be too late," she said. "Pipal has lost consciousness."

While the others waited in the front room, Areena ushered Tenzing and Taylor into Pipal's bedroom. Black curtains draped the barren walls. Aghast, Tenzing immediately set himself to the task of removing them. Taylor moved to the side of Pipal's bed and knelt beside her. Her eyes were closed. She was barely breathing. Taylor looked over his shoulder for the lama. Instead of the Rinpoche, he saw James Nielsen removing the last of the black drapes. Taylor turned back to Pipal and whispered her name in her ear. Her eyes fluttered. "Pipal, can you hear me?"

Her eyes opened and penetrated his.

"How can I talk you out of this?" he pleaded, tears forming at the corners of his eyes.

Her eyes diverted to James Nielsen, now seated at the end of the bed. James spoke. "Don't you understand, Roger. Her death is already written. I wasn't meant to be reborn. We went against the current of the Tibetan beliefs. It's time for the karmic debt to be balanced."

"That's why you are here, Roger," murmured Pipal, struggling with each word. "The frustrations you feel now are the same ones you tried to deny when James died. For you, this moment completes a cycle that had been artificially held up. My death is the shadow of James' years ago. In a sense, it has already happened and can not be reversed."

Taylor didn't really understand. He gave in to a sob, but gathered himself to whisper as forcefully as he could. "What of this futile chain of fasts? Certainly they aren't irrevocable. Are you sure you want others to go through this ordeal? Is your death not enough?"

Pipal seemed to hear his words but didn't answer. Taylor looked back to James for help. "No, Roger, the others do not have to die. In this, you are right."

Taylor looked back to see if Pipal heard what James had said, but Pipal's eyes had closed. He turned again to James, but James was just an effigy, now seated in the corner of the room. When he turned back to Pipal, she was also but an effigy with a paper face. In his frustration, he ripped the paper face from the pillow that was her head and tore it into shreds.

Downcast and confused, he exited the room. Seeing Areena, he pushed the scraps of the *spyang-pu* into her hand, then, wordlessly, continued out the door with Edwin, Gopal, Carolyn, and his mother following. When he stepped into the street, he noticed the mongrel dog motionless on the ground. It was dead. Its one working eye finally closed. He reached down and stroked the dog's head before moving slowly on down the street.

After a few blocks, Gopal Dutta disappeared down an alley. A block later, Taylor turned to face his mother and Carolyn trailing several yards behind with his grandfather. He advanced to the women and embraced them as one. "I'm sorry, Carolyn. I'm sorry, Mother. All along I did what I thought I had to. I don't regret those choices so much as I regret not communicating with you at those times I was pulling away. I should have done that no matter what. And Mother, I should have attended your funeral. There is no excuse for my missing that. I'm sorry." Tears were rolling down his cheeks as he spoke. His grandfather put a comforting hand on his back. "I'm sorry," he was saying again when he woke.

It was eight-fifteen. Taylor quickly climbed from bed, a visit to Pipal foremost in his mind. He ran a bath and got out his shaving kit. As he waited for the tub, he shaved. Once he settled into the bath, it felt so good he soaked for almost fifteen minutes, reviewing the end of this latest dream and sorting out the events of the last two weeks. That the course of his life should bring him here to meet Pipal, in this way, after exactly ten years in India, was so completely unlikely, yet also so eerily synchronistic, he felt the ordeal he was going through must hold some kind of deep personal meaning and insight—as suggested by this latest dream. How else could he have fallen for Pipal so quickly if he weren't feeling James in her? And the dates of her birth and James' death were so suggestive. Plus all the repeating dreams. Yes, he had to see Pipal one last time, and he wanted her to give him the understood password, *Tenzing Chogyam,* without his prompting her.

The more he thought about it, the more the urgency of the situation pressed upon him. He got out of the tub and dressed in his khaki pants with a white shirt, then hurried down to the lobby. He had a quick cup of tea and on the way out asked the concierge for directions to the nearest hospital. Not only was Taylor intent on clearing his mind of the reincarnation question, but he'd also decided, despite the message within his latest dream, to save Pipal's life. Such a beautiful young woman should not be allowed to die!

He hailed a taxi and was soon coaxing the driver to Haridwar's Government Hospital with utmost haste.

It took only a few minutes to get to Government Hospital. "I have no idea how long this is going to take," Taylor said to the cabbie as they pulled to a stop in front of the plain rectangular building that was both a hospital and a medical school. "Maybe a few minutes, maybe longer. Wait for me."

The driver's eyes betrayed some uneasiness with this directive. "There are very few taxis in Haridwar, sahib. I can't wait for a single customer, even should I leave the meter running."

Taylor pulled out his wallet and produced several large bills, probably enough to cover the driver's time for a week. "Be here when I get back. Even if it's tomorrow." The driver's wide smile was answer enough, and Taylor dashed up the stairs to the hospital.

Taylor's intent was to procure whatever equipment was required to save Pipal's life. He wasn't exactly certain what he would need, though he expected some kind of intravenous feeding system was necessary, electrolyte solutions, glucose, possibly plasma, perhaps some antibiotics.

Government Hospital was built in 1922 and had originally been staffed with English doctors and nurses, but over the years, native Indians, many trained in England, had taken over operation of the entire range of health care services. The Hindu nurse at the reception desk balked at Taylor's request. It only incited him further. "What do you mean I can't just come into a hospital and demand I.V. equipment? I'm a special emissary from the Governor-General. I can pay you twice, three times what it's worth. I have an emergency that is of vast concern to the British government—and the people of India."

"I don't understand, sir. Please tell me what this is for," the nurse asked in English.

"Christ, woman, get me your supervisor. No, get the hospital director. I'm in a hurry. We have a life at stake." He was pushing it. He was about to break orders from New Delhi just going to Pipal's house. Now he was using the Governor-General's office as a point of leverage for what had become a personal mission. He was way out of line and he didn't care.

As the nurse stammered before him, he turned and walked down the hall to the administrators' offices. He entered the director's office without knocking, nearly bowling over another doctor standing before the director who was seated at his desk. Both were Hindu males who listened with increasing disbelief as Taylor rattled out his needs and his credentials to expect these things.

After excusing himself to the other doctor, the hospital director addressed Taylor, speaking in English. "Could you possibly shed some light on this particularly difficult situation to which you allude?"

"I would rather not. I'm in Haridwar on classified orders from New Delhi."

The hospital director politely asked the other doctor if he might have some time alone with this man who had interrupted them. The doctor left, and the director, Doctor Abhay Bhandary, spoke more candidly. "Mr. Taylor, my first impression is that you're out of your mind. Barging into my office, making demands for things which you can't fully explain, and expecting me to believe that you are some kind of special agent with special orders from Lord Mountbatten—how can I possibly say yes to these requests?"

Taylor sighed with exasperation. "Doctor Bhandary, you're right. I'm wrong in expecting anything. But," again his emotions began to run ahead of him, "I'm up against a wall. I have a life and death situation that I can't explain. What can I say? What can I do to get what I've asked for? Money is not a problem."

Doctor Bhandary was a handsome man in his mid-fifties, wearing a white medical jacket over a suit and tie. His eyes were large and full of feeling. He spoke softly and evenly. "I don't know why, Mr. Taylor, but I'm going to give you this equipment you've requested, but with one stipulation. If, as you say, this individual is in immediate need of intravenous sustenance, then you also need someone qualified to diagnose and administer whatever is necessary." Taylor started to interrupt, but the doctor raised his hand. "I understand you have advanced Red Cross training and experience, but if you want this equipment, with as little as you have offered as explanation, then you must take a qualified person with you."

At a loss, Taylor could only shake his head.

"This is the only way, Mr. Taylor. The only way."

Taylor stared in futility at the ceiling, then faced the doctor. "The situation could be dangerous. This medical intervention may not be wanted—might even be fought."

The doctor raised his brow.

"If I'm to be accompanied, it must be without any show, without any medical dress," he paused, reflecting on the difficulty of the situation, "and with no questions asked."

Now it was the doctor who sighed. "Then it must be me that accompanies you."

Taylor had no choice. "Fine. I have a taxi waiting out front. You get the equipment and I'll tell the driver we're on the way."

More than slightly uncomfortable with the provision to bring the doctor with him, Taylor rethought his strategy as they taxied across town to Pipal's home. Having the doctor did have its advantages, but the logistics became more complicated. These Taylor explained as they bounced through the rough back streets of Haridwar.

"When we get there," said Taylor in the front seat, turning to Doctor Bhandary in the backseat with the medical equipment. "I will have the taxi park a few blocks away. I will be welcomed at the house, but not by those outside in the street. So I will take an alley to the back door. Unfortunately, Doctor, I am uncertain how the patient will respond to my bringing you there. Once that is worked out, I will come back to the taxi and take you to the patient."

The doctor nodded.

When they turned onto the street of Pipal's home, Taylor told the driver to stop. From a distance, he could see the long line and many other pilgrims who were camped out in vigil along the street. He pushed open the taxi door, then turned to Doctor Bhandary. "I'll be back as soon as I can."

The doctor nodded, then spoke. "Mr. Taylor, I would have to be living in some other country not to know that you are trying to save Areena Kaur's daughter, Pipal. I am a Hindu and all along have been an opponent of partition. I have respect for what this woman is trying to do." He paused looking Taylor squarely in the eyes. "But I do not agree with the death fast. If she has been at this for as long as I think she has, we may well be too late. I can tell your intentions are honorable, but I will do nothing without the young woman's full and conscious permission. I'll be waiting. Good luck."

Taylor stepped out into the street and hurried into the alley that traced through several blocks to the back entrance of Areena Kaur's house. When he reached the back door, he knocked twice. By the time Areena reached the back of the house, Taylor was already inside.

"Mr. Taylor, the end is very near. I have not allowed her a visitor since last night. The few times she has woken she has refused even the water." Areena paused and bowed her head. "The ordeal is becoming too much for her. She wants death to come quickly now."

"May I see her?"

"Yes," said Areena, leading him to the front room. "I believe she would like that."

"I have brought a doctor, Areena." He had to tell her. "I want to save her life. I can't bear to see her die."

Areena was unprepared for this. A tide of hope washed across her face, then her brow tightened. "Mr. Taylor, no one would like to see Pipal out of that bed more than me. I don't even know if it's possible to save her now, but regardless of what I think, it's her mind that must be changed first. And considering the extreme state of her health, I don't think there's any reasoning with her now."

"It's not too late. With intravenous fluids we can give her sustenance even if she hasn't the strength to lift her head. Just let me talk to her. There's still time. I'm certain."

Areena was not. She sought Taylor's eyes for his deepest motives.

"Areena, even if she's sleeping, with your permission, we could put a tube into her arm and get this going immediately."

Areena shook her head. "I would certainly like to see her saved, but not without her permission."

"In the name of Christ, woman, think about what you're saying. She must be half, no, entirely out of her mind by now. It can't be left to her. It's for you—and me to decide."

Again Areena said no.

"Fine, but I will try to change her mind."

"You can not press her, Mr. Taylor. It will bring too much turmoil to her final hours."

The priest who would be her *hpho-bo* was seated on the floor meditating. He opened his eyes and spoke in Hindi. "Sir, please, you may not be entirely aware of what you're asking. I'm also a dear friend of Pipal's and am not eager to see her die. And yet, if this is her wish, allow her that. She knows what she's doing. Besides the act of putting a needle into her arm is against the code of nonviolence. On those grounds alone, I doubt she will allow it."

Taylor took a deep breath to contain his ire, then turned away and stepped through the curtain into the back room.

Pipal was sleeping. All the flowers had been removed from the bed and arranged around the room. Taylor knelt by her bed, awed for the moment just to see her. Despite her pallor and horrible thinness, he saw her as she must have looked prior to the fast. He saw her through the eyes of love. A love he was still trying to understand.

He lifted her light bedcover and took her hand. It wasn't warm like he expected, but cold. Her body was struggling to maintain its heat. He held her hand between both of his and gazed down the length of her arm, imagining where they might insert the IV tube, knowing he had the power to reverse the situation. He dared to think of forcing this on her. He imagined rushing out to the street, calling to the doctor, and brusquely pushing all aside to save her.

As these thoughts raced through his tortured mind, he became aware of another presence in the room. Turning his head ever so slightly, he saw the apparition of James Nielsen sitting at the end of the *charpoy*. James was the one ghost in his life with whom he had yet to reach some kind of closure. James' presence made the truth horribly evident. Even if Pipal were not the incarnation of James, she was, as James had been long ago, a life that he could only know in passing, a lesson in death for a cynical man struggling to find a reason to believe.

The apparition spoke softly, yet with clear intent. "Your coming here with that I.V. equipment, Roger, means you don't take this woman's commitment to the fast seriously. That her way of thinking is secondary to yours. Give her the faith in her beliefs that you could not give to mine. Trust in her convictions. Let her die."

Taylor bowed his head, unable to look into the apparition's eyes for the truth just spoken. When he lifted his eyes, James was gone. A moment later, Pipal moved her head. Her eyes fluttered then opened slightly. Taylor pressed her hand and she smiled.

"I'm glad you're here, Roger Taylor," she said with a tremulous voice, just above a whisper.

In spite of the profound sadness of the immediate, a moment welling with the past, he returned her smile. "Are you in much pain?"

"No, Roger, I am fine," she said, calling him by his given name for the first time. "I welcome the end," she continued. "It is time."

He stared into her eyes, wanting to ask her about the I.V. tube, wanting to ask her about James.

Pipal smiled. "Will you take my story to the West?"

Taylor struggled to respond. His thoughts ran this way and that. "I can't," he heard himself say.

"But I think you will. I think this story will be told," she said, still holding the last glimmer of a smile.

Taylor clung to her hand and poured himself into her eyes, then finally asked what he'd needed to for so long. "Pipal, do you remember your past lives?"

Pipal smiled warmly. "Why would you, a westerner, ask such a question?"

"You remind me so completely of a friend I lost almost twenty years ago, I can't help but wonder if you could be him reborn."

"And you believe such a thing is possible?"

Taylor again lowered his head, then muttered softly, reluctantly, "I don't know. I just feel him so strongly when I am here, I had to ask." He paused, his heart suddenly beginning to pound. "Does the name *Tenzing Chogyam* mean anything to you?"

Pipal's radiant smile seemed to be her answer. Taylor felt this like an opening in his heart, but before Pipal could say a word, her eyes diverted. Taylor turned his head and it was Areena, who having heard the soft voices, decided to look in on them.

"How are you, Pipal?" asked her mother.

"I am tired, Mother, but I am also ready." She turned her head on the pillow and her eyes closed, then they opened again slowly. Looking at Taylor, she spoke a few lines of poetry in Sanskrit that Taylor didn't understand. She smiled at him, then her mother, and fell back to sleep.

For some time, both Taylor and Areena remained quiet. Then Areena said, "Come, Mr. Taylor, let her sleep."

Taylor lifted the bedcover over her arm and stood. Areena held back the curtain as he exited the room. Lost in a maze of thoughts, Taylor walked across the front room. He was about to leave the house without another word, but caught himself as he reached the door. He turned back to Areena, while also meeting the eyes of the priest who had spoken before. "You were right. It had to be her decision to accept a doctor's intervention." He paused, still clearly distracted. "And she would have said no. It was obvious. I didn't even ask."

Taylor used the front door to leave the house. Many of the pilgrims watched him walk slowly down the street. No one said a word. Without looking back, Taylor continued on until he reached the taxi where Doctor Bhandary was waiting. The doctor started to climb out of the car, thinking it was time, then he saw the look in Taylor's eyes.

"Were we too late, Mr. Taylor?"

"No. But bringing you here was a mistake," he said looking off to the east and one barely visible snow capped Himalayan peak in the distance. "Thank you for coming with me. I'm sorry for any inconvenience I have caused you." He pulled his wallet from his pocket and gave ample sums to both the driver and the doctor. The driver chuckled with glee at the cash. The doctor tried to refuse it. Taylor wouldn't let him and told them both to be off. He would walk back to his hotel.

It was a long slow walk through the now packed streets of Haridwar. Taylor arrived at the hotel in the middle of the afternoon. After an early dinner, he retired to the lounge as had become his habit. The place was almost entirely full. Chuluun was at the bar with a second bartender. Taylor was served by Chuluun. As he paid for the drink, he told Chuluun that he had seen Pipal one last time. "She won't last another forty-eight hours."

"Will there be a fast to follow?" asked the Mongolian.

"As far as I know." A disconsolate Taylor took his drink and headed to a seat in the corner of the lounge.

It was over. He would stay long enough to watch what happened in the next few days, but that would be all. He had one drink and retired to his room.

Roger Taylor climbed out of bed the next morning feeling unusually clear headed and rested. He'd slept through the night without a dream or an interruption. He drew a bath and soaked for twenty minutes. During that time, he entered into a soul-searching self-examination, really a recounting of his last visit to Pipal. Two things stood out.

The first was a realization that came to him through the words spoken by James Nielsen as an apparition: *Give her the faith in her beliefs that you could not give to mine.* It was a shortcoming he had known all along but had denied. His inability to fully take part in James' funeral had drawn from the goodwill of the so-called experiment. It would have been better if he hadn't attended. Instead he had been a source of negativity in a sacred ritual. And, if he could believe the messages sent to him within the psychic storm of the last few days, not only had Tenzing Chogyam known this then, but so had James.

The second was the admission that he was the one who had spoken the password, *Tenzing Chogyam,* when it should have come from Pipal. It was too easy to dismiss all that he had felt so strongly in that moment as nothing more than his own projections—James' words included. Lying there in the tub, with only himself to judge, could he say that he now believed in the Tibetan metaphysical philosophy? Had his ten years in India changed him in the way Tenzing Chogyam had anticipated? Had Pipal really answered his question about reincarnation? Or did he simply want so badly for her answer to be a yes that he'd imagined it was? That seemed to be the bottom line. Could he really say that he had received any solid piece of information, any factual proof of reincarnation from outside the psychological container of himself? And if not, did that really matter?

He looked around the bathroom. He let his eyes pause on the ordinary things, the soap, the towels, the electric light bulb, the sweating window pane, the stark, plain surface of the plastered walls. He lifted his right hand from the water and, turning it this way and that, stared at its subtle detail, the veins, the pores, the tiny hairs. A drop of water fell from his hand into the tub with a barely audible plop. He watched the tiny circular waves propagate outward on the surface of the water. There was something dwelling in the moment he had never noticed before, some fuller potential he had long denied or missed.

Taylor bowed his head, and in the overwhelming silence of the now, prompted by a viscous sense of opening from within, he felt something, someone, calling him from without. No words, no voice, just an overwhelming sense of gaping cognizance, as in hearing the first few notes of a familiar piece of music one can not yet identify. Beyond all ordinary reason, he wondered if in that moment Pipal had just expired.

Taylor went down to the dining room holding on to a profound internal quiet. He had a cup of tea and some toast. During that time, he wondered if he should go across town to see Pipal. It seemed too much. For all the good feelings he'd received from Pipal and her mother, he still felt like an outsider. Yes, he wanted to go, but he wouldn't. Instead he had a second cup of tea.

Halfway through the cup of tea, Chadi came running barefoot into the dining room with a hotel employee calling after him to stop. Chadi reached Taylor's table just as the employee collared him. Taylor immediately told the employee that Chadi was his friend and it was fine. The employee reluctantly turned away as Chadi, gasping for breath, sputtered out his news in Nepalese. Taylor didn't catch all that was said, but the tears in the boy's eyes made the message obvious. Pipal had died. Chadi had run to the hotel as soon as he'd heard. It couldn't have been more than an hour ago.

Taylor walked unhurried through the streets of Haridwar with Chadi by his side. The sky was brilliantly clear and had gained its full azure by the time they came in sight of Pipal's home. As they neared, Taylor felt a thickened sense of solemnity in the vigilant pilgrims camped along the street. A few looked up to watch him pass, but most seemed absent in their murmuring of chants and prayers. He slowed his pace as he reached the house and told Chadi he wanted to go in alone.

As one might approach an altar after many years absence from the church, Taylor, full of premonition, quietly stepped up to the door. Through the window he could see two candles on the table. The door opened before he knocked. A Buddhist priest he hadn't seen in his previous visits told him that the house was closed because of a recent death.

Taylor asked if he might talk to Areena. She heard his voice from inside and came to the door before the priest could respond. Areena told the priest that this man was her friend, then asked Taylor to come in.

"Areena, I'm so sorry to hear that Pipal is gone." He advanced to Areena and gave her a hug. "I guess it was inevitable after yesterday. Maybe it's just as well the ordeal is over."

Areena, looking very tired, nodded. She led Taylor to the table and they both sat down. "You just missed her, Mr. Taylor. She died this morning, not long ago." Areena spoke full of withheld emotion. "The *hpho-bo* is in with her now. He is to be alone with her until the swoon has ended."

The curtain that provided privacy to Pipal's bedroom was not entirely closed, allowing Taylor a glimpse into the room. All he could see was the priest kneeling beside the bed and the faint definition of Pipal's body beneath the covers. A white cloth covered her face. He recalled the same scene years before when Tenzing Chogyam whispered into the ear of James' motionless body. It had nearly turned his stomach then. Today, though he could barely hear the faint intonations of the *hpho-bo's* recitations, it seemed meaningful and profound.

"The priest who met you at the door did an astrological reading for Pipal at the moment of her death," said Areena. "It's supposed to tell something about her life and where death will take her."

Taylor's expression asked the obvious question.

"According to the priest, it was a confusing reading. He said that her life was very pure and that her death was like that of a yoga master or an avatar. As such, she should take the great perpendicular path, which means immediate liberation and transference at the moment of death. This also means there should be no break in consciousness and no swoon, and yet the *hpho-bo* still remains with her. He says that despite the reading, her consciousness is still present, almost as if she were waiting for some sign or signal to ascend to her natural path."

Recalling that moment in the bath when he thought he'd felt her passing, Taylor couldn't help wonder if maybe she had been waiting for him. "Areena," he said, still thinking of James Nielsen, "what were her last words?"

"I don't think Pipal ever woke again after your conversation with her yesterday," replied Areena. "As far as I know, she spoke her last words to you then. I was just peeking into the room at the time, but I recognized her favorite lines from the *Bhagavad Gita*."

"Yes," he said, recalling the moment. "She spoke those lines in Sanskrit. I didn't quite understand them."

"She quoted them directly from the ancient text."

Taylor needed no further help. "Many lives you and I have lived," he began, "I remember them all, but thou dost not." As he spoke the lines, he could hear James saying them in the cottage at Oxford in the spring 1930. The hair stood up on his neck and a shiver passed through his body.

For the next hour, Taylor sat outside Pipal's room with Areena, who had gradually come to find solace in Taylor's presence. Neither said a word and the atmosphere of the ceremony began to replace the stark emptiness of the word *dead*. The steady chanting, the quiet recitation of the *hpho-bo* to the corpse, the incense, the chimes, the air was fraught with the otherworldly. The two weeks of restless nights and excess drink, the provoking dreams, the stress of the death watch, all served to heighten Taylor's susceptibility to the moment. Emotionally drained, tired to the bone, his head floated. He felt apart from his body—earth into water—almost like he was watching from above. He didn't fight it. He took in every detail of what was happening around him—and to him.

He gushed with feelings and memories, a watershed of his entire life funneling into this moment—water into fire. He reflected on the fact that this was the second time he'd witnessed the sacred Tibetan death ritual, and it struck him heavily as meaningful coincidence—and deja vu.

He saw now as the initiate not the scholar, and the awkwardness of the Buddhist symbols that had never rested easily within the Christian orientation of his upbringing gave way. He saw through the pasteboard nature of all symbols and caught a glimpse of the invisible trinity, master glyph behind it all. A powerful sense of opening within—fire into air— telescoped the moment with an awareness—opening without—that he'd been touched deeply.

At that moment, the *hpho-bo* exited from Pipal's room. "The swoon is over," he announced soberly. "Her liberation is complete. You may view the body if you like."

Areena stood and motioned to Taylor. She led him into the room.

Pipal lay on her right side. The sunlight had just reached the room's windows and a rectangle of light framed her head and shoulders. Though her face was still covered, the light shone through the white cloth like it was gauze, illuminating a countenance of serenity and calm.

Areena knelt by the bed and began to pray. Taylor could not take his eyes off the tranquil face beneath the cloth. After a moment, he noticed that Areena had stopped praying and was also looking longingly at the face beneath the cloth. One last question arose in Taylor's mind.

"Areena," he said softly. She looked up at him. "Who's the next in line to fast?"

A faint smile graced Areena's solemnity. She stood and reached into the pocket of her skirt. She withdrew her fist and extended it to Taylor. He opened his palm and she dropped a cluster of paper scraps into his hand. "It *was* to be the woman from Calcutta, Sumitra."

"But what's this?" he asked as he used a finger to inspect the tiny pieces of paper, apparently once a single sheet.

"It is—or was—the list of volunteers for the fast."

Taylor looked at her still unsure what this meant.

"The *hpho-bo* found these beneath her pillow this morning just after he realized she had died and turned her on her side. She'd kept this list by the side of her bed ever since the third week of the fast. I noticed it was gone yesterday before your arrival, but I thought nothing of it. I fell asleep after you left, and the *hpho-bo* stayed with her all night except for a few moments. No one saw her wake, but as I far as I can tell, she decided sometime last night or possibly the night before to cancel the chain of fasts. She said nothing to me, but that is the only way I can interpret the shredding of the list."

Mystery within mystery suggested solution. Taylor pressed the scraps of paper back into Areena's hand and flashed upon that moment in the dream two nights ago when he pressed the scraps of Pipal's *spyang-pu* into her hand. Giving in to everything, he wrapped his arms around Areena, tears rolled from his eyes, freeing his deepest feelings and years of regret in the way they always must. Amid the hug, he also remembered the end of that dream two nights ago—hugging his own mother and Carolyn, the tears, the release of guilt, the release of grief, the release from the shackles of his past.

Shortly after Areena had shown Taylor the remains of Pipal's list, the old woman from Calcutta appeared at the doorstep. Areena brought the woman in and told her of Pipal's decision to end the death fasts. Sumitra had known she would be next and found the news devastating.

"But, Areena," she said, her eyes straying to Taylor's, "I needed this fast for the cleansing of my soul."

"No, you have served your penance," said Areena. "What was done to your body years ago, does not affect the soul if you fought the insult at the time."

"Did Jesus say that Areena?" asked Sumitra in all sincerity.

"No," said Areena with a soft smile, "I did."

The old woman began to cry silently. Taylor advanced to her, taking her hand. "Good woman, don't underestimate who you are and what you've done. You did much good for me in the past two weeks. And your tipping us off to the presence of RSSS that day of the kidnapping attempt may have saved twenty lives."

She looked up at him through tear glazed eyes. "But what will I do now? All that I have planned for was the end."

Taylor could not resist. He kissed the woman lightly on the forehead. "If it is not to be, trust that there must be something more for you to do."

After Taylor said goodbye to Areena and Sumitra, he headed back to the Queen's Imperial. As he walked, he noticed that he was seeing the city much differently than he had before. The Hindu sculptures and Buddhist mandalas that he'd purposely ignored before, now stood out like beacons in the street. New meanings, new understandings, softened his glance everywhere it fell.

As he neared the west side of Haridwar, groups of Hindu men and women were running through the streets, yelling and laughing and emptying cups of red and yellow water on one another or streaking red powder on each others faces or their clothing. The festival of Kumbh Mela had begun.

Taylor smiled as he watched the people in wild celebration. He recalled being told many years ago that it was a time when all grudges and ill will were to be forgotten. It seemed somehow personally relevant to him, and as that thought sank in, a passerby splashed his white shirt with a cup of red water. A week ago, this would have set him off. Today, he felt included.

When Taylor reached the Queen's Imperial Hotel, he remembered that the *ghats* all along the river's edge in Haridwar were the focus of the festival and the crowds. Instead of going into the hotel, Taylor set off for the Hari-ki-pairi *Ghat*, the most famous of the bathing locations, where Vishnu's footprint was memorialized in stone.

When he reached this most sacred part of the Ganges, he stood back on the bank and watched a swarm of pilgrims go down the *ghat* stairs and wade fully clothed into the water up to their waists. Several thousand people were there, standing side by side, splashing about like happy children. After a while, Taylor proceeded down to the river. Up and down its banks as far as he could see the *ghats* were full. Without a thought for his clothes or the cleanliness of the water, he waded in up to his navel. He dipped his hands into the river, and using them as a cup, splashed his face and head with the healing waters just as the other pilgrims did. This was, at last, his real baptism to India.

CHAPTER 25

After a full ten minutes in the scared river, Roger Taylor climbed the *ghat* stairs and proceeded dripping wet up the slight incline to the street, intent to walk the ten blocks back to the Queen's Imperial Hotel. Before he reached the street, looking up ahead of him, he saw Captain Rantanbir standing beside his patrol car. Taylor smiled as he got within speaking range.

"So, Captain, I take it you are still following me?"

"Mr. Taylor, it's not an easy task trying to protect an agent of His Majesty's intelligence service. When I saw you go into the water just now, I thought you were going to drown yourself. Even worse," he added, appraising this man who was always so immaculately dressed, "I thought, after all the trouble you've caused me, it would be best to just let you drown."

Taylor laughed. "Do you know that it's over?"

"I heard Pipal died, but wasn't sure what would come next."

"She stopped the chain of fasts."

"Was this something you inspired?"

"I don't really know, Captain. I might have had something to do with it."

Rantanbir reappraised the condition of his friend, looking him up and down, noting the red streaks on his shirt and that Taylor had not even removed his shoes prior to entering the water. "May I ask what prompted you into the river?"

"A new appreciation for what it means. I needed to be cleansed."

Rantanbir nodded, clearly impressed. "What's next for you?"

"I'm not sure yet. I have to clear some things up with Mountbatten. I'm still on the books for two more months in India."

"Hopefully not in Haridwar."

"I'll make a special request, Captain," laughed Taylor, who was now entertaining the idea of staying for Pipal's funeral.

"Need a ride back to the hotel?"

"If you don't mind a wet seat."

"Let's go."

The two men climbed into the patrol car and minutes later were pulling up in front of the Queen's Imperial. Taylor spoke before getting out of the car. "Captain Rantanbir, thank you for putting up with me. And allowing me to take part in the stakeout. I would have made a real ass of myself if you hadn't given in to my request."

"I knew that, Mr. Taylor," said Rantanbir. "I wasn't sure if it would be more difficult to have you with us or against us."

Taylor nodded. "Well, I appreciate your tolerance." Taylor offered the other man his hand. Rantanbir gave Taylor's hand a firm shake. "You're a good man, Rantanbir." Taylor pushed open the door to the vehicle.

"And you've been quite an ass, Mr. Taylor," said Rantanbir with a chuckle. "But I'm thinking that dip in the Ganges might have done you some good."

Taylor laughed. "I'm sure it did." He climbed from the car and ascended the stairs to the hotel.

Taylor called Mountbatten that afternoon and gave him an abbreviated report of what had transpired. Seemingly unconcerned about the death of the young woman, Mountbatten was pleased with the news that the chain of souls had been broken and complimented Taylor highly for his work, even apologized for his doubts in him earlier.

The Governor-General told him to return to New Delhi and they'd begin the paper work to get him out of India. Taylor thanked Mountbatten for this, then asked for permission to stay in Haridwar to witness the rest of Pipal's funeral. Mountbatten found the request a bit odd, but granted it.

Then Taylor asked Mountbatten an even tougher request. "Sir, I need your approval to give this woman's story to the newspapers."

"What? The entire purpose of the mission was to keep the thing quiet."

"I know that, your lordship, but it's over."

Mountbatten allowed a moment of silence at his end to penetrate his anger. "It may be over, Taylor, but even a story could incite violence at this time. You must know that."

"I understand that, sir. But I won't give them the story for a year. It was a promise I made to the woman to get her to break the chain," he lied. "She wanted the world to know that Gandhi had not approved of partition." Taylor tightened his jaw after saying this, knowing what Mountbatten would be thinking.

Again there was a long silence at the other end of the line. "When you get back, we'll talk about it," said the Governor-General, closing the discussion.

When Taylor put the receiver down, he noted to himself how distant Mountbatten's voice seemed, not just many miles away, but seemingly many worlds apart. He would get Pipal's story published, even if he had to wait five years and write it himself.

CHAPTER 26

Though Pipal's transference occurred three hours after her death, the funeral ceremonies continued for forty-nine days. Roger Taylor stayed in Haridwar the entire time, stopping by Pipal's home periodically to pay his respects to Areena and to observe the funeral process. Throughout this seven-week period, Taylor was reminded of James Nielsen's Tibetan funeral, and how extremely difficult that experience had been for him. In retrospect, that first funeral seemed like necessary preparation for this second vastly different experience—because, at some level, he had broken through his life long devotion to strict empiricism and his eyes were open in a way they never had been before; life was more than what could be rationally explained. And apparently he'd needed all of those ten years in India, as foreseen by Tenzing Chogyam, for this to occur. He even felt that those repeating dreams, where he was lost in Victoria Terminus, were a form of real communication with the Rinpoche, wherever he might be now—dead or alive, and that something in the nature of those lucid dreams—that is, his being aware within the dream that he was dreaming—was also an important incite into the nature of consciousness and reality. It was the same incite that Tenzing had tried to impart to him years ago in his seminar when Taylor had argued so vehemently against the Tibetan beliefs.

When the funeral rites drew to a close and the effigy of Pipal was disassembled, Taylor asked to watch the burning of the *spyang-pu*. Any last doubts he may have harbored for the occult mysteries vanished like the *spyang-pu* when the *hpho-bo* lit the paper mask in the butter lamp and the flames rose high and clear without a ruffle or a twist. Whatever life was, he thought, it was not random; it held meaning within meaning.

That night Taylor ventured down to the basement lounge for the first time since Pipal's death. Kumbh Mela was long over, and the place was empty but for three patrons. Chuluun was behind the bar, working on a cigarette. The two men had not spoken in a long time. The husky Mongolian almost smiled as Taylor took a seat in front of him.

"Gin and tonic?" asked Chuluun, reaching for the bottle of gin.

"Not tonight. I'm off the stuff for a while. I just came by to say goodbye and thank you for your help."

"You stayed for the entire funeral?"

Taylor nodded. "My time here has been quite different than I expected that day I first came down here looking for information about the fast."

Chuluun took a pull from his smoke and looked off momentarily before exhaling. "You didn't exactly win any points with me that night."

"But you'd already seen what it would take me two weeks to figure out. Pipal was not of this world. She really was a holy woman, a woman Jesus, as the pilgrims have called her."

Chuluun looked down a moment at the thin trial of smoke rising off the end of his cigarette. "That's why I wished I'd never said anything in the first place." He looked up at Taylor. "But now that it's over, maybe it was all right."

"I think it was. Things worked out as they had to. The chain of fasts is over. That's a good thing. But Pipal is gone." Taylor paused remembering the first time he saw her beneath the neem tree talking to the pilgrims. "I think that was beyond anyone's influence—certainly yours or mine."

Chuluun nodded then crushed out his cigarette. Taylor recalled Mountbatten doing the same when he'd referred to Pipal as a burning ember on the deck of a ship full of explosives. Taylor extended his hand. "I'll be on the train tomorrow headed to New Delhi, Chuluun. Thank you for your help—and your understanding."

Instead of taking Taylor's hand, Chuluun placed his palms together, bowed his head, and uttered a soft, "*Namaste.*"

Taylor greatly appreciated this and returned the gesture, then walked out of the bar.

Fifty days after Pipal's death, a renewed Roger Taylor boarded the train bound for Ambala. His mind was so at ease he barely noticed the long tedious trip. But during the second leg, Ambala to New Delhi, one final awakening occurred. He opened his briefcase and pulled out the flask James had given him so long ago. It was empty and he didn't open it. He just reread the rugby score etched on its side, recalling that last trip to Twinkenham. And in that moment, he remembered the rest of the promise he'd made to James and Tenzing the night of the wager—should the proof bear out, he would spread the word. Without a second thought, he decided to quit the C.I. D. and return to the United States to start a new life, teaching eastern philosophy at an American university—and while there, he would make a special effort to see his father.

Taylor filed his official report on the mission in Haridwar two days after arriving in New Delhi. Mountbatten wasn't there, so he returned to Bombay and gave his boss at C.I.D. his resignation papers. He wasn't asked to complete his final two weeks in India, so he booked passage on an ocean liner bound for New York that would be leaving in four days. He took the time to clean out his apartment and pack the few things he owned.

The night before he left, he attended a big state department party at the British Embassy, hoping to catch a few of his friends and business acquaintances and bid them and India adieu. The embassy in Bombay, like Victoria Terminus and the Queen's Imperial Hotel, was excessive. The party was the same. Everyone in black tie or evening gowns. More food than could be eaten. Liquor flowing like water. Taylor had been to a thousand such parties and had always enjoyed them, flourishing in the society of the rich and famous.

On this night, however, the scene disturbed him, perhaps because he'd had nothing to drink. Seeing India through new eyes, he saw a room full of Englishmen and their wives drinking like fish and babbling about trifles. For the first time, the culture that was colonial India truly offended him. It made him sad, but at the same time relieved him—because he was leaving. Clearly it was time.

Taylor didn't stay long at the party. Being sober in a room full of drinkers reminded him how banal parts of his old life were. As he walked out, the Maharani of Gwalior was just stepping out of a limousine. As was her way, Naija was alone and dressed traditionally in a beautiful burgundy *sari* and matching *choli* that showed off her figure and left her stomach bare. The *sari* neckline and hem were embroidered in gold. A red ruby was set in her navel. She wore her hair free, hanging down past her waist like a glistening black cape, and an ensemble of diamonds on her neck and wrists fit for a princess. She could not have looked more stunning—and her manner showed that she knew this.

Taylor extended his hand to her as she reached the top of the embassy stairs, uncertain of her response. Naija smiled graciously and gave him her hand. "Please, Roger, would you escort me in?" The way she said it sounded like an invitation for the rest of the evening.

Taylor offered her his arm and led her into the party. As they entered the room and walked into the noisy crowd, Taylor spoke, "You know, Naija, I'm glad to get this chance to see you—and you do look absolutely ravishing, but I would never have allowed myself to be seen in public with you tonight if I weren't leaving the county tomorrow."

Naija suddenly stopped and let go of his arm, shocked by his tone and what was beginning to feel like a horrible snub.

"You blew my cover when I went to Haridwar. It nearly cost me my life. And you had to know that, Naija. You had to." Taylor paused looking her in the eye. "So now that I have properly escorted you into this party, I'm sorry to say, I must leave."

Apparently having already plotted out an evening with Taylor that would last well into the morning, Naija took this as a direct insult. She reached out and slapped him across the face. Taylor simply put his palms together and bowed. "Good night, Naija." Then turning to all those who had heard or seen the slap and were now staring at him, he called out, "And good night to all of you," and then said quietly to himself, "Goodbye, India. Thank you for having me."

GLOSSARY

Aparigraha- the practice of non-possession, non-attachment to the material.

Charpoy- a wooden bed frame, strung with ropes covered by a thin straw-filled mattress.

Choli- a midriff-baring blouse often with short sleeves and a low neck, cut to fit tightly to the body.

Churidars- pants shaped much like riding breeches, loose at the hips, tight at the calves, often worn with a sherwani.

Coir- a mat woven from the fiber of coconut husks.

Darshan- to experience the presence of a holy person.

Ghat- stairs at a river's edge to allow bathers easy access to the water.

Hpho-bo- the extractor of the consciousness principle.

Khadi- a coarse, homespun cotton cloth.

Namaste- a greeting or salutation, meaning "I bow to you."

Pagri- a turban-like head cover.

Pallu- the loose end of a sari that is draped over the shoulder or over the head like a scarf.

Sangsara- the realm of wandering souls, a place between earthly existence and nirvana.

Santhara- the Jain religious ritual of voluntarily fasting to death.

Sari- a long piece of cloth that is draped around or over the body in various styles and often worn like a skirt.

Satyagraha- the belief of sacrificing ones own desires for the benefit of others, devotion to truth.

Sherwani- a collarless Indian jacket that reaches down past the knees.

Spyang-pu- a paper face placed upon a Tibetan funeral effigy.

Tulku- someone who can remember his or her past lives.

Tonga- an animal-drawn, two-wheeled cart.

THE AUTHOR

Dan Armstrong is the editor and owner of Mud City Press, a small publishing company and online magazine operating out of Eugene, Oregon. He has written extensively in both fiction and non-fiction. Access to his books, short stories, political commentary, humor, and environmental studies is available at www.mudcitypress.com.

Made in the USA
Charleston, SC
13 July 2011